ROMANCE AT THE SWEET
SHOP OF SECOND CHANCES

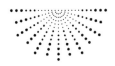

HANNAH LYNN

ALSO BY HANNAH LYNN

Standalone Feel Good Novels

The Afterlife of Walter Augustus

Treading Water

Erotic Fiction?

The Complete Peas and Carrots Series

Peas, Carrots and an Aston Martin

Peas, Carrots and a Red Feather Boa

Peas, Carrots and Six More Feet

Peas, Carrots and Lessons in Life

Peas, Carrots and Panic at the Plot

Peas, Carrots and Happily Ever After

The Holly Berry Sweet Shop Series

The Sweet Shop of Second Chances

Romance at the Sweet Shop of Second Chances

Turmoil at the Sweet Shop of Second Chances

The Grecian Women Series

Athena's Child

A Spartan's Sorrow

Queens of Themiscyra

Alternatively sign up to my newsletter and receive a free book.

Sign-up to Newsletter

For Peter and Dee,

a lot had changed for Holly Berry over the last ten months. She was no longer working in a job she disliked, sitting at a computer all day inputting data until her back ached. She was no longer living in London, paying crazy rent while she scrimped and saved to get together a deposit for her own place. And she was no longer with Dan, her now ex-boyfriend, who had strung her along year after year, with empty promises of settling down together. Six years she had spent believing him that they would be together forever. That he was the man she was going to spend the rest of her life with, that she would have a family with. That was until she found him cheating on her with someone five years her younger and in her own bed, of all places.

Thankfully, that life was long gone.

Now, she was her own boss and the proud owner of one of the most fabulous things in the world. A sweet shop. But not just any old sweet shop. *Just One More* was the same one she had worked in as a teenager. A jar-filled jewel in the centre of the beautiful village of Bourton-on-the-Water, in the heart of the Cotswolds.

It wouldn't be too much of a push to say that *Just One More* had been her first true love. And it was thanks to her that the place was still standing. In fact, it was better than standing. It was thriving. It hadn't been easy. To say the shop had been in a dire state when she took it over, would be an understatement. Between a leaking roof, out-of-date stock and a cat that kept bringing her *presents* of the most undesirable kind, it had been touch-and-go whether she would be able to keep the place at all. But somehow, she'd got through it all.

She now spent her days laughing and joking with customers, weighing out bags of peanut brittle and other favourites and indulging in one-too-many chocolate eclairs or rosy apples. She had regulars she knew by name and suppliers who would always get her the best deals on treacle toffees and marzipan teacakes. And work colleagues—well, employees technically—who were more friends than anything else.

As well as her work life, her personal life was also much improved, lodging with one of her new best friends for a very reasonable rent, although Jamie, her "landlady", had stipulated that she bake for them at least once a week.

And then there was her upcoming date. Yes, Holly Berry was going on a date!

Ben Thornbury was the village Bank Manager and she would be the first to admit that initial impressions had been less than favourable—on both sides. His opinion of her had been somewhat influenced by the fact that their very first meeting had taken place when she'd knocked him off his bicycle—accidentally, of course—but it had definitely been her fault, and her lack of road safety awareness did nothing to enamour her to him. He'd also made no attempt to hide the fact that he thought her purchase of *the shop*, with no business experience, was utterly insane. She, unsurprisingly given his initially unfriendly attitude, found him pompous, cold and self-righteous.

But somewhere along the line, things had changed. Ben had been the one who'd stepped in at the last minute and saved her from losing *Just One More*, securing a mortgage deal for her after that rat, Giles Caverty, had tried to ruin her forever.

Like the leaky roof though, Giles was a thing of the past and she had heard on the grapevine that he was now working in Monaco and would be there for an indefinite period. She was just glad he was no longer anywhere near Bourton, giving her the head space to get to know Ben a little better.

Spending time with him was fairly easy. They lived next door to one another. They would walk to work together in the morning, and then at the end of the day, he would wait for her, often helping to straighten up the jars or sweeping the floor, if it had been particularly busy and she was still cashing up. The fact that they were neighbours, and he was also a close friend of Jamie, meant that the three of them often spent their evenings together: sometimes at her and Jamie's house, feasting on a meal she'd cooked up for them all or playing board games, sometimes in one of the countless pubs in Bourton and the villages beyond.

But spending time together like that was not the same as going on a date— just the two of them.

It had been months since he'd first proposed the idea. She'd accepted the offer almost immediately. After all, if there was one thing she knew about Ben, it was that he was a good guy, and after the previous two men in her life—Dan the cheat and Giles the snake—she felt she deserved someone trustworthy for a change.

But for weeks, every attempt to find a mutually convenient

day kept falling through: he'd have to work late; she'd have a commitment with Jamie or her other good friend, Caroline; his sister would need a babysitter; he'd have to go away with work; his nephew would need help with coursework. By the time they'd got to mid-October, nearly two months later, Holly was starting to think that he wasn't that interested after all. But finally, they settled on an evening. If she was honest with herself, she expected it to fall through, too, like all the others had.

The day in the shop had seemed to go on for ever, as she continually stopped to check her phone, wondering at what point a message would ping, saying he wasn't able to make it after all. And yet, when it finally ended, the only one she'd received from him was to say that he had to stay half an hour later than he'd intended at the bank, so she should head home without him, but that he was very much looking forward to their date. It was actually happening!

By six o'clock, she'd shaved her legs, settled on a top borrowed from Caroline and applied a fraction more makeup than she normally would. She'd considered getting her hair cut, too, particularly as it hadn't seen a pair of scissors since she'd moved to Bourton, but that seemed a bit like over-kill, especially as she knew that hair styles and makeup were probably at the bottom of the list of what Ben found attractive in a woman.

"So, it's actually going ahead at last, is it?" Jamie asked, coming into the kitchen and taking a seat opposite Holly at the table. Her nervous tension wasn't being helped by the deep frown on her friend's face.

"You could look a little bit excited for me."

"It's not that I'm not excited. I'm just worried, that's all, in case anything goes wrong."

"Why would that happen?" Holly queried. It was hard not

to feel deflated by this negative attitude. "It's a first date, that's all. We're not agreeing to marriage or anything."

"It's just that I care about you both. You know that. And I like our little group as it is."

There was a part of Holly that wanted to be cross with her for this lack of enthusiasm. Jamie hadn't been keen on her seeing Giles either, although admittedly, she'd been right on the money with that one. Still, she understood why she was concerned. If this thing with her and Ben worked out, it could change the group dynamics. Then again, it might make them even better and she had a feeling in her gut that they could be good. Really good.

"I promise. Whatever happens, our little gang will be just fine. Worst case scenario, we stay friends."

Jamie pursed her lips, then relaxed them into a half-smile.

"Okay, I guess it would be kind of cool for you to get it together, after what you've both been through before."

This was the first time she'd mentioned anything at all about Ben's past relationships. On more than one occasion, Holly had been tempted to ask her, but as Jamie and Ben had been friends for so long before she'd arrived on the scene, it didn't feel quite right. She'd always assumed he was such a workaholic that he'd never found the time to do much dating. But now that she'd brought it up, the urge to learn more was overwhelming. As she was trying to think of a way of phrasing it, Jamie was speaking again.

"So, tell me. Do you know where he's taking you?"

Holly frowned, looking down at the pair of trainers on her feet.

"I don't know, but he said I might have to run."

Jamie raised an eyebrow questioningly.

"Do you know how to run?" she asked.

CHAPTER TWO

*H*olly already knew that Ben paid attention to everything. Not just things that were said to him in conversation but the slightest, most innocuous remark that most people would forget only seconds after hearing it. Like the time Jamie had mentioned that she had a sudden craving for Becherovka, a drink that had apparently been a staple when she'd spent six weeks travelling in the Czech Republic but had never managed to find since.

Three days later, Ben had appeared on their doorstep, with a bottle he'd sourced from some obscure website. Naturally, they finished it that very same night.

Then there was the time that Caroline had mentioned how her oldest child was devastated after scratching the paintwork on his bike. The next afternoon, he'd turned up at her house with a bag full of metal paints and some swanky stickers to give the whole thing a revamp, in true pimp-my-ride style. It was constant little kindnesses like this that made Holly like him. But why would he suggest wearing running shoes on a date? Surely, he knew her well enough by now to realise that jogging to get to the baker's before it shut was enough exercise to last her a week.

She was still mulling this over, when a knock at the door brought her back to reality.

"Well, whatever it is, I guess you're going to find out soon enough. Go on, you'd better not keep him waiting. And I suppose I should tell you to have fun," Jamie grinned. "It's possible you two could be quite cute together."

Holly jumped off her seat and darted around the table to give Jamie a hug.

"Just don't do anything I wouldn't," her friend advised.

"Is that even possible?" Holly asked.

Her heart was pounding as she slipped her coat off its hanger and opened the front door. Normally, if a man standing in front of her were holding flowers, they would be the first thing she'd pay attention to, but after the most fleeting of glances at the bouquet, her eyes skipped over it and settled on his attire. Ben was the type of person who seemed most at home in a suit and tie. This look was beyond even a normal level of casual for him and certainly more informal than she would have expected, given that it was a first date. His cargo trousers and grey hoodie top looked like he was about to go on a bike ride.

His eyes went immediately to her feet.

"Great," he said. "I was worried you might have thought I was joking about the shoes."

"I know you better than to think you'd make a joke," she replied.

His eyes met hers with a hint of surprise and she felt the blood rise to her cheeks.

"Sorry, I didn't mean …" she stammered.

"No, it's fine," he replied, now blushing himself.

Great. Less than three sentences in, and they were already

almost unable to converse. Maybe they should cut their losses and call it quits.

"These are for you," he said, breaking the silence and thrusting the orange calla lilies and purple thistles at her.

"I should just put these in water quickly," she murmured, then hesitated as she took the flowers from him.

Should she invite him in? Normally she would, and he probably spent as much time in their house as he did in his own. But Jamie was there, and it was clear she had concerns about this whole dating thing. Maybe it would be better if he waited outside.

"I'll just be one second," she said, turning and hurrying back to the kitchen.

"Over already?" Jamie asked when she reappeared.

"No. We're just going. Could you look after these for me, please?"

Jamie took the bouquet, a smile once again teetering on her lips.

"Don't go breaking any hearts tonight, okay?"

"Have you met me?" Holly replied. "I'm not exactly the heart-breaking type."

"I wouldn't be so sure about that."

Five minutes later, and they were in his car, heading towards Cheltenham. Neither of them speaking.

"Can I guess what we're doing?" Holly said at last, breaking the silence.

"I don't know, can you?" Ben replied, pedantically.

Fiddling with the sleeve of her jacket, she thought through the options. If they'd been dressed like this in the daytime, she'd definitely think they were going on a hike or a bike ride. But it was already dark, so that was out.

"Indoor skiing?" she speculated, simultaneously thrilled and anxious. She'd never tried it before and suspected she'd be terrible at it but was excited by the thought of giving it a go.

"No," he immediately replied, and her enthusiasm dropped. A second later, it peaked again.

"An escape room! Are we doing an escape room?"

This time, a smile flickered on his lips.

"No, it's not that. But if you'd like a hint, I'll give you one."

Did she want one? It would hurry things up.

"Okay, then."

He ran his tongue across his lips before speaking.

"Okay. We're going to be in a room."

"A room? That's it?"

"Yes."

"That has to be the worst clue possible!" she laughed. A second later, he was laughing, too. It was as if a spell had been broken and things were back to normal again. He still wouldn't tell her where they were going, but at least the tension had gone, and in its place, a sense of excitement bubbled anew and then surged when Holly found out where they actually were going.

He was right. It was a room. A large room full of obstacles, neon lights and smoke machines

"Laser Quest!"

"You once mentioned you'd never got to do it as a child. That you'd missed out on a couple of chances because ... well, you know."

"Because we couldn't afford it," she finished, to save him the embarrassment.

"I thought maybe now you'd like to give it a go."

Holly found herself rendered speechless, partly by the fact he'd remembered what she'd considered such a simple, throw-away comment, and partly because of the way she still felt about missing out on all those treats that other children had so often taken for granted.

"This was a bad idea, wasn't it?" he said, suddenly looking ashen. "You hate the idea, don't you? I'm sorry. I just thought that—"

"It's perfect," she said, her voice quivering. "It's absolutely brilliant."

His face broke into a relieved smile.

"You're sure?"

"I am. Now, who are we shooting?"

The teams were four against four. A couple in their early twenties joined them and together they faced off against a group of teenagers. Teenagers who, it appeared, were pro laser taggers.

"Behind you!" Holly yelled for the umpteenth time, frantically waving her gun in the air.

"I'm got! I'm got!" Ben called back.

I'm got, quickly became the catchphrase of every member of their team. By the time they were done, Holly was dripping with sweat, her hair plastered to her scalp.

"I can't believe how good they were," she said, as they stepped out into the street, the evening air seeming even cooler than normal against her over-heated skin. "Did you see the girl leap off that bridge?"

"I leapt off a box. I feel that was pretty impressive."

"You jumped off a step and nearly twisted your ankle. She literally swung on the underside of the overpass."

"It was a pretty high step," he protested, with a mock huff. "And the reason I nearly twisted my ankle was because I was trying to block you from getting shot, if you recall."

"How could I forget heroics like that?" she grinned back.

It felt like she'd been grinning all night. So much so, that her cheeks actually ached.

They ate dinner in Cheltenham too, at a sushi restaurant off the High Street, so small that they had to wait outside until a table became available.

"Sorry, they don't let you book," he explained, glancing nervously through the window yet again. "We can go somewhere else, if you'd prefer."

"I don't mind waiting," she replied. "Besides, you said it was good here, right?"

"I like it."

"And you do have exceptional taste."

"I like to think so."

"I think I'm evidence of that."

His cheeks coloured as he finally caught onto the fact that she was flirting with him. Or at least, attempting to. The truth was it still felt odd to her. It wasn't that she didn't find him attractive. In fact, if anything, all the fun they'd had that night had made her realise just how much she did, and the conversation was flowing like they were old friends. But as much as she pretended otherwise, she did share Jamie's worry about what would happen if this didn't work out. How would it be with Jamie and Caroline on nights the four of them got together, if she and Ben ended messily? Still, she'd spent almost her whole adult life worrying about all the *what ifs* that could be waiting around the corner, and she was done with that. She was living her best life now, doing the things that made her truly happy and tonight that was very definitely spending time with Ben.

The restaurant door swung open into the night, bringing with it a blast of warm air and the sound of laughter and chatter from inside. A couple, arms around each other's waists, stepped outside. The door was just swinging shut again when a waitress caught it and pushed it open again.

"We've got a table ready for you now," she said.

Ben took the door from her and stepped back, holding it for Holly.

"After you," he said.

CHAPTER THREE

*T*he sushi was sublime, as was the conversation, which was full of laughter and reminiscences of their shared secondary school experience, although Holly had no memories of Ben there, whatsoever.

Because he was driving and couldn't drink, she opted for a virgin cosmopolitan, not that it made any difference to her enjoyment of the occasion. Giggling fits constantly erupted from their table, and it was only at the end of the evening that she realised her chair had shifted and she was sitting with her knee touching his. It felt completely normal to be so close to him. In fact, everything about the night felt natural. Added to which, each time his hand accidentally brushed against hers, her pulse skyrocketed.

"Sorry guys, we're closing up now," their waiter said, looking apologetic. Behind him, at the bar, the only other member of staff still present was yawning and rubbing his eyes.

Holly glanced down at her watch.

"Wow, it's five past eleven."

"We should head home," Ben said. "I know how busy Saturdays are for you. I probably shouldn't have kept you out so late. I'm sorry."

"Don't apologise. I've had a wonderful time."

"Me too. I've had a lot of fun," he said.

His eyes met hers and she felt a fluttering start somewhere behind her belly button.

After splitting the bill, at her insistence, they ambled back to the car park. It felt like she should put her hand in his, but the pavements were narrow and walking like that would mean one of them would be in the road. Then again, it wasn't like there was much traffic at that time of night. She quickened her step a little to move alongside him, stretching out her fingers to reach for his, only to draw them back at the last moment. No, if he wanted to hold her hand, then he would. As they reached the car park, his hands were sunk deep in his pockets, sadly.

They spent the journey back to Bourton in companionable silence, conversation replaced by a string of eighties hits drifting from the radio.

Unable to stop herself from yawning, Holly clicked her neck from side to side.

"Everything all right?" he asked.

She covered her mouth and yawned again.

"I think maybe I need to do a bit more exercise, if running around with a load of teenagers like that wears me out so much. It's a bit embarrassing."

"You and me both. I can already feel the muscles in my shoulders seizing up."

"Perhaps, next time, we should go for something more relaxing. Like a spa day."

He wrinkled his nose.

"I'm not sure if sitting in a hot tub of man soup would achieve that," he commented.

"Man soup?" she laughed, but now that the phrase and image had entered her head, it was a hard to shift them. Bodies bobbing up and down in a big bowl of steaming water. Yup, man soup felt like a pretty accurate description.

Had it been a normal date situation, he would have dropped her off at home, or she would have made her own way back to her house, but the fact that their front doors were within feet of each other, meant that when Ben drew into his driveway and cut the engine, Holly was left wondering exactly what was going to happen to next. He wasn't going to walk her to her front door, was he? That seemed ridiculous. Then again, he had picked her up there, and it didn't feel any sillier than sitting in the car like a pair of teenagers.

With the radio now off, silence engulfed them for the first time. Only one question was floating through her mind. Was he going to kiss her? That normally happened after a successful evening, didn't it? She'd spent so long out of the dating loop, she wasn't sure. Besides, did she even want him to kiss her? Or maybe she should be the one to kiss him. But she'd taken the initiative like that with Giles and look how that ended—with him sprinting out the door.

Ben didn't look like he'd be rushing anywhere, right now. He hadn't even undone his seat belt. But maybe seeing her aggressive, competitive side on display against a group of teenagers with laser guns earlier, had convinced him that she wasn't relationship material. If that were the case, then why hadn't he got out of the damned car yet? What was he waiting for?

"I had a really nice time tonight," she said, feeling that one of them had to say something.

"I did too," he replied, but he seemed tense.

"We should do it again."

"We should do it again."

Their words came out simultaneously, as did the laughter that followed. They both seemed uncertain where this was going.

"It should be my choice," she blurted, in an attempt to fill another silence.

"Sorry?"

"The date. I don't mean if we go on another. I'd like to do this again. I already said that didn't I? I mean I'll choose where we go next. If that's all right with you?"

Great, she thought, wanting to gag herself right there and then. As if the end of the evening wasn't proving awkward enough, she was now babbling like an idiot.

"That would be great," he replied. "Next week?"

"Okay, next weekend then."

Yet another silence. How many of these were they going to have to endure? she wondered. Maybe that's what it seemed like to him—an endurance test. Oh God, how could something go from spectacular to train wreck in just a few seconds?

"Okay," she said, again. "I'll see you before then though, obviously. I mean we do live next door and we walk to work together. If you still want to, that is?" (Oh good Lord.)

"Of course."

"Okay, so I'll see you tomorrow?"

"See you tomorrow."

There was nothing left to say. It was now or never. Either she took the plunge and kissed him or she needed to get out of the car. One second passed. Then another.

"Holly …" he started, just as she hurriedly opened the door and jumped out onto the gravel pathway.

A moment later, he too jumped out and bounded around the car towards her.

"Holly," he tried again.

She stopped, holding her breath. Turning to face him, her heart was thudding against her rib cage.

"Yes?"

He took one step forwards, then another. After three steps, he was only inches away from her. Close enough for her to smell the wasabi from dinner.

"Good night," he said, then leaned in and kissed her on both cheeks, before turning away, unlocking his door and stepping inside, before she'd had a chance to utter a response.

CHAPTER FOUR

*J*amie was still up, ready and waiting for all the gossip.

"So how was Laser Quest?" she asked, accosting Holly in the hallway before she'd even removed her shoes.

"You knew?"

"Of course, I knew. You don't think I'd let Ben take you somewhere without running his plan past me first, did you? I thought it was a sweet idea, choosing something you'd always wanted to do."

"It was. It was really sweet."

"And the rest of the date …? You two looked quite cosy out there."

It was only when she stretched out her hand that Holly realised she'd been holding a glass of wine ready for her. She hesitated. It was half eleven, with work the next morning. What the heck? She took it and gulped down a large mouthful.

"It was good. Great, actually. I think."

Jamie's brows furrowed.

"Great, you *think?* What does that mean?"

"It means I think it was great. I enjoyed myself. We had fun."

She didn't know how much detail to go into, although it was obvious her friend would badger Ben later, if she didn't satisfy her thirst for information. While she contemplated how she could bring up the issue of the lack of kissing or hand holding, Jamie was already in with her next question.

"So, are you going on another date or not?"

She was relieved this was a question she could actually answer with confidence.

"We are. Next weekend. Maybe Sunday. Ben won't be working, and that's the easiest day for me to get Caroline to cover the shop. The only problem is, it's my turn to pick what we do."

Jamie's eyes glinted with mischief.

"I believe I can help you think of something entertaining," she winked.

"I thought you weren't even sure you wanted us to date?"

"Well, if you're going to do it, I might as well have some say in it. Plus, I'm pretty good at planning. Tell me, what sort of thing do you have in mind?"

What did she? Nothing. That was the truth of the matter. A perfect second date was what she needed to come up with. But the Cotswolds in October didn't exactly lend itself to the same sort of exciting and interesting options you'd have in London. Regardless, she was confident that she'd think of something that would blow him out of the water.

*T*he air was rich with the familiar aroma of fresh fudge and Parma violets.

"You do know we've had customers, don't you?"

It had been non-stop all day, people in and out as if on a conveyor belt. Many of the jars needed topping up and there were gaps on the shelves. When she looked up from her phone, she saw Drey, her part-timer, glowering at her in what seemed very much like a reversal of roles, considering Holly was the boss.

"You've been glued to that thing the entire time I've been here," the teenager complained.

"I'm trying to find something," she said with a huff, shoving her phone back into her pocket. "Besides, there aren't any here now."

"That's because I've served them all. And now I need to restock, which means I'll have to leave you in charge of the till."

"Last time I checked, I was the owner of this place actually, you know."

"Yes, one who spends all her time daydreaming about her new boyfriend." Drey smirked, arching an eyebrow. "So, how did the date with Mr Bank Manager go, anyway? I'm guessing badly from the mood you've been in all day."

That girl was such a smart-arse. When Holly had first met her, she'd been going through a goth/punk stage, with dyed hair and heavy eyeliner. Her style had started to lighten up a little, recently. She was still all in with the brightly coloured hair, but there was a definite mellowing in her clothing choices, less angry. In fact, the other week, she'd been dressed almost totally in pastels.

Appearances aside, she'd been a godsend, to her and the

shop. Not that she'd realised it when they'd first met. In fact, she'd been on the point of calling the police to have her arrested for shoplifting. As it turned out, Drey was as passionate about keeping *Just One More* in business as Holly. She'd been doing most of the heavy lifting, keeping the place going for months before Holly had taken over from Maud. Darling Maud, who'd never quite managed to retain her love of the place after her wife, Agnes, had passed away but who, just like Holly, had been lucky enough to have Drey there to help. Which was brilliant, apart from on days like this when she insisted on sticking her nose in where Holly definitely didn't want it.

"No, the date did not go badly, actually. It went very well. And how did you even know we'd been on one, for that matter? I certainly didn't tell you."

"Caroline told me. Her and Jamie were taking bets on who'd cancel this time."

"Seriously?"

"In their defence, it did take you months to get your act together."

This was quite true. The hard part was behind them now, but trying to think of something good to do for their second date had her stumped. She'd thought of little else in the last four days but had come up completely empty. Now she only had another four left. It didn't help that Ben seemed to know she was struggling, either. That morning, as they'd walked to work, he tried to goad her into confessing.

"There's no shame in admitting it," he'd said, when they'd reached the riverside. "Don't worry."

"I'm not worried," she'd replied, rather curtly. "Actually, the only thing I'm concerned about is that you're going to be upset when you realise that your date wasn't as good as mine."

"Is that so?"

This was as close to flirting as the two of them had come these last few days, but it was definitely flirting. The fact that he was continuing to talk about a second date and was still walking to and from work with her each day, felt like a good sign. So what that they hadn't held hands or kissed on their first date? It wasn't as if she'd been particularly forthcoming herself. In fact, maybe she'd given him the wrong signals. Or perhaps, knowing about her previous relationship history, he hadn't wanted to rush her into anything. Yes, that would be it.

"So?" Drey asked, startling her from her reverie as she tipped aniseed balls noisily onto the scales in front of them. "Have you got any idea where you're going to take him yet?"

She was about to say something defensive, when the words disappeared and all that left her was a sigh. Wearily, she stepped from behind the counter and reached up for the jar of fizzy cola bottles. She removed the lid and tipped a couple into her hand, then threw them into her mouth.

"No, I don't," she said, chewing. "I don't have a clue what to do. But it's got to be really good and that he won't have done before. But not too far away."

Drey stopped what she was doing and leant her elbows on the counter.

"You should let me help. I'm excellent at coming up with things to do. It's a fact."

Holly groaned inwardly. What was it with people trying to take over her life? Didn't they think she was capable of running it herself?

"Do you want it to be serious, or a laugh?" Drey continued.

"Fun," she immediately replied, remembering how much her cheeks had ached after the Laser Quest. "Definitely fun."

"And you could drive there? Travel a bit if you needed to?"

"I suppose so," she answered.

"Great," she said, a smirk spreading across her face. "Now, how do you feel about getting wet?"

CHAPTER FIVE

*H*olly was excited. This was going to be a brilliant date. Possibly even better than getting shot at by a bunch of random teenagers and then eating amazing sushi. And the weather, which had been her biggest concern, was perfect for it. They could still do it in the rain, the chap had said when she'd made the booking. It would just be a bit trickier. Some people actually preferred it that way, he'd assured her, although she suspected that was just a sales pitch. She didn't want them to spend their afternoon like that. Thankfully, they weren't going to, although it had been a close call. Thursday to Saturday, it had been wet from dawn 'til dusk and she'd gone to bed each night with her stomach anxiously churning. But when she'd opened her eyes that Sunday morning, it turned out to be the clearest day of the entire week.

"You'll need a change of clothes," she'd told Ben the night before, as they'd stood together on the patch of gravel between their two homes. "And you need to be okay about getting the first set pretty dirty."

She'd picked her words carefully, wanting to make sure he didn't get too many clues.

"Is there anything else I should know?" he'd asked.

"Nope," she'd replied, unable to suppress a grin. "Just come prepared to have fun, that's all."

He'd nodded, his eyes locking on hers. "I think I can manage that."

They were leaving just after midday. Caroline had taken the afternoon shift at the shop, joining Drey for what was almost certainly going to be a hectic time.

"Let us know how it goes," Caroline said, taking down a jar of liquorice jellies. "I want the complete lowdown tomorrow."

"Will do," she replied, butterflies already swarming in her stomach.

"You're going to love it," Drey added, enthusiastically. "And take some mints with you. You know, in case you decide to snog."

She felt guilty leaving them to it and they practically had to push her out the door. They stood there and waved her off.

She groaned, as she checked the sky for clouds once more. There really were no secrets in Bourton, she thought. With that in mind, she wondered if Ben knew how much their friends were itching to see if they actually managed to make this work or not? Like there wasn't enough pressure to be dealing with already.

Perhaps she would have felt a little better had she been able to dress up for the occasion a little, but there was just no point. She'd packed a dress for afterwards, though. Something nice that she could wear when they went for food. She'd located a couple of pubs close to the activity that they could choose from, based on how hungry they were.

With a flurry of excitement hastening her every step, she was surprised to find that Ben was already outside the house waiting for her when she arrived home, despite it still being five minutes before their arranged meeting time.

"Let me just run in and grab my stuff," she said, pulling her keys out of her pocket. "You've got your change of clothes, have you?"

He sniffed, indignantly. "You know you've already sent me a text message reminding me this morning."

"Is that a yes or a no?" she asked.

"It's a yes, and don't you need to get a move on? I thought you wanted to leave by one. It's two minutes to."

"It's okay. I've factored in plenty of extra time. You pick the radio station," she said, throwing him her car keys. "I'll grab my bag and the snacks."

"Snacks?" he said, looking momentarily concerned. "How far are we going?"

"What does it matter? Every good outing must start with snacks. Didn't you know?"

Then, offering what she hoped was a flirtatious wink, but more likely looked like an awkward blink, she disappeared into the house.

Her activity clothes and shoes were ready in a rucksack by the front door. After giving her hair the most manic of quick brushes and checking her appearance in the mirror, she added sweets to the bag and headed back out to the car. This was her turn to drive and his to wonder where they were going.

"Time to get started," she said with a grin.

They began their journey heading up the Roman road that led past Northleach and Chedworth and dozens of other little villages that she still didn't know the name of, despite having lived in the area her entire childhood. Since moving back, she'd wanted to get out and about more. Perhaps cycle to some of the nearby places of interest, like she and Ben had on a trip to Lower Slaughter during her early days at the shop. But running the business had turned out to be all-consuming, even with Drey coming in several extra afternoons a week. Half days off, like this, were as rare as hens' teeth. On her one regular weekday off, when Caroline took the helm, Holly found herself having to catch up on paperwork and household chores or simply sleeping off the tiredness that came from being on her feet all day. Not that she regretted her choice. She loved it. She just wished she had a little more free time and a bit more energy. Still, this was nice. Maybe she and Ben could make a habit of going out for drives when she finished work on a Sunday, while it was still light enough. She could even pack a late picnic. Or just bring sweets from the shop to snack on.

"I almost forgot," she said, do you want to open up the rucksack on the back seat?

Ben reached over, pulled the bag onto his lap and unzipped it.

"Lemon bonbons?" he said, throwing her a grin.

"And sherbet lemons and lemon super-sours. Help yourself."

"You know I never say no to lemon-flavoured sweets," he said.

"I do. Open them up and put them in the middle, would you? I fancy a bonbon."

Being in the car next to him felt so easy, so relaxed, and more than once, she found herself wishing he'd rest his hand on top of hers on the gearstick, the way Dan used to when they went out together. That was in the early days, of course, when they'd been happy and before he'd started criticising her driving, muttering that she was going too fast or too slow or telling her to watch out for random obstacles. This wasn't like that, though. Ben was nothing like Dan to start with. Her left hand remained on its own.

As they reached the roundabout at Cirencester and turned off, she hoped he wouldn't notice what was on the signpost. South Cerney was home to the Cotswold Water Park and the biggest lakes in the region. When she'd been growing up, there'd been various school trips, with the standard water-sport offerings of kayaking, canoeing or building rafts out of old oil drums and bits of rope, none of which her parents could ever afford for her to go on.

She had seen online that, in recent years, the place had evolved into something truly remarkable. There was still the kayaking and canoeing, of course, but now there were other things, like paddle-boarding and windsurfing and even wake-boarding, where you get pulled along by a massive cable. She thought it looked rather good fun, although she doubted she'd have the upper body strength for it. Maybe next time they came, they could try it. Today, she wanted to make sure they'd finish the activity she'd booked with plenty of time to go some-where nice to eat, afterwards.

When they came to the next roundabout where, once again, the brown tourist sign for the water park was on display, she realised that Ben had stopped speaking.

"Is everything all right?" she asked, taking the slip road and the first of the lakes came into view. "You've gone very quiet."

"Have I?" he replied, his eyes locked on the road. "I'm just thinking."

"Oh, right," she said.

The lakes looked truly impressive from here. Light glinted off the water, which reflected the autumn tones of the surrounding trees. Ben, she noted, was staring at them intently. A little too intently. A surge of nerves flooded through her.

"You are okay with water, aren't you?" she asked, suddenly panicking that she might have missed an exceptionally important factor in her date planning.

"Water?"

"You know, that wet stuff. You can swim, can't you?"

Whatever response she'd been expecting, it wasn't the high-pitched, nasal laugh that came from him now.

"I'm a grown man. A fully grown man. A responsible adult."

"So, is that a yes?"

His eyes, still fixed on the road, appeared to be almost bulging.

"It's been a while," he said. "How much swimming is involved, exactly?"

"None, well, hopefully none."

A sigh of relief came from his lips.

"Oh, that's okay then. What exactly are we doing?"

At that moment, she slowed the car to take a tight corner, and it came into view as the roadside trees ended. It was bigger than she'd expected. Higher and wider. Pretty damned massive, in fact. Pillars and platforms of blue and green inflated plastic, created an over-water obstacle course the size of a small palace. The photos really hadn't done it justice. They'd made it look little more than a large bouncy castle. This was immense.

Dozens of people were currently on it, in the process of racing from one end to the other, and they all seemed to be doing really well. The course went from a starting platform to a second, over an inflatable bridge. The next section consisted of large inflated balls suspended above a narrow walkway. As they attempted to navigate this bridge, the balls swung back and forth. The man in the lead hesitated and was overtaken. The new race leader made it another two steps, before one of the balls sideswiped him, sending him high into the air and then back down to the lake with a huge splash.

"That," Holly said, feeling half terror, half excitement, "is what we're doing."

CHAPTER SIX

"*I*f you don't feel comfortable doing this, you really don't have to," Holly said, for the umpteenth time. "We can just get lunch. There are some great restaurants around here. In fact, there's a pub less than two miles away which has incredible reviews. It's where I thought we'd go afterwards. But we can go now, if you'd rather."

Ben shook his head. "Are you kidding? This looks … brilliant. Brilliant. Look at all the people having fun."

She gazed out at the obstacle course. There were two families on it now. One of them was well over halfway around, screaming with delight as they pulled each other back by their T-shirts, trying to overtake. The other family was—well, she tried not to dwell on them—dripping wet and sobbing. And that was just the adults.

This wasn't eliciting quite the reaction she'd hoped for. Even as she confirmed their booking, he remained transfixed on the Wet-and-Wild-Water-Wipeout course, swallowing frequently and wincing each time someone fell in.

"Okay guys. Gather around for the safety briefing, please."

The activities centre was in a large wooden boat shed that had various kayaks and canoes stacked up along the walls. There were several other types of boats that Holly wasn't familiar with, too, although judging by the way the young woman in the Water-Centre uniform was tapping her foot impatiently, it probably wasn't the ideal time to ask.

Sunday, Holly was coming to realise, was probably not the best day to choose for an adult visit. Everyone else standing there waiting, apart from the member of staff, looked even younger than Drey and they were enthusiastically ignoring the woman.

"Guys," she shouted again, above the racket. "Do I need to remind you that if I don't think you've taken this safety information on board properly, then I'm within my rights to stop you from going on the course? And you will *not* get a refund."

The group quickly fell silent, although their sullen looks made their annoyance plain.

"Okay, so the first thing is, you have to wear a life jacket, no matter how strong a swimmer you think you are. So, please bear with me while I find you all the correct sizes."

One by one, she handed them out, starting with the teenagers before reaching Holly and Ben.

"What standard do they meet?" he asked, taking the jacket offered to him.

"Sorry?"

"The life jackets. Do they still meet the old EU standards, or has something else been put in their place? I assume they're fully tested."

"I guess so. They float."

"Okay. Okay."

He nodded repeatedly, swallowing visibly as he checked the

label inside the jacket, before slipping his arms into it and tightening the buckle, then pulling at it several times.

As Holly accepted hers, she was completely distracted by him. She wanted to say something. Check he was definitely happy with it. This was not the enthusiastic reaction he'd had from her when they'd arrived at the laser tag event. In fact, she hadn't seen him look this stressed since she'd knocked him off his bike, all those months ago. But she'd already asked him if he was okay so many times, it had become embarrassing. The last thing she wanted to do was play the nagging girlfriend, particularly as she'd never been like that with Dan, and she wasn't even Ben's girlfriend yet.

With everyone now sporting a suitable life jacket, the young woman stepped back to reiterate the safety rules.

"So, just to go over things one last time. The aim is to enjoy yourself, have fun and try not to get too wet. But if anyone deliberately pushes someone into the water, they will be removed."

A couple of kids gave each other sly looks. In Holly's opinion, that seemed like pretty difficult law to enforce, although she'd heard a klaxon blast several times while they were getting ready. Maybe that had been because someone had broken the rules. All the same, having seen how slippery and wet the whole thing was, she doubted she'd be able to balance well enough to keep herself upright, let alone think about pushing someone else into the water at the same time.

"As I mentioned before, it's a one-way course," the girl continued. "Don't backtrack. Ahead only. And if you are at the front, please keep moving so as not to hold up the others. If you fall in the water, there are ropes to help you get back on. If you don't use them, you're just going to slide back in again. So please, use the ropes. And just one last check that you're all comfortable swimming fifty metres?"

She looked first at the group of teens, who immediately rolled their eyes.

"I've been swimming for the County since I was fourteen," one girl said, tossing her hair back.

"And the rest of you?"

"We've *all* been swimming for the County since we were fourteen."

"Great."

The woman somehow managed to keep a smile in place, despite the annoyingly condescending attitude of the youngsters.

"And are you a county swimmer too?" she asked Holly, her eyes sparkling with good humour.

She must have the patience of a saint, Holly thought, having to deal with kids like this all day.

"No," she replied, "but I can swim fifty metres. Probably not as fast as these guys, though."

"Great. And you?" She turned to Ben. "Everything good here?"

"Of … of course," he stammered.

"Fantastic. Then let's walk down to the start."

The first challenge came before they'd even got onto the course. A floating platform lay between the edge of the lake and the starting point, which they had to traverse before they could begin. The group of county swimmers barely waited for the signal to go before they were racing off onto the platform, then bounding over the first obstacle: a high wall, with ropes to help you climb up the near side and then a slide on the other.

Sensing that Ben didn't want to be crowded, Holly hung back, waiting until everyone was well on their way, before turning to him.

"You want to go first?" she asked.

"After you," he said. Whether he'd actually turned pale, or it was just the reflection of the water, she couldn't be sure, but she hoped it was the second.

"Okay, wish me luck."

Taking a deep breath, she leapt onto the platform which, thankfully, wobbled only slightly.

"It's fine," she said, bouncing over to the wall. "It's good."

Steeling himself, Ben followed her. His feet barely grazed the platform as he landed next to her.

"Impressive," she said.

"I did the long jump at sports day in Year 8."

"That explains it," she laughed. "Right. Ready for the next bit?"

As they scaled the wall side by side, she wondered when she'd last been on anything like this. Then she remembered. A couple she knew had a bouncy castle with a big slide at their wedding reception a few years ago. She'd only had one go, before Dan had insisted it was only for the children and that she and the other adults were making spectacles of themselves. She didn't think that was the case at all, but she didn't want to cause an argument, and so she'd stayed sipping an overpriced glass of wine, watching others careering around and laughing their heads off.

"So, what do you think?" she asked when they reached the top of the wall and prepared for the slide down the other side. "Having fun?"

"Too soon to say, but it's sturdier than I imagined."

"Which I'm taking is a good thing?"

"Maybe. Ask me at the end. I'm a man who likes safety standards. I actually looked into becoming a safety analyst once. I was offered a graduate post after leaving university."

"You know what, that doesn't surprise me at all."

He punched her playfully on the shoulder, his nervous demeanour teetering on a grin. At last! This was more like she'd been hoping it would be.

Over on the other side of the course, two of the county swimmers were already in the water and a third looked about to dive off the trampoline there. Beyond that, rolled the green hills of the Cotswolds, divided into a patchwork of irregular shapes by hedgerows and lines of trees.

"Isn't it a beautiful view from up here," she said blissfully, despite the chaos around them.

"Yes, it is," he replied, but when she turned to him, she discovered he was gazing straight at her not the scenery, and a swarm of butterflies took flight inside. She shifted her position ever so slightly. Surely this was the perfect time to share their first kiss. Ben was beginning to move towards her, too, when the klaxon blasted, destroying the moment.

"No loitering on the stations!"

The young woman's voice was amplified by a megaphone as she yelled from the shore.

"Please keeping moving forwards!"

Pursing her lips, Holly shook her head.

"Okay, I guess we're going down. You ready?"

"After you."

"We can probably do it together."

"It's fine. I wouldn't want to push you off accidentally. It's safer going down one at a time."

Knowing she wouldn't win this, Holly pushed herself off, slid down and bounced at the bottom. There was actually a fair amount of room this side, she found, managing to stop a good-few feet from the edge of the inflatable.

"It's fine!" she yelled up to Ben, who waved back nervously before starting his own descent.

It would be wrong to describe what he did next as sliding. He was on a slide and Holly and the others had definitely slid. He somehow managed to dig his heels into the plastic with such force that she was amazed it didn't burst. So, rather than arriving gracefully at the lower level, his body jerked and bumped down in the most ungainly manner, while the surface emitted a high-pitched screeching sound in protest.

"Well, that was better than expected," he said, breaking into a smile as he hoisted himself up onto his feet. "What's next?"

What was next, was a tubular beam you were meant to walk across. Holly made light work of it as she skipped to the other side. Ben, however, decided to get down and straddle it, then shuffled forwards inch by slow inch. Holly bit down on her lip, trying to suppress her laughter.

"It's wider than you think," she called from the far end. "It's honestly not that hard to do standing up. Give it a try."

"Is there another rule that says I have to stand up to traverse this?" Ben called back.

"I don't think so."

"In that case, I'm quite all right as I am, thank you."

Further obstacles followed. Climbing frames. More slides. Trampolines too.

The county swimmers had already finished one circuit and were coming back behind them on their second, as Holly and Ben tackled another wall. This one leaned back towards them from the vertical, creating an overhang. Here, they'd provided handles to assist you, but it still looked like a tall order – literally. She'd noticed it from the road. It had been the one that had caught her attention from the shore, too. This was the pinnacle of the obstacle course. The ultimate challenge. And they were standing right in front of it.

There was no way she was going to make it, Holly thought. The last time she'd managed monkey bars had been in primary school. While carrying heavy boxes of sweets up and down stairs had probably increased her upper body strength, the last thing she wanted to do was plummet down into the water from the very top. Still, that was all meant to be part of the fun, wasn't it? And they had stayed dry so far. Besides, she could use her feet too on this. It was a case of balance and determination.

This time, she didn't even bother asking Ben if he'd like to go first. She'd attempted everything else before him, and there was no reason to believe this would be any different. Without waiting for any more doubt to creep in, she grabbed the first two handles and lifted herself up, planting her feet firmly against the plastic to give her leverage.

The next hand hold was within easy reach and she soon found herself climbing at pace. Adrenaline surged. Her arms were holding out. She was going to do it! She was going to reach the top of the biggest obstacle in the course!

Feeling increasingly optimistic, she swung for one of the uppermost loops. It was a stretch, but she'd make it. However, as her fingers grasped the plastic, a foot slipped. Only a tiny slip, but it was enough. She flailed about frantically for the next handle, but missed it and spun one handed for a moment, then all strength and hope gone, she plummeted straight down.

She hit the icy surface with a smack and gulped in a mouthful of water in shock. The cold seemed to penetrate all the way to her bones. She could only have been submerged for a couple of seconds, before the buoyancy of the life jacket pulled her up again.

"Holly!" she heard Ben yelling, as she blinked water out of her eyes and coughed repeatedly. "Are you okay?"

He was crouching on all fours, leaning over the edge of the inflatable.

*S*he coughed out a laugh, along with more water. Now she was getting over the initial trauma, she found it wasn't anywhere near as cold as she'd first thought.

"It's actually quite nice. You should come in for a dip."

"I'll take your word for it. Are you getting back on?"

She looked up at the wall.

"Yeah, I think I'll give it another go. I was so close."

"There's a rope here."

As she swam towards it, her determination increased. The shock of the cold water had given her just the rush of energy she needed. Yes, she would definitely make it this time. She grasped onto the rope, ready to yank herself back up.

Maybe it was because she was so busy thinking about the extra force she was going to use to scale the wall this time, or maybe the whole thing was just less substantial than she'd expected, but the moment she tugged on the rope, she knew she'd made a mistake. Knew it but at the same time could do nothing to stop it.

"Ben!" she shouted, trying to warn him, but it was already too late. One moment the plastic base was flat and the next it was tilting alarmingly, sending her back into the water, swiftly followed by a splash, as he joined her.

CHAPTER SEVEN

"*Y*ou know I could have been responsible for you drowning? You should have told me you couldn't swim."

"Of course I wasn't going to tell you that. It's embarrassing. Besides, you'd gone to all the effort of organising the trip. And under normal circumstances, I could see that it would be a very good idea."

Holly appreciated him saying that. It had been, after all, a pretty good idea, if she said so herself.

"Was telling me you couldn't swim less embarrassing than having half the Gloucestershire Under Sixteen County Swimming Team dragging you to shore?"

"Okay, no. Probably not. God, what an idiot."

Ben shook his head which, rather like a dog trying to dry its fur, sent a spray of water droplets over her, then wiped his face with the back of his hand. Thankfully, the place had plenty of spare towels and the young woman had provided them with several. If anything, she looked even more pale than he did, presumably worried that she was going to get into trouble for allowing a non-swimmer onto the course.

He probably hadn't needed four teenagers to rescue him though, Holly had reflected, particularly as his life jacket had functioned perfectly adequately and he'd stayed well afloat. But despite all his protests, they'd all rushed to be the first to reach him. It was a scene no one involved was likely to forget. Ever.

Holly and Ben were now sitting on their borrowed towels on a grassy slope outside the boat shed, watching the next group tackle the course. To be honest, she was a little annoyed that she wasn't going to get the opportunity to tackle the massive over-hanging wall again, but that didn't seem the right thing to bring up in the circumstances.

"I think it's sweet," she said instead, reaching over and squeezing his knee.

"You think it's sweet that I can't swim?"

"No, that you didn't want to tell me. Although I am a little surprised that you can't. I thought that would definitely be some-thing you'd know how to do. You're so outdoorsy, what with all the cycling and everything. I thought you'd be the triathlon type."

"It could be my mother's fault. Actually, it *is* her fault. She's terrified of water. It was probably that incident in Spain, I think."

"So you never went swimming as a child, at all?"

"Our holidays usually consisted of city breaks—train trips exploring Europe, that type of thing. We did lots of hiking, too, although preferably not in areas with lakes. If there any, we could only ever paddle in them."

"And you never wanted to learn as an adult?"

He shook his head again, which sent another spray of water over her.

"It's not that I haven't wanted to. More a question of time, I suppose. My sister learned when she had her own children. She didn't want them to miss out on things like we did, so actually had swimming lessons alongside them. It's just never made it to the top of my priority list."

"That's a pity. It's fun, and it's good for you. Relaxing, too. Well, normally," she added, a little shamefaced. "And there are so many other things you can do once you've learned. I was looking at the wake boarding earlier."

Ben looked back out at the view.

"You are right. They do lessons at the leisure centre in the village. Maybe I'll make enquiries."

He turned to her, water still trickling down his cheeks.

"You know, Holly Berry, you make me want to experience new things. It must be something about your reckless nature."

"I'm not reckless."

"You bought a sweetshop with zero business experience."

"You're never going to let me live that down, are you?"

"Not as long as you know me, which I hope will be a very long time."

The fluttering was back and had reached a whole new level. He was looking at her, shoulders tilted forwards, like he was about to go in for the kiss. Or maybe it was just the best angle to stop the water from running into his eyes. She wasn't sure. But the feeling that this was the moment, had returned, and she felt herself leaning towards him. He was leaning in more, too, and then … he rocked himself to his feet and stood up.

"So, shall we get changed and head off?" he asked, throwing a towel over his shoulder. "I think I'm ready for food."

Holly blinked. Had she misread him? She must have. Suppressing the fluttering in her chest and a definite feeling of embarrassment, she stood up, too.

"Food sounds good," she said.

*T*he meal was delicious. A proper pub, with chunky chips covered in salt and gravy thick enough to stand a spoon upright in. One hour flew past and then another, and when Caroline messaged to say that all was good at the shop, and she had cashed up, Holly saw no reason to rush back. So they had gone for a stroll around Cirencester, with its impressive Abbey and higgledy-piggledy High Street.

"I was offered a job here a couple of years ago," Ben said, as they passed a large bank. "Head hunted to manage the place."

"That's pretty impressive. Why didn't you take it?"

"I did think about it, but I was happy with the life I'd got, you know, being able to walk to work each morning, knowing all the clients. I didn't like the prospect of starting from scratch again. And I didn't want to move from Bourton, so that would have meant commuting. Why change a good thing, right?"

"So, you don't think you'll ever leave the bank?"

"I wouldn't say never, but I don't have any plans to. Would you leave the sweet shop?"

Holly offered him the most withering look she could manage.

"Are you serious? After all the effort it took to get it?"

She dropped her eyes and let out a wistful sigh. The truth was, she'd stopped thinking beyond the here and now and she liked it that way. All that time she'd spent with Dan she'd focused on what they *would* do when they bought a house, when they had children, when they got married, when, when, when. And when that bubble burst, she'd felt cheated out of a future she'd spent so long planning. But at some point, she would have to start thinking more long term. After all, she doubted Jamie would still want her as a housemate when they were in their nineties. Although things hadn't worked out with Dan, that didn't mean she'd given up on all her dreams.

"I suppose, like you said, you should never say never, but I bought it because I could see myself growing old in it, like Agnes and Maud. Maybe, one day, having a couple kids who could help me out behind the counter when they were old enough."

"Free child labour. Excellent forward planning," Ben joked.

Despite the humour, a thought popped into her head. It was probably far too soon to bring it up, but it was there now, and if they were actually going to become a couple, she was going to have to ask at some point.

"So, what about you?" she said, trying to sound as nonchalant as possible. "Do you want children?"

He didn't reply immediately, and she found her stomach churning in anticipation.

"I don't know. There was a time when I was absolutely certain that my future would involve them. But now …" He pressed his lips together.

"What changed?" she asked.

After what Jamie had hinted at, she was certain there must have been something to cause his change of heart. He shrugged his shoulders.

"Life, I guess. I look at my sister and her three, and she does an amazing job, but it's full on. Every day. It's not easy and doesn't seem to let up at all as they get older. There are always new things to worry about. It's gone from stressing about whether they're eating enough to whether or not they're going to be able to get a job one day or if they're safe on a night out. I feel for her. And I sometimes doubt I'd be responsible enough to have them."

"Really?" She raised her eyebrows. "You're the most responsible person I've met in my entire life. If *you* don't think you should have children, I'm pretty sure every adult in the whole world should stop procreating. Wow, you not responsible enough for children? I dread to imagine what you'd think of me having one, then."

It was just a throw-away remark that slipped out without any thought, but when she looked up, she found him looking at her utterly seriously.

"I think you'd be fantastic," he said, slipping his hand into hers. "I have no doubt that you would make the most wonderful mother."

Heat rushed to her cheeks, turning them a bright fuchsia. Had Dan ever told her that? She was sure he must have said something along those lines at some point, but it certainly never felt like this. And taking her hand like that at the same time, too. This was a definite signal, wasn't it? Either way, she didn't let go.

They continued to stroll around Cirencester for another hour, before stopping for hot chocolate, complete with whipped cream and marshmallows. Finding a quiet bench by the Abbey they sat and watched as people milled about most, it seemed, dressed in the requisite Barbour jacket and Hunter wellies. A sports car went by and she couldn't help but think of Giles. The first time he'd taken her out had been in his very fancy vintage model to a very fancy restaurant. Yet she would forgo any of that luxury for another day like this.

It was only once they were heading back to her car that she realised they were no longer holding hands. She couldn't remember when they'd stopped. It was obviously before they'd bought the drinks but how much before? Did it really matter? No, of course it didn't. He was taking things slowly, that was all.

Conversation flowed on the way home to Bourton, and every now and again, his hand would rest on hers on the gear stick or he would catch her eye and smile and she would once again feel a surge of happiness. And while she wasn't certain, she couldn't help but think that he was feeling the same way.

As they pulled into their shared driveway and she cut the engine, her pulse was hammering loud enough to burst an eardrum.

"I had a great day," Ben said, speaking first. "It's always a great day when we're together. Have you noticed that?"

"I have."

"I think I'd quite like it if we had a few more."

"I would too."

This wasn't like last time, Holly thought. If she kissed him now, he would surely kiss her back. She was ninety-seven percent certain of it. She just needed to pluck up the courage to do it. Or did she? He was closer now, a nervous smile on his face. She could smell the chocolate from earlier, which fortunately was stronger than the underlying scent of lake water still clinging to his skin. A grin was making her cheeks ache. Any second now, she was going to kiss Ben Thornbury. Could she manage that while she was smiling so much? She inched towards him, about to close her eyes for the magical moment, when something moved in the periphery of her vision outside the car. Turning, her jaw dropped.

"Dan!" she exclaimed.

"I think you mean Ben," Ben said, moving back with a look of pained confusion on his face.

"No, I mean Dan. He's here."

CHAPTER EIGHT

*H*er break up with Dan had been far from amicable, predominantly because she'd caught him in their bed with another woman. They'd been together for over six years, and he'd been the first man she'd ever lived with. The only man she'd ever lived with. And only the second boyfriend she'd ever introduced to her parents. He was the one she'd planned on spending the rest of her life with, putting everything else on hold to save up enough money so they could buy their *forever home* together. But this had been months and months ago, and apart from a few weeks of unsuccessful telephone calls, apologising and begging her to come back, followed by a fair few angry ones, demanding that she give him money for the upkeep of the flat she wasn't even living in anymore, all communication had ceased. No text messages. No voice mails. Nothing. And yet there he was, standing on her driveway with his hands in his pockets.

Holly whipped away from Ben, fumbling with her seat belt, which she finally managed to undo. With trembling hands, she pushed open the car door and got out.

"Dan?"

A look of relief spread across her ex's face as he took a step towards her. "Phew, Hols. I was starting to worry I'd got the wrong place."

She couldn't move. She couldn't speak. The trembling had been replaced by a feeling of numbness and her throat had turned the sort of dry that could only be fixed with a really stiff drink. All she could do was stare at him. Dan was here, on her driveway, smiling at her. He was actually looking rather good. His hair was neatly cut and swept in a wave to one side, and he was wearing a shirt she didn't recognise. His shoes were polished, and he seemed to look a little broader around the shoulders, too, not like he'd put on weight, more like he'd been working out. Finally, after trying twice unsuccessfully to clear her throat, she managed to utter something that was almost intelligible.

"But ... how ... did you know where I live?"

The last time they'd been in contact, she was staying at Maud's cottage, and she hadn't even told him that. As far as she was aware, she'd never even mentioned that she'd returned to Bourton.

"Oh, I just asked around a bit."

He sounded casual, although he was digging his toes into the ground, nervously.

"Asked around a bit. What does that mean?"

A slight colour rose to his cheeks.

"Well, I tried your parents. I'd guessed they'd still live in the same place, so that was cool, but I'll be honest, Hols, they were rather hostile. I don't remember them being quite so rude."

"You went to my parents?"

"It does happen, I know," he continued, obviously not listening. "People get ruder when they get older. Happened with my Nan, too. Changed, you know."

Holly was struggling to keep her mind on track. Had Dan always been so evasive, she wondered?

"So, my parents told you where I live?"

"Well, no. They told me to message you, but then that would have ruined the surprise, wouldn't it? And I didn't want to do that. You remember Jean, who I used to work with? She'd mentioned that you were running a sweet shop. She'd seen you on Facebook, I think. I knew how crazy you were about that old place before. I always found it a bit weird, actually. So I went there. I was amazed I actually remembered where it was. I'd forgotten how small it was. It's cute. I get why you'd want to work in a place like that. Not as a career, but as a kid. Anyway, I asked a woman there."

"Caroline? Caroline told you where I live?"

Holly's head was starting to ache, partially because of the shock of Dan turning up out of the blue like this but just as much at this unwelcome news. Caroline knew all too well how she felt about him. They'd all been friends at secondary school and though they'd lost touch over the years, she'd been the first person Holly had reconnected with on returning to Bourton. It was hard to believe that she would do something like that.

"Is Caroline the woman behind the counter?" he asked.

"Yes."

"Then no. Definitely not. When I told her my name, she got strangely angry. A bit like your parents, actually. I told her that I'd deleted the message you'd sent me with your address, but she still wouldn't tell me."

"What message? I never sent you my address."

"But she didn't know that, did she?"

Holly squeezed the bridge of her nose and tried to ignore

the throbbing that had started up in her head. It was bad enough that he was here, but the lengths he'd gone to, to find her, were bizarre.

"So how *did* you find out where I live?" she asked. "Can you please just tell me exactly how you tracked me down?"

A self-satisfied smile spread across his face as he pushed his chest out a little. Yes, he'd definitely got bigger since she'd last seen him. More muscular.

"It was luck really, I suppose. I was waiting outside the shop, thinking you might just turn up, despite the fact that miserable woman had said you wouldn't, when some old woman asked if I was okay. Well, I spun her the same line I'd tried inside, you know, about having deleted the message and whatnot, and what do you know? She pointed me in this direction. Couldn't remember what the number it was, but she knew the colour of the door. Said it was one of the semis with a shared driveway. I checked all the way down the road but figured it could only be this one and came back to wait, and what do you know? I was right! Great, eh?"

Bloody marvellous, Holly thought. No doubt the old lady thought she was doing a good deed. Who it could have been was anyone's guess. Everyone in Bourton seemed to know everyone else's business, not to mention their address, date of birth, long-lost relatives and probably whether they had a wheat intolerance.

"Is everything all right, Holly?"

Ben was now out of the car, too and standing on the other side, a look of concern on his face.

"I … I … this is Dan."

"Dan Hampton," Dan said, stretching out his hand.

"Ben Thornbury," Ben said, making no effort to come

around the car and shake the other man's hand. "Holly, are you okay? Do you need anything from me?"

She swallowed, repeatedly. Somehow, in all the rigmarole of Dan getting his story out, she'd entirely forgotten about Ben being there. She'd forgotten about how, only moments earlier, they were going to have their first kiss. She had the sudden urge to hit Dan with her best left hook and follow it up with a kick to the shin, hard enough to send him flying all the way back to London. But she didn't feel that would make a great impression on Ben. Besides, her head was still pounding, and she wasn't sure her aim would be up to the task.

"It's fine. Really. I'm fine."

Ben's eyes lingered on hers in a way that made her wonder if he could actually read the chaos in her mind. She didn't want him to go. She wanted him to stay right there with her. But at that same time, she didn't want to appear unable to handle the situation, which she most definitely could. Yes, she and Dan had parted on bad terms, but she knew him well enough to deal with anything he had to offer.

"It's fine," she said again, forcing herself to smile. "You go on inside, and I'll give you a call later."

"I'll be in all evening. Just knock on my door if you need me?"

She could hear his reluctance at leaving her. Would it be wrong to kiss him now? she wondered. Yes probably. The temptation to reach out and take his hand was so strong that she had to clench her fists to her sides. The sooner he was gone, the sooner she could use every expletive known to man to find out exactly what the hell Dan was doing on her doorstep and get rid of him, once and for all.

"You go on," she repeated.

This time, he didn't question her. He hesitated for a

moment longer, then opened the back of the car and retrieved his bag of sodden clothes. He looked at her one last time and then walked to his door and opened it.

"Remember, I'm just here if you need anything," he said, hovered a moment longer, then disappeared inside. As the door closed behind him, Dan's smile widened.

"Seems like a nice neighbour," he said. "Did you give him a lift from somewhere?"

"Sorry?"

Her eyes were still on Ben's front door.

"I guess you weren't working today. I thought you shop-keepers worked every hour you could. I guess you've got it easy. So, are you going to invite me in, then?"

He dug his hands back into his pockets, shifting his feet in the gravel driveway and making little divots in the stones.

"I could do with a cuppa. It's been quite a long day. Wasn't exactly a two-minute job getting here, you know. I decided to take the train. Thought it would be easier. But the bus service isn't up to much around here, and then there was a rainstorm. I think I've just about dried out. I packed some spare clothes and everything but didn't have anywhere to get changed. Never been keen on doing that in public toilets, as you know."

That was when the real difference between this Dan and the one she remembered struck her. It wasn't the clothes or the physique. He was rambling, just like she always did when she got nervous. But he never did anything that made him feel uncomfortable, including putting out the rubbish, or clearing dishes waiting in the sink to be washed.

"What are you doing here, Dan?" she said, finding her voice again. "Is it money? Do you think I owe you for something? I thought you eventually agreed that you'd pay the rent on our old place yourself. And I'm afraid it's too late to change your mind. I've sunk every penny I had into the business."

"I'm not here for money."

"Then why?"

The divots had now become holes, and she made a mental note to fill them back in the moment he left. Jamie hated it when the driveway stones became untidy, even just from the bikes. If he didn't stop soon, he was going to get down to the concrete below.

"You're not going to make this easy on me, are you?" he said.

"Make what easy?"

"Fine, you want me to say it? I will."

She had no idea what he was going on about, and she was about to say as much when he held up his hand to make it clear he wasn't finished speaking. The words tumbled out in one long stream.

"I made a mistake, Hols. I know I did. A horrible, big mistake. But I've changed now. I promise I have. And I want you back. I want you back for good."

CHAPTER NINE

They were in her kitchen, the kettle boiling for Dan's tea, while Holly poured herself an extra-large glass of white wine. She hadn't asked him if he would like one. This was Jamie's good stuff, far too nice to waste on him. If there'd ever been a moment when she'd felt like a stiff drink, it was now. After his declaration of remorse outside, she'd been almost too stunned to speak or move. Even now, she struggled to know where the hell to begin.

"Can we talk?" he asked.

He was perched on one of the stools the other side of the breakfast bar and had been staring at her intently since they'd stepped into the house. Technically, she hadn't actually invited him in. She'd been too dumbstruck to tell him to sling his hook. As she'd opened the door to get away from him, he'd slipped in behind her, protesting that they just needed to talk and then offering to put the kettle on which he'd done, even when she hadn't replied.

She knocked back the last two mouthfuls of wine before dejectedly resting her elbows on the worktop. The kettle clicked off, but she didn't stir to open the cupboard and get a tea bag out for him. If she didn't do something soon, he'd end up sleeping in the kitchen, and that was the last thing she wanted.

"Dan, I haven't heard from you in months. You've made no attempt to get in contact. No attempt to even apologise."

"I did apologise!" he said, his calm demeanour suddenly gone. "I did. I sent you a hundred text messages and voice mails. You know that."

"I hate to tell you this, but text messages and voice mails don't count as an apology for having sex with someone else. Did you think that would make everything all right? Really?"

He pursed his lips, as if actually considering this.

"I'll admit it. I wasn't in a great place back then. I didn't know how else to say I was sorry. My head was all messed up. But I'm here now, aren't I? Isn't that what counts?"

"I think it's a massive case of, 'too little too late'."

In a sudden motion, he grabbed her hands and pulled them towards him, looking pleadingly at her. She found herself going rigid at his touch and yanked them away again.

"It's not, Holly. Don't say that. I know it's not too late. Whatever you need. Whatever you want me to do. Here …" He reached into his pocket and pulled out his phone. The screen saver was an old photo of the pair of them. One taken at a wedding years before. From the tense smile on her face, it could well have been the one where she wasn't allowed to go on the bouncy castle. But despite that, they did look good together. He tapped the screen. The picture vanished and another appeared, and Holly blinked away the memory.

"Here."

He passed her the phone. This shot was of a yellow front door, a bog standard one. It looked like the sort you'd probably find on any new housing estate around here and, she suspected, in much of the UK.

"What am I looking at?" she asked, wondering what the significance could be that she wasn't able to grasp.

"Keep scrolling."

She did. The next photo was of a hallway, beyond the now-open yellow door. The third was of a modern kitchen, all white, with sparkling new appliances and a fridge large enough for a catering company.

"It's on that new development just outside of Ilford. I know we were never that keen on the houses, but this one's got a great-sized garden, and there's a superb primary school within walking distance."

Because of her slight addiction to looking at houses, she kept scanning through the photos. He was right about the size of the garden. It had been nicely styled with patio plants and even a large trampoline in a back corner.

"I should probably confess that I spent quite a bit of my share of the deposit money we'd been saving, when you left. Letting my hair loose, I guess you'd say. But there's a promotion going at work, and the boss has already said I'm a shoo-in for it. And I can ask my mum and dad to lend us a bit of money, too, if we need it."

She put the phone down on the table, half expecting to look up and find she'd been transported back to their London flat. That's certainly what it felt like. Dan talking about deposits and money and basically acting like nothing had changed. Like she didn't have an entirely new life now. One that she happened to really like.

"Is this some kind of joke?" she asked.

He frowned.

"Of course not. I promise you. If you're not keen on this

house, there are some others I looked at. In fact, one came on market just down the road from that three-bed semi with the green en-suite you liked. And it's not a bad price, either."

She shook her head, still struggling to believe what she was hearing.

"Dan, even if I entertained this ridiculous notion, you should know that I no longer have my deposit money. I spent it. Every penny. On the shop."

"Not to worry. It shouldn't be too difficult to sell, should it? It looked pretty busy when I was there, earlier."

Her jaw dropped. This had to be a bad dream, a truly torturous one. Any second now, her alarm clock would blast her rudely back to consciousness and this ludicrous nightmare would be over. Yet time ticked by, and Dan was still standing there, looking at her expectantly. What was she supposed to say? She picked up her wine glass to take another sizeable gulp, then realised she'd already finished it and plonked it back down again. Fortunately, at that moment, she came up with exactly the right thing to say.

"You need to go now, Dan."

A wounded look flashed across his face.

"But we haven't had time to talk properly."

"Okay, let me end this for you quickly. You're insane. You're obviously having yet-another midlife crisis—or maybe it's an extension of the first one. Who knows?—but I'm not selling my business and I'm not even remotely considering getting back together with the man who cheated on me. It's not happening. Not now. Not ever. Now, please, *please*, just go."

"Hols—"

"No. Don't you dare Hols me. My name is Holly. And whatever else it is you want to say. I don't want to hear it."

He wrinkled his nose. This had been a habit of his whenever he was about to say something he knew would annoy her. It was usually accompanied by a waggling motion of his jaws. Today, though, it was just the nose. But it seemed he'd finally run out of things to say. He opened his mouth, as if to try again, only to be forestalled by her telling him she wanted him out of the house ASAP. Jamie had texted to say she'd be home soon and the last thing Holly wanted was to have to try and explain to her what the hell was going on here.

"Please Hols, I mean Holly," he whined.

"What?" she spat, feeling her temper fraying.

"Do you think I could sleep on your sofa tonight?"

CHAPTER TEN

*H*olly considered it an extreme show of restraint on her part that Dan left the house that evening with all his limbs intact. In fact, she thought she'd acted unbelievably generously in the circumstances, writing directions to the Seven Hounds, the pub she'd stayed in when she'd first arrived back in Bourton, all those months ago. At the time, she hadn't expected that her stay there would be the start of a whole new life for her. It was going to be a very different story for him.

Before he left, she'd checked the bus and train timetables on her phone and jotted down the exact times and numbers that he would need to get out of Bourton and back to London in the morning. By ten-thirty the next day, he was going to be out of her life for good. Again.

When the front door finally closed on his retreating back, she fell against the wall and sighed. Eyes closed, she rubbed her temples, trying to alleviate some of the pressure that had been building since she first saw him on the driveway. Jeez, of all the ways she'd imagined the day might end, this had not been one of them. Her thoughts returned to what she'd hoped for and to

Ben. She must see him straight away and apologise. But after glimpsing herself in the hall mirror, she hesitated.

Despite thinking she'd cleaned herself up adequately after her dunking earlier, she was still a mess. Her hair was sticking out at strange angles and there appeared to be lines of grime around her neck. She was so grubby, in fact, it was hard to believe they'd been allowed into that nice pub for a meal. And even more surprising that Dan had made his declaration of undying love. He'd always been quick to criticise her if she'd had a hair out of place or her makeup was anything but flaw-less. Still, she was thinking about Ben now, not him. It seemed like a good idea to have a bath before she went round.

She was still soaking when she heard the door.

"Up here!" she called down to Jamie.

"How did it go today?" her housemate-cum-landlady called back up.

"I'm afraid I drank the rest of your nice wine."

"Wow, that good then."

"So, ignoring the fact that your ex is a total dick—which, to be fair, we already knew—tell me how the date went. Are you and Ben officially a thing now, or is my friendship group in tatters?"

They were slumped on the floor against the sofa, demolishing a packet of cinder toffee between them.

"I wish I knew. Despite him nearly drowning, it seemed to go pretty well. It was a great day, actually."

"So?"

"So … I don't know. After this Dan fiasco. I've tried messaging him, but he's not replied."

Jamie's jaw clicked as she rolled it around.

"What did I say about breaking his heart?"

Holly grabbed another sweet.

"This was hardly my fault, besides …"

Her voice drifted off. She was torn. Part of her wanted to tell Jamie more details of the date, like how every time she thought they might be close to kissing, Ben seemed to back away. How she was worried it was actually going to be her heart, not Ben's, that got broken. But then her friend was already feeling awkward about it all and the last thing she wanted was to put her even more in the middle of it all. She let out a long sigh.

"I just hope Ben knows that I didn't expect or want Dan to turn up."

"He's a reasonable guy. Explain it to him, like you've just done to me. I'm sure he'll understand."

Holly crunched another piece of the honeycombed sweet. She would find out soon enough.

*T*he habit of walking to work together each morning had started by accident. It just so happened that they left their houses at around the same time. The first occasion they'd opened their front doors in unison, there'd been some slightly embarrassed discussion of the weather, but by the third or fourth time, things had settled down to an enjoyable routine and they looked forward to the short journey in each other's company. And if one of them happened to be running a little late—which was inevitably Holly as opposed to Ben, then the other would perch on the wall outside and wait.

She looked forward to these little moments more and more.

Each meeting gave her the chance to learn something else about him. And it made a pleasant change to know that someone was listening and genuinely interested in what she had to say.

When she went to step outside that next morning, she was nervous that maybe he wasn't going to be there. Or worse, he would be and ask about Dan. So, when she found him sitting on the wall as usual, waiting, briefcase in hand, a sigh of relief rippled through her.

"How are you feeling after yesterday?" he asked, jumping down.

Wow, straight to the big question. But it was probably a good thing that he wasn't skirting around this issue. They started walking.

"To be honest, it was pretty screwy. I mean, who does that? Turns up out of the blue after eight months, offering undying love and a happy ever after. Even wanting to buy a house together. It definitely messed with my head."

Ben cleared his throat. "I meant, how are your muscles feeling? You know, after the obstacle course. The climbing walls and all that."

"Oh."

If a manhole had opened up in front of her at that exact moment, she would have had no qualms about stepping straight into it and disappearing. An awkward silence ensued as she tried to rearrange her thoughts and make a sensible reply.

"Uhm, they're okay, I guess. A bit stiff," she finally managed. "What about you? Do you ache?"

"Only slightly," he replied. "I did some yoga last night to stretch everything out before I went to bed."

"I didn't know you did yoga?"

"Why? Do you do it too?"

She wanted to say yes, that she really enjoyed it, and then

they could arrange a yoga date and talk about all their favourite positions or ashrams or whatever they were. But that would have been a huge lie. The only ones she actually knew and could do without straining something, were Child's Pose and the one where you lay on your back and closed your eyes and basically went to sleep.

So, all she could say was, "No. I don't."

After that, an awkward silence settled in, and reluctant to make any further faux pas, she kept quiet. After all, he was just as capable of thinking up topics of conversation as she was. Or apparently not, as the High Street came into view, and they were still not speaking. When they reached the shop and she fumbled in her handbag for her keys, all she could come up with was:

"I guess I'll see you at the end of the day, then?"

"Sounds good."

"And maybe we could go to the cinema if you'd like to? If there's something you fancy on?"

He offered a half smile.

"Great. I'll text Jamie to see if she's free, too," he said.

CHAPTER ELEVEN

"*H*e friend-zoned me. He completely and utterly friend-zoned me."

"I thought you three went to the cinema together all the time?"

"We do, but that was before, you know, I thought we were going to be a thing."

Drey placed the jar of humbugs back on the top shelf.

"What, so you were just going to dump your friend when you two started dating? Is that what you're saying?"

Holly scowled. This had been her go-to facial expression of the day whenever there weren't any customers in the shop. And occasionally when there were, too. She'd even made a small child cry after he'd asked for sweet peanuts without saying please.

"Why are you here, Drey, aren't you supposed to be at college? It's a Monday."

"Staff Development Day."

"It is? Wasn't there one of those last week?"

"No, that was a Wider Learning Day."

"Right, and you don't have to be at college for any of these?"

"Nope. Lucky for you. You get the pleasure of my company all day."

Holly's scowl hardened. Sulking on your own was one thing but having a teenager confirm your bad temper only made things worse. She'd already told herself the exact same thing about them all going to the cinema together. Maybe she should text him and ask if he fancied doing something later in the week, like dinner or anything else obviously romantic, with just the two of them. She picked up her phone and switched to messages, only to put it back down again. He could contact her. After all, she'd arranged the last date. The ball was in his court.

On the other side of the shop, a young girl had just picked up a jar of cherry lips and was shaking it up and down as if it were a percussion instrument.

"Can you stop that, please?" she snapped. "We're not a music shop. If you break that jar, you'll have to pay for it."

Muttering apologies, the mother seized the jar, replaced it on the shelf and hauled her daughter out of the shop, much to Holly's satisfaction. Her gratification was short-lived as Drey strode up to the counter.

"What was that?" she said, with a distinctly unimpressed look.

"What do you mean? We're lucky she didn't drop it. Do you know how much hassle it would have been if we'd had to clear up sweets and glass from all over the floor?"

"Really? And what about Agnes' rule? No bad moods on the shop floor, remember?"

Holly felt a shiver of guilt. She was right. That had been her old employer's number one dictum, which she'd told Holly on her first day there and one she'd been fairly good at upholding.

"Maybe you should go out for a while," Drey suggested, in a somewhat condescending manner, considering she was over ten years her junior and her employee.

"You know I am your boss, right?"

"I do, and maybe after a nice walk, you'll start acting like one again."

With a huff, Holly picked up her bag from behind the counter.

"I'm not paying you for today, by the way," she said as a parting shot as she headed for the door. "You can't just turn up randomly and expect extra wages."

"I'll eat a ton of sweets, then, while you're gone, shall I?" she responded with a smirk.

A minute later, Holly was out on the High Street, wondering if she'd simultaneously got the best and worst part-timer possible.

Outside, Autumn was in full swing, without a green leaf left in sight. Most had already succumbed to the wind and drifted to the ground in endless varieties of amber and orange. Soon it would be Christmas. She'd been looking forward to it since she'd first arrived back in the village. There would be the giant tree placed right in the middle of the river, decorated with glittering baubles and multi-coloured lights. And the shops would have fake snow and swathes of cotton wool in the windows, together with artificial icicles and snowflakes that would light up at night.

Seasonal displays had always been one of Agnes' fortes. Holly suspected that was one of the other things Maud had let slip when Agnes died. But this year, she was going to blow all the other shops out of the water. She would buy white fairy lights in bulk, some for the shop but also for the house. She had convinced Jamie that they should decorate it entirely with white lights and was already planning where to put them. They had a couple of old sets that they'd used in the garden, to decorate the gazebo in the summer, when weekends had seen endless barbecues and late-night board games out there. They should probably replace those, too. One set kept flicking on and off for no apparent reason and Jamie thought they were probably a fire hazard.

It didn't take long to realise that Drey had been right; the fresh air was helping to clear her head. Of course Ben wanted to keep including Jamie in their activities. She did too. Their friendship was one of the most important things to her. The last thing she wanted to do was risk sacrificing that for a relationship which—if her track record was anything to go by—might not last. And was it really that surprising that he'd been put out by Dan's surprise visit? How would she feel if his ex had turned up on their doorstep? Not that she knew anything at all about his exes. He was a closed book on that issue. Maybe, on their next date, they could talk a bit more about each other's pasts. It might help them both feel a little more secure.

She picked up cake and a coffee at the bakery and sat on a bench by the river, one of her favourite things to do, just sitting and watching the world and the ducks go by. She didn't do this often enough, she thought. She was going to have to get into some better habits and take regular breaks when Drey was there. She was perfectly capable of holding the fort by herself for a while. After all, she'd been doing that before Holly had turned up. And she would have to pay her for today, especially as she'd just left her to it on her own.

After thirty minutes, she decided it was probably time to head back. Coffee cup in hand, she headed back via the bakery again and picked up a stuffed croissant for Drey as a thank you. On her return, a glance through the window told her there were only a couple of customers in the shop, which was a relief. She would expect an apology and the fewer people there were to witness it, the better.

"Sorry," Holly said, the moment stepped through the door. "You're entirely right. It was Agnes' rule, and I was being utterly selfish. But no bad moods from now on. I'm not even going to think about—"

She stopped, the words frozen on her lips. All the calm that had been restored during the last half hour instantly evaporated.

"You have to be joking," was all that she could say.

Her throat was dry, her pulse increasing, and a red-hot anger was building inside her.

"Ten-thirty, Dan. You were meant to be getting the ten-thirty train out of Moreton. What the hell are you still doing here?"

CHAPTER TWELVE

*D*espite Holly's outburst, and clear distress at seeing him in her shop, Dan looked perfectly happy. More than happy, in fact. He was wearing the same smart clothes as yesterday, although his shoes were not quite so polished and his hair not quite so well waxed into position. As she approached him, his smile widened, and he stretched out his hands towards her.

"Hols, honestly, it's fine. I get it. I completely get it."

She was trembling now, quivering, partly with rage, partly in pure disbelief. Why was he here? Again. Could he have missed the bus? No, because Dan didn't miss buses or trains. Not unless he was deliberately trying to avoid something, like the time she'd wanted to visit a friend down in Poole and he'd spent an unfeasible amount of time looking for a book he needed to take with him, meaning they'd missed their train by two minutes. No, everything he did was considered and deliberate.

"Excuse me, would I be able to get some help here?"

Behind Dan, an elderly man with a flat cap and a walking

stick was looking up and down the shelves, seemingly struggling to find what he was looking for.

"Of course. I'm so sorry. How can I help you, Mr Craven?" Holly said, shoving Dan to the side. "Are you after something for yourself or the grandchildren today? We had a delivery of those jelly worms they like, earlier in the week."

"Hols, please, just hear me out. I promise you'll love this."

She was struggling to hear what her customer was replying over Dan's racket and her own pounding heart. Drey stepped out from behind the counter.

"Why don't you come over to this side of the shop and tell me what it is you want, Mr Craven?" she smiled, before glowering at Holly and muttering, "Then you can deal with your other little issue," at her, making no attempt to disguise a dismissive gesture towards Dan.

Holly was about to disagree. She was far more aware of which sweets Mr Craven's grandchildren liked, but the last thing she wanted was Dan hanging around, scaring off other customers. Once again, she followed Drey's suggestion, trying to hold onto the promise she'd made only minutes before not to be in a bad mood in the shop. She gritted her teeth and clenched her fists, marching not just out of the shop but all the way across the road to the river's edge.

"You were meant to be gone by now," she spat, when she finally turned to confront Dan. "You were meant to be on the train. I even wrote down the times for you."

"I know you did."

"Well, you've missed the one from Moreton, now. You'll have to go from Cheltenham instead. I don't care how many changes that entails. And don't even think of suggesting I give you a lift there."

"No, no." He shook his head. "I didn't miss the train. Well, I did, but deliberately. I was on the platform when it arrived, in fact. I just didn't get on. It all suddenly clicked into place, you see."

She shook her head, not sure what she was supposed to say to that.

"What clicked?"

"You, me. I get it, I was such a dick."

She lifted her eyebrows at the first thing he'd said that she couldn't disagree with, but it still didn't explain why he was smiling like a fool.

"Of course, you don't want to leave this place. Look at it. It's gorgeous. I didn't realise until I was on the bus. You know, all this green, all this fresh air. And you've put so much work into the shop. I can see that. It looks brilliant."

"Thank you."

Her rage subsided just a fraction. Whatever she'd expected him to say, it wasn't that. Maybe this was why he was still here. To clear the air before he left. Even she could appreciate that. Given how their relationship had ended, this did seem a better way to finally draw a line under things.

"Which is why, when I saw the train arriving, I rang the office," he continued, "and asked them to put in a transfer for me. To Cheltenham."

"What?"

Holly's jaw dropped, but he didn't seem to notice.

"They said it will take a couple of weeks to formalise but shouldn't be any problem at all. Actually, there might even be another promotion in it for me. I can't believe I didn't think of it before. It makes perfect sense. On the bus back, I had a quick look online and there are some fantastic little villages between Cheltenham and here. We could buy something straight away, or rent if you'd rather. Not forever, obviously, but I don't think it'd take us that long to find the perfect place. And I don't mind a bit of a commute, if that works better for you. I was thinking maybe somewhere like Cold Aston? That looks rather nice. Northleach would be good travelling-wise for both of us, but I'm not sure we'd really want to live in the same village as your parents, would we?"

The trembling had stopped but Holly was filled with pure and utter disbelief. Still watching his lips move, she blinked a few times. This had to be a joke. Maybe there was someone secretly filming them, and she was going to find herself on one of those candid-camera shows.

"I don't understand what it is you're saying?" she said eventually, the pounding in her ears making it almost impossible to think straight.

He grinned, cocking his head to the side like a dog who was proud of the fact that it had just chewed up your expensive new work shoes.

"I'm going to move here. I'm going to move to the Cotswolds, so we can be together again."

"*A*pparently, he's spoken to his mum and dad, too, and got them to agree to lend him some money, so I don't even need to sell the shop to help with the deposit."

"That's very decent of them," Jamie said, pulling out a Tupperware container with left-over cottage pie from the fridge.

Holly had been so furious, she hadn't said another word to Dan after his big announcement, just turned straight around, stomped across the road into the shop, slammed the door and turned the sign around to Closed, even though it was twenty minutes too early and Mr Craven still had to pay for his jelly worms. She'd cashed up and not uttered a single word to Drey or any of the bemused locals she met on her way home.

"No," Holly replied. "It's not at all. It's creepy. What's wrong with them? All of them. What an earth would have made him think I'd want him to move up here?"

"Are you sure you made it clear enough?" Jamie asked, unclipping the lid and placing the bowl in the microwave. "You know you tend to ramble a bit when you're on edge. Maybe you just didn't say what you meant intelligibly."

"I told him that there was no way, before hell froze over, that we were ever getting back together. I'm not sure what I could've said that would have been clearer than that."

"Maybe it was the tone you used?"

"Really?" She picked up a tea towel and threw it at Jamie. "You're not taking this seriously. Obviously, he's lost his mind. Either that, or I'm in some kind of nightmare, and I'll suddenly wake up and find Dan never left London."

"Can you smell that food in the microwave?" Jamie asked, apparently ignoring everything she'd just said.

With a groan, she replied, "Yes, of course I can."

"Well then, you're not dreaming. I'm pretty sure you can't smell in dreams."

With an even bigger groan, Holly dropped her head onto the table. Had he always been like that? she wondered. Not taking no for an answer. She guessed he must have, and she'd just got used to it and accepted it.

"Can we please go to the pub? I need to get out of here," she muttered.

"You can. I'm helping at the care home."

Holly looked up from between her elbows.

"On a Monday? I thought Thursday was your night."

"It is, usually, but we took on this new regular volunteer

who's turned out not to be regular at all. Second week in and she's cancelled on us. On bingo night, of all nights."

"So why do you have to be the one that covers for her?" Holly asked.

It was hard not to be aware of how much Jamie was doing. Not that she'd ever say it to her face — she knew exactly what the reaction would be if she did—she was worried her friend sometimes took on too much. She took on every job that came her way as a roofer, ran Anne Summers parties and volunteered at half-a-dozen different places in the village. Some weeks Holly felt exhausted on her behalf, just looking at the entries on the calendar in the kitchen. But Jamie seemed to like it that way. However, Mondays were usually set aside for their girls' night, and she would be sad if that went by the board.

"Paul's on a night shift," Jamie said, starting to explain why she'd drawn the short straw. "Graeme's got to stay in with his kids. It's Tess and Andy's wedding anniversary and Jess is up in Leeds for a friend's hen do. So, either I go, or they'd have to cancel. And they really love their bingo, even more than the bridge or Cluedo nights. I don't think it's fair if they have to miss out just because other people are flaky."

This was why Holly loved Jamie and the rest of her group of friends in Bourton. Back in London, most of the people she'd known had all been, as Jamie would put it, *flaky*. If she was honest, so had she, often cancelling at the last minute if she was worried that a night out might cost too much, or Dan had persuaded her she'd have more fun staying in and watching a film with him. Jamie, and Caroline and Ben, made her want to do better, to be her better self.

Which was why Holly found herself saying, "Why don't I come with you?"

CHAPTER THIRTEEN

*T*he Weeping Willows Care Home was on the outskirts of Bourton, on the road that led up the hill to the group of villages called the Rissingtons, and about the limit of Holly's walking ability on a chill autumn evening. The area had expanded substantially since her childhood, with new housing estates spreading out into what had previously been open fields. But the Home had maintained an impressive-sized plot which, unsurprisingly given its name, had two large weeping willows in the front garden. A wide gravelled driveway led to a three-story main building with several one-story wings.

"This place is massive," Holly said, the brisk walk having warmed her nicely by the time they reached the entrance. "I don't know how I never noticed it before."

"This one's actually quite small. I wish you could have seen the one Giles and his uncle bought up. It was lovely. Such a nice old building, and it even had a stream running through the grounds. This place has plenty of room outside for the residents in the summer, though."

While Jamie chatted to the man on the front desk, Holly had

a quick nose up a corridor. It was much as she'd expected, with light-peach walls displaying local scenes in gilt frames. It smelt strongly of disinfectant and floral air fresheners, with undertones of fried meat and vegetables.

"Come on, this way," Jamie said, tapping her on the shoulder. "Bingo is held in the Birch Room."

It didn't take long for Holly to discover that the various communal rooms were all named after trees. They passed wooden plaques announcing Oak, Elm and, unsurprisingly, Willow. After the third set of double doors, they took a left down another peach-coloured corridor to a final pair, with a sign outside telling them they'd arrived at Birch.

She hadn't spent much time considering what to expect at the bingo or what the people who attended it would be like. Maybe a dozen or so men and women, likely all dressed in the same colour beige or peach, like the walls, possibly with one or two dressing gowns on display and probably a couple of them sleeping, too.

But when Jamie pushed open the door, she was hit by a wall of noise that sounded more like a youth centre than a care home.

"About time. We were about to start a revolt," a man piped up from somewhere.

"Margaret was threatening to start singing."

"You said you like it when I sing."

"No one likes it when you sing, Margaret. There are dying cats that can hold a tune better than you."

Holly stopped in her tracks, quite taken aback. It reminded her of a secondary school classroom. There were tables and chairs, which looked as though they had at some point been set in neat rows but were now all over the place. Some people were sitting, and some were standing, and although she was sure she must be mistaken, she could have sworn there was a faint aroma of cigarettes in the air.

"All right, all right, settle down." Jamie swept in, raising her voice above the racket. "Let's get these seats sorted. Come on guys. And Sid, if you're selling ciggies again, I'm going to report you to nurse Donna."

"Why do you always think it's me?" said an old man at the back of the room indignantly, before promptly bursting into a coughing fit that had him doubled over in his chair.

"I don't think it's you. I know it's you. And you should start looking after yourself."

"Are we here for a lecture or to play bingo?" one of the women piped up. "Because if I wanted a lecture, I could ring my daughter up."

"Fine," Jamie said, with a mock sigh. "You get yourself into seats and I'll set up the balls. Everyone, this is Holly. She's offered to give me a hand this evening, so don't scare her off."

There was a general murmuring of, "Hello Holly."

"She's going to come around with the cards and dabbers."

Holly wasn't exactly sure what dabbers were, but she followed Jamie across to a cabinet, where she pulled out all the paraphernalia involved, starting with an ancient-looking cage full of numbered balls, a large tray with holes—also numbered —and packs of cards.

"We tried doing it the modern way, you know, using an app to randomly select the numbers, but no one liked it, so we're back to this," Jamie said, as she heaved the contraption over to the table at the front.

Next, she handed Holly a small cardboard box. Dabbers, she discovered, were felt pens, only chunkier than normal. When applied to—or dabbed on—the cards, they produced large coloured circles to cover the numbers that had been called.

"Don't give out the cards until they're all sat down. And watch out for Sid. He always tries to swipe more than one."

"It's my arthritis!" protested the offending gentleman. "It makes it difficult to take just one at a time."

"Doesn't make it difficult to get those ciggies out of the pack though, does it?" Jamie countered, with a raised eyebrow.

The old man muttered something into his chest, but it seemed good natured enough. It was wonderful to see the relationship Jamie had built up with them all. It felt as if they'd stepped into an old family member's house for a Christmas get-together.

As Holly handed out the cards, she had no problem smiling hello to everyone. She was enjoying herself already. Some days just turned out like this, she'd found since moving back to Bourton. Particularly working in the shop. At first, she'd been aware of her cheeks aching from grinning so much. They seemed to have got used to the change now. It was the way people behaved and treated you that was so lovely. How Dan had ever thought she'd consider leaving, showed just how little he knew her. Then to turn up at the shop and say he was going to transfer jobs. It was either the most insane or most romantic thing anyone had ever done—and she tended towards the first option.

"Call off the search party, I'm here!"

Holly's stream of thought was broken as the door burst open and in swept a woman who couldn't have looked more out of place had she tried. Her long white hair was pinned up in large curls, over which she wore a teal hat with three enormous peacock feathers flying from the top. The teal theme continued down through the rest of her outfit which was complemented by a pearl necklace and earrings set and a pair of heels that Holly was fairly sure she herself wouldn't manage to walk in. The whole ensemble wouldn't have looked out of place in the ballroom of the Titanic. Her arms flowed languidly by her sides, as if she were waving to adoring fans, and when she reached a table with an empty chair, she waited until one of the men there pulled it out for her, before sitting down and arranging her skirts.

"Verity," Jamie said. "I was beginning to worry you'd got lost in your wardrobe."

"There's nothing wrong with taking care of one's appearance. Besides, the fact that my nephew has dumped me here must mean I've got limited time left and I plan to make the most of it."

She put a small, beaded handbag on the table and undid the clasp, before pulling out what appeared to be a bejewelled dabber. Holly's eyes widened at the sight. She knew she was gawping, but it was hard not to. The old woman caught her staring and her grin widened.

"We have a visitor. Good thing, too. I knew that other gal wouldn't last the course. You could tell by her shoes. You." She pointed at Holly. "Come here. Let me see yours."

"Sorry?" Holly started in surprise.

"Your shoes. I want to see them."

"Ignore her," Jamie murmured, counting the balls. "As someone who's sartorial inspiration comes from the early nineteen hundreds, she has very strong views on people who wear more modern fashions."

"Fashions!" coughed Verity—who obviously had no problem with her hearing—in obvious disgust. "Please don't tell me you consider those overalls you turned up in the other week any form of vogue. Unless the look you were going for was Victorian chimney sweep."

"I came straight from work, as you are well aware. And they are very comfortable and practical."

"That is no excuse. I know you have much better items in that wardrobe of yours. I gave them to you. It never hurts to be prepared and pack an extra outfit, you know."

Jamie rolled her eyes.

"Do you want to play bingo or not? Because if not, I've got a pint waiting with my name on it. And Sid, don't think I didn't just see you pass Glennis one of your cigarettes. Really, Glennis, you know the doc is worried about your oxygen levels. I would have thought better of you. Now, can we begin?"

While Sid and Glennis grumbled at the back of the room, the rest of the residents let out a cheer, ready to start, and once again, Holly felt that now familiar ache in the apples of her cheeks.

It was unlike any game of bingo she'd ever experienced, not that she'd actually taken part in one before. But she'd seen enough on television to have a pretty good idea what they were normally like. People usually sat in silent concentration, so as not to miss a vital number, until there was the sudden burst of noise as the winner shouted *house!* and waved their card above their head, excitedly. Holly had no idea how they knew which numbers had been called or how Jamie would hear if a winner declared themself, over the racket. Apart from one couple, who sat quietly holding hands all evening, the rest of them seemed to be enjoying a free-for-all.

"I tell you, there's no four in that machine! I've got a four. I can't win. I want to swap. I want a new card!"

"It's rigged!" someone else yelled, when Jamie called out another number. "It's all rigged!"

"Do you know that bingo was invented in Italy?" someone else said.

It was absolute chaos and utterly exhausting but incredibly good fun. Verity, with her grand entrance and aloof manner, was one of the few who took the game seriously. She sat with a posture that reminded Holly of a barn owl, shoulders back and not a hint of a curve in her spine. She was almost jealous. The old lady obviously hadn't spent a large chunk of her life hunched over a computer, inputting data.

At one point, Jamie suggested Holly took over operation of the ball machine, but quickly got booed off as she didn't know any of the proper calls.

"You can't just say the number. It's snakes alive, fifty-five! What are you doing? That's half the fun."

"Twenty-five, Christmas Day," she tried.

"No, no, no! It's twenty-five, duck and dive!" they yelled.

And when they told her twenty-six was two and six, half a crown, she had no idea what they were on about and gave up. It didn't even rhyme!

"You should probably bone up on it, if you're going to come again," Jamie advised, taking over, much to Holly's relief.

They continued to play in the same chaotic manner.

At twenty past eight, a nurse came into the room.

"Time to wrap it up, ladies," she said. "These guys need to get ready for bed."

"Ridiculous," Verity piped up. "What we need is to get the party started. Where's the Champagne? The Chambord? Lord, I'd even settle for a disco ball and some of that modern techno music."

"How about you settle for a hob nob and a cup of camomile tea, instead," said the nurse.

Verity scowled and sniffed in disdain, before turning to Holly and Jamie.

"You know, just one little party, that's all. Is that really too much to ask?"

"They're so much fun," Holly laughed, on the way back home. "I just hope I have that much energy when I'm their age."

"You're telling me. You try being there on a quiz night. We can only do one a month, it's so draining."

"And Verity. The outfit."

"That was nothing, believe me, compared to some of the things she wears. Not to mention her shoes. She had too much to fit into her room when she arrived and had to give a lot of it away. I'm pretty sure selling her collection would have raised enough to pay off my mortgage."

"Maybe we should try stealing a pair of her heels next time, then," Holly joked.

"She'd probably give you a pair, if you asked," Jamie said, "especially if you turn up in trainers. She hates them."

When they reached the pair of semis, Ben's side still showed a light burning. The good humour Holly had been feeling subsided with a thud.

"Shit."

"What is it?"

"I didn't wait for Ben after work. I locked up early and forgot to let him know."

It probably wasn't a massive deal, she tried to convince herself. He would have seen the shop was closed and guessed that she'd needed to leave quickly. But he hadn't texted her to check if everything was okay, and that was something he would normally do.

"So, what's going on with you two?" Jamie asked as Holly looked up at his window with substantially more longing than she'd expected. "Is date number three in the pipeline? You know you'll have to shave your legs for that one?"

The heaviness she was now feeling prevented Holly from reacting to her friend's taunt. Maybe Jamie had been right all along. Perhaps they should call it quits before either of them got hurt. But she had the distinct feeling it might already be too late for that.

CHAPTER FOURTEEN

$\mathcal{T}$he next day was a Tuesday, which was Holly's official "day off", which she always said using air quotes to signify the theoretical nature of the expression. It was true she would normally get a couple of hours to herself, sometimes to do the shopping or pop in and visit her parents, but it was difficult to think of it as an actual rest day, when most of the morning would be spent doing shop work, be that catching up on invoices, making stock checks or running to the cash and carry to replenish the shelves. The shop was never far from her mind. But at least on Tuesdays she got a lie in. That was something.

This week, she'd planned to recuperate from the mental exhaustion of the last couple of days and emerge from bed as late as possible. But when she woke up at just gone eight, she found herself itching to start moving. She pulled the pillow over her head, hoping that blocking the sunlight filtering through her curtains might help her drift off again, but after a further five minutes, she knew it was pointless. She was well and truly awake. She might as well get up and do something useful. Before that, however, she checked her phone.

The good news was that there were no messages from Dan saying he'd bought the house next-door—not that she'd put anything past him right now. The bad news was that there weren't any from Ben, either. She'd texted him when she got in from bingo to apologise for not letting him know that she'd gone home early from the shop and that she hoped he'd had a good day at work. He'd replied with an impressively impersonal, *It was fine thank you.* Since then, nothing.

How on earth was she supposed to interpret that? Did he not want to know why she'd closed early? Or would he have thought it was a private matter and she would tell him if she wanted to?

There were no kisses, but then there never were on his messages. And looking back through their previous exchanges, she could see they were all in the same formal style. And yet this felt different. Colder. Was it possible for a text message to feel cold? She was probably reading too much into it—and she knew that Jamie and Caroline would both say that she was—but it just didn't feel right. She wanted to talk to him, to set things straight about her and Dan, but marching into the bank and demanding a one-on-one with the Manager wasn't going to do her any favours. So instead, she had a shower, got herself dressed and headed over to her parents.

I have to say, I never thought that Daniel had it in him," her mum said over a cup of tea and home-made shortbread. "Didn't think he had a romantic bone in his body, if I'm honest. Said so much to your father more than once."

"It wasn't romantic, Mum, it was demanding. Trust me on that."

"Well, you know your heart, my love, and I think you're well clear of him. Your dad was always romantic, you know. Not in big ways, but in the little things. They add up over the years. Bringing me a cup of tea in bed every morning. Putting my slippers by the radiator when the weather turns cold."

"Walking you home from the shop every day," Holly muttered to herself.

"What was that, dear?"

"Oh nothing. Nothing. Just thinking out loud, that's all. Where is Dad by the way? I thought he was going to cut back on his hours?"

"Him, cut back? You have to be joking. He's been saying that every day since you left home. No, he's working as much as ever. I think he's a bit worried, you know, with all the redundancies that are happening round here at the minute."

"At his place?" Holly asked, a familiar churning sensation starting up in her. It sometimes felt like her dad and redundancies had a closer relationship than rhubarb and custard, although nowhere near as enjoyable.

"No, not there yet, but you know what he's like. I keep telling him we'd be fine. We don't need much at our age. And I could always up my cleaning hours, but you know what he gets like."

Holly did, and then she thought of those old people in the care home the previous night. Her mum and dad were way off that, of course, but there would come a time when they wouldn't be, and those places were expensive. Maybe she'd have to move back home to look after them. But then that wouldn't work if she had a family of her own by that stage, although the chances of that happening were growing smaller by the year. Even if she found herself in a committed relationship in the near future, it would probably be a long time before they'd even consider having children. And what about the shop? She'd only just started to turn a profit on the place, and it certainly wasn't enough to pay someone to cover her full-time, while she took maternity leave or looked after her parents, come to that.

"Are you all right, love? You look miles away."

"Sorry? Oh, just thinking about stuff, that's all."

"Well, don't think about it too much. It might never happen."

No, Holly thought with sadness, *it might never happen at all.*

She stayed for lunch, but then her mum had to head off to one of her cleaning jobs, over at a big house near Cold Aston. This left her wondering how to spend the rest of her afternoon off. This was ridiculous, she thought. Normally, she craved time off, a chance to get a brief respite from work. And yet today, she was unable to focus on anything.

So, she did the one thing she always enjoyed. She baked.

"*J*esus!" Jamie said, when she got home at five o'clock. "Are we hosting a banquet that no one's told me about?"

"I was just feeling a little stressed," Holly replied, now feeling embarrassed at the state of the kitchen, where almost every surface was covered with plates of cakes and breads. There was even a jar of jam, that she'd made with blackberries from the garden. She was especially pleased with the breads, in particular a sun-dried tomato and olive loaf that she hadn't made in years. Now the problem was how they were going to eat it all before it went stale, particularly as new regulations dictated that the feeding of bread to the waterfowl was officially banned in the village. They could now only be given oats, seeds or defrosted frozen peas, of all things.

"What would you like? What can I get you?" Holly asked. "I think the jam would go really well with the date and walnut loaf. I've made a lemon drizzle cake, too. And apple turnovers."

Jamie's face contorted in a way that was most unusual where food was concerned. In fact, it had been specified before she'd moved in that Holly would be in charge of cooking.

"I'm sorry, I'm out for dinner tonight."

"Oh, I didn't realise. That's okay. I'll eat some of it and we can have sandwiches for lunch tomorrow. And the day after. And the day after that."

She could hear the self-pity in her own voice. This wasn't like her at all, but she was struggling. Maybe she should just call it a day, have a long bath and an early night. She was about to say as much when Jamie spoke again.

"You could always take some next door. You know what Ben's like. His stomach is bottomless. And there's a nice bottle of wine in the fridge. You could get drunk and confess your undying love."

"That's not funny."

"It's a bit funny. Look, as much as I'm not sure about this relationship, I know you like him, and I suspect he likes you, too. And there's no way the two of us are going to get through this much food."

Holly stared at everything she'd created and chewed on her lip. It was true that he was always very complimentary about her food and having a normal evening together might be just what they needed to reset their awkward situation.

"You're right," she said, pulling off her apron and grabbing the nearest loaf. "I can do that. I can take some round to Ben. We're friends. Neighbours. Neighbours take each other food. It's what they do, even if they haven't been on a date. I'm going right now."

Holly expected Jamie to be pleased she was agreeing to her suggestion, but her nose was crinkled.

"What? You said I should go."

"Oh, you definitely should," she replied. "I'm just not sure you'd want him to know you wear Harry Potter pyjama's this early in the relationship."

CHAPTER FIFTEEN

*I*t then took twenty minutes for Holly to get ready. She decided that a shower wouldn't go amiss, particularly as she was covered head to toe in flour. Next, she had to decide what to wear. After three changes of outfit, she was finally standing in front of Ben's door holding fresh cakes and loaf of bread, with a bottle of wine tucked under an arm, dressed in the same jeans she wore ninety-five percent of the time and a top that came out at least twice a week. It was a wonder she bothered to keep so many other clothes in her wardrobe.

Jamie beeped goodbye as she pulled out of the driveway.

You can do this, Holly said to herself, taking a deep breath. *You can do this.* Although she immediately identified a problem. How was she going to knock on the door? She didn't have a spare hand. She leant forwards and pressed the doorbell with her nose.

A minute later, Ben opened the door.

"Hi," she said.

"Hi," he replied, before immediately springing into action. "Let me give you a hand. Shall I open your front door for you?"

"Oh, no. These are for you. If you want them. I did some baking."

His eyes widened as he took in all that was on offer. Maybe she had gone a little over the top.

"You did quite a lot, didn't you?"

"If you don't want it, it's fine. I can drop a few bits and pieces off to Caroline."

"I don't mind. I mean, it's very nice of you, but if you'd prefer to take it to Caroline and her family …"

How did every conversation they had end up being quite so awkward? Neither of them moved. Her cheeks were growing redder by the second. She should go, she thought. Just turn back around to her own house. Not that she'd be able to open the door like this.

"I've got plenty more for Caroline. Here, have this. If there's too much, you can always take some into the bank."

"Okay. Thank you."

He took her baked gifts, plate by plate, to his hall table.

"Was there anything else?" he asked.

She was rooted to the spot in his doorway, wondering why everything was so difficult. It hadn't been this bad since she'd run out in front of his bike. Any second now, he'd disappear back inside, and yet another opportunity would have slipped through her fingers. There was no way she could let that happen. So instead, she pulled out the bottle of wine from under her arm and blurted out the first thing that came to mind.

"Do you fancy playing a board game?"

*S*he and Dan had hardly ever played board games. She quite enjoyed them, but in his opinion, if you were going to have a games night, you should invite others around to make it more interesting. In that case, you'd have to offer dinner and make sure you had enough drinks in. Then you'd need nibbles for later, and when all the expenses were added up, it just wasn't worth it for ninety minutes of entertainment. Particularly not in his case, as he was such a bad loser. So, she was pretty much out of touch with latest developments, believing that Monopoly and Cluedo were still the height of popularity.

Since moving in with Jamie, all that had changed. Caroline was the biggest fan, always bringing a new one around for them to try, and Holly found that they were really good fun. Unfortunately, when she was given a pile of cards or a stack of counters, a level of competitiveness she never knew she had came to the surface. Tonight's game of Scrabble was proving no different.

"Equalise," Ben said, adding seven tiles to the stray E Holly had carelessly provided him with on the board. "Seventy-six points."

"What? You have to be joking!"

"Add it up for yourself."

She was tempted to. How on earth could you get so many points from one short word? He could, apparently. Still, she had a good one to follow up with.

"Fidget," she said, proudly, using the E that he had just put down.

"Good word," he said. "Eleven points."

"No way. How come you got seventy-six and I only get eleven? Fidget is a great word."

"I agree, just not if you're trying to get a top score at Scrabble."

The first time they'd played in a group, he'd used all sorts of fancy words, like circadian and quixotic, that she'd insisted on looking up online at the end of the game, not believing they were real words at all. They were, of course.

Waiting for him to make his next move, she shuffled the letters around on the rack in front of her, hoping to find something good. She'd got an H, a J and a W which meant, with only Us and Os for vowels, she was looking at three-letter words, tops. Glancing up, she scanned the board again, in case there was anything there that might help. Of course, she'd have to see what he came up with, first.

It was in that brief moment that something caught her eye through the back window. A light was flickering from behind the hedgerow, over in Jamie's garden.

"Cakes. With a triple letter and a double word, that's twenty-eight points. And it seems rather appropriate in the circumstances, don't you think? Holly? Holly, is everything all right?"

"Sorry, did you say something?"

"I was just saying that cakes is an appropriate word, given all the baking you did today."

"Oh, yes."

"Are you sure you're okay?"

He put down the bag of tiles and looked at her. She should be focusing on her next move, but she couldn't take her mind off the flickering. She sighed.

"It must be those bloody fairy lights switching themselves on again. I think I'll have to go and unplug them."

"Sorry, did I miss something?"

"The garden lights are faulty. They're on again. I should probably bin them. Jamie's convinced they're going to start a fire one day."

She was starting to agree. They were plugged into the mains, with a timer that you set so they'd switch on and off when you wanted. The problem was that they'd developed an annoying habit of completely ignoring the timings, for no apparent reason that they could fathom. She'd tried resetting them. Jamie had tried resetting them. It made no difference. At random times, day and night, the bloody things would suddenly start flashing. She really thought they'd finally sorted it out the other night, but apparently that wasn't the case, and the last thing she wanted was to be responsible for a fire at her friend's house.

"Oh, don't worry, it'll be fine," he said in a casual, most un-Ben manner, possibly just high on his Scrabble score. "You ready with your next word?"

She glanced down at the crisscross of previous offerings on the board and then back at her tiles and knew there was no way she could win.

"I really do think I should just pop around and unplug them," she said, already on her feet. "Why don't you pour us another glass of wine, and I'll be straight back. And maybe choose another game for us to play?"

"Three glasses of wine on a weeknight. Look at you—such a rebel," he said, with a twinkle in his eye.

Holly smiled to herself. It had taken a bit of time, but they were back to where they'd been before Dan put in his unexpected appearance. Maybe the extra glass of wine would be just what she needed to pluck up enough courage to mention a third date.

"Actually, why don't we curl up on the sofa and watch a film," she said with a grin, heading for the lounge door, her confidence growing. "You can pick. Just make it something good."

They had often discussed the idea of joining their two back gardens with a gate. Or better still—given how much time the three of them spent together—getting rid of the hedge altogether. Unfortunately, at present, she still had to go out of his front door, across to her own and through the house. Thinking that she'd grab a cardigan while she was there, she headed upstairs first and took one from the pile on the chair by her bed, before returning downstairs to unplug the offending fairy lights for the final time. Cardigan on, she went through the kitchen and opened the back door. Her jaw dropped at the sight in front of her.

"What the hell is this?"

CHAPTER SIXTEEN

$\mathcal{I}$t was like a scene out of a romantic comedy film. In fact, exactly like one. The fairy lights she'd come to turn off weren't on. Instead, there were dozens of tea lights and candles positioned all around. They were on the bench, in the rock garden and precariously close to Jamie's wooden shed. Some were resting on the wall, clustered together in groups of three or five and others placed in large glass lanterns near the back door. How many were there? There must be over a hundred, without a doubt. Possibly more than two hundred. How long must it have taken to light all these? And why on earth would anyone do such a thing? She found herself wondering if she was somehow in the wrong garden. But nope. There were her fruit bushes and there was her vegetable patch at the back. Not to mention the fact that she'd just stepped out of her own kitchen.

Then she noticed a figure standing in the shadows. Dan. He was dressed far more formally than the last couple of times she'd seen him, in a shirt and jacket, worn over smart jeans.

When he realised she was there, looking at him, he seemed surprised.

"So, I've been getting things wrong a lot lately," he said.

She registered the fact that he was talking but couldn't bring herself to move. She was speechless. Breathless. The entire scene was incredible. Beautiful.

There was no way he could have organised this, she thought, noticing small details, like the crystals scattered around that were reflecting the candlelight and making it look as if the whole garden were starlit. He didn't do romantic, and he certainly wouldn't have spent a heap of money on candles and accessories. He wouldn't even buy cut-price supermarket flowers on Valentine's Day, proclaiming the whole thing a load of rubbish, orchestrated by big business to cajole people into spending ridiculous amounts of their hard-earned cash. No, this couldn't possibly be down to him. And yet there he was, dressed impeccably and looking at her with anticipation. Finally, after clearing her throat, she managed to speak.

"Dan, what are you doing? What is going on h-?"

"Sorry," he interrupted. "Can I say something? Please? If you don't mind. I want to get this right. I've been sort of … practising, so could you just hear me out? Would that be okay?"

Holly found herself even more taken aback by the way he was speaking. The nervousness. The babbling. However, unable to form a single sentence of her own, she let him say his piece.

He closed his eyes and took several deep breaths before opening them and trying again.

"I've been getting a few things wrong of late," he said. "Actually, I've been getting a lot wrong, but you know that. I was doing it for a long time. Hols—Holly, I know I have made mistakes. And I don't just mean the big one. That was a huge mistake, I know that, but I made mistakes before that too. I made a mistake not appreciating you. I made a mistake not telling you I loved you every day. Not kissing you and telling you how beautiful you looked every morning when we woke up. It was a mistake not to chase after you when you came here. I know I sent text messages and rang and things, but I should have stood in the rain and banged on your door and begged you to return to me every single day."

Her heart was aching now. What was he doing? It was so completely out of character. In fact, she couldn't remember a single time when he'd allowed himself to be this open, this vulnerable.

"Holly, if you'll let me, I want to spend the rest of my life making up for all those mistakes."

He was swallowing repeatedly and as he put a hand into his jeans' pocket, she wondered if he was going to pull out a tissue, he looked so close to tears. But when it removed it again, he was holding something quite different. He dropped to one knee, opened the small box and held it out to her.

With trembling breath, she took a half step forwards, squinting in the pale candlelight.

"Is that …"

"My grandmother's engagement ring? Yes. I spoke to my parents about it the other week and they were thrilled. You know how much they love you, and they've been furious at me for being such an idiot. But if you don't like it, you can choose something else. You can pick whatever you like. I want to do this properly, with the perfect ring and everything."

Dan was now not the only one with a lump in his throat, as Holly gazed at the beautiful diamond solitaire glinting in his hand. She'd always had a thing for antique jewellery. Not that the new ones in the shop windows weren't very pretty, but there was something so much more romantic about a piece that had history and probably a story to tell, if it could. A love story, hopefully. Someone's life, encapsulated in a golden hoop. More than once, she'd imagined that, if Dan proposed, he might do it with the family heirloom his mother had told her about. And there he was now in front of her, down on one knee, with the ring in his hand. But he couldn't be proposing. It just didn't make sense. Months had passed, and they hadn't even spoken. This had to be something else.

"Dan ..."

"I'm asking you to marry me, Holly Berry. I'm asking you to spend the rest of your life with me."

She was glued to the spot, her heart thumping so much, she could hear it pounding in her head. This was ridiculous. Beyond ridiculous. She couldn't possibly marry Dan. She'd forged a new life for herself. And yet still no words left her lips. He looked just as he had in their early days together, when they couldn't keep their hands off each another.

He slowly rose to his feet, came up to her and slipped the ring onto the third finger of her left hand. It was a little loose and tipped to one side slightly because of the weight of the stone, but it was beautiful. Perfect, in fact. The most perfect ring and proposal she could ever have dreamed of.

Dan moved even closer. She could feel his warm breath on her skin as their lips moved towards each other. How long had it been since someone had kissed her properly? she thought, as they were barely a hair's breadth apart. Months. And before she knew it, that's what they were doing. Kissing.

It was a strange sensation. She was kissing her awful ex, and it felt ... pleasant. That was it. It certainly wasn't unpleasant and there was a nice familiarity to it. But there was no spark. No tingles flooding through her, even with the romance of the moment. If anything, it was rather dull. Her mind drifted away and she wondered what it would be like if it were Ben standing there instead. If it were his lips against hers. And she felt a sense of warmth returning. But this wasn't Ben, she suddenly remembered. This definitely was not. It was Dan, the last person in the world she'd ever thought she'd do this with again. The last person in the world she ever wanted to.

With a shake of her head, she broke away. Dan stood there, with a massive grin on his face. She was about to speak, when the back door creaked behind her. And as she turned back to the house, she saw him there, the look of hurt on his face as clear as day.

"Ben!"

CHAPTER SEVENTEEN

or a split second, time seemed to stop. The candles continued to flicker, and the cold breeze still chilled the air, but for Holly, everything stood still. On one side, Ben was staring at her, looking as if all the blood had drained from his face, while on the other, Dan was flushed with colour.

Then, in a blink, everything changed. Ben was smiling.

"Sorry, I didn't mean to interrupt. You'd been a while. I just wanted to check everything was okay."

"It's … it's …" She seemed to have lost control of her tongue, as if she was trying to work out how to speak. It didn't help that her heart appeared to have jumped so far up her throat, she was having difficulty breathing. "It's … he's …" She wasn't even managing her normal babbling nonsense. She couldn't get anything out at all.

"It's okay, mate." Dan moved past her, stretching out his hand. "You're the neighbour, right? I think I met you before, outside."

"Possibly," Ben replied with a casualness that didn't match the rigidity of his shoulders.

"Dan."

"I know."

"Holly's fiancé."

At this, Ben's eyes widened, and he looked past Dan to Holly, who was still struggling to follow what was going on. Time had started again for her, but now seemed as tangled as a ball of wool after a kitten has found it, and she couldn't find the place to start unpicking what the hell had just happened.

"Her fiancé?" Ben said, turning to Holly. "Then I guess congratulations are in order."

This time it was the sight of Ben that had sent her pulse rocketing.

"What?" she said, finally twigging what had been said. "Fiancé?"

"Yes," Dan laughed, taking her hand and squeezing it. "That's what you're called when you've agreed to marry someone."

"What? I … I …"

"I should go," Ben said. "Leave you two to celebrate."

"No!" Holly finally found her voice again. "No, it's not. I'm not. I didn't …"

"Hols, grab some glasses, will you? Might as well get one for Ben too, as he's here. Turn it into a proper celebration."

From behind one of the blackberry bushes, he pulled out a bottle of fizz, and proceeded to loosen the cap. The cork shot up into the air with a loud pop and bubbles fizzed out onto the lawn.

"I should go," Ben said again.

"No, stay, mate. Come on. If I'm going to move down here, I should probably get to know some of Holly's friends. You guys are friends too, I take it?"

"We're …" Holly looked to Ben for help. She wanted him to

say, no, they weren't just friends. They were much more than that. They were the people whose company they enjoyed the most. Who laughed and joked together and whose hands felt empty if they weren't holding each other. She wanted him to tell Dan that they were dating. That they were a couple, even, but as he started to reply, she already knew he wasn't going to do that.

"We're really just neighbours," he said, and Holly felt her heart shatter into sharp pieces. "But you two enjoy your special moment. Congratulations."

And with that, he turned around and walked back into the house.

Tears stung her eyes and her stomach felt as though it had turned to lead. There was a pain in her chest that felt as if someone had pierced her to her very core.

"Hols? Glasses?" Dan said, the foam from the champagne now dripping off his hands, as he looked at her expectantly, eyebrows raised.

A second later, the shock passed, and spinning around, Holly raced inside.

"Ben! Ben! Wait!"

He was already through her front door and opening his own.

"Ben, please. I didn't know this was going to happen. He was just there."

"I understand."

"No. No, you don't. I had no idea at all. I didn't want it. I didn't want …" Him. That was the word that should come next. So why wouldn't it leave her lips?

"It was a beautiful proposal," Ben said. "Obviously heartfelt."

The colour drained from her cheeks.

"You were there."

"I was. I wasn't spying or anything. Like I said, I just came to check that you were all right. And there he was, on one knee and then … well, you know …"

He'd seen them kissing. And there was no way he could know that it was him she'd been thinking of, not Dan.

"Ben, it was all a mistake. Dan and I … we're over. We've been over for months. You know that."

"Really? Then I think you ought to go and tell your fiancé that, don't you?"

Of all the conversations she'd ever had in her life, this was probably the worst. No, not probably, definitely. At least when she and Dan had ended it the first time, there had been no hour-long, tear-filled heart-to-heart, or bitter accusations, at least not in person. She'd simply grabbed some things and left. Maybe if they'd gone through all that back then, it would have made this easier.

"I'm sorry. I was just overwhelmed. What you did out there was really wonderful."

Most of the candles had been blown out by the night breeze. Only a few of the lower ones remained alight, probably scorching the grass by now.

"I meant every word, Hols. I will spend the rest of my life making it up to you. Whatever you want. Kids? I'll have twenty. You want to keep the shop -you want to start a chain of stores— I'll support you."

"That's sweet of you to say."

"It's not just words, Hols. I mean it."

"I know. But it's so easy to say things—and I do believe

you'd try—but achieving them is quite another thing. If you'd done this a year ago, I would have said yes without a flicker of a doubt, but I'm not the same person I was then."

"A year's not that long."

"Maybe not, but I'm different. I can't explain it, but I know it wouldn't work. My heart wouldn't be in it. I don't love you anymore, Dan. And I sometimes wonder if I ever really did."

A flash of anger crossed his face. Perhaps she was being too honest with him, but she was only telling the truth. When she arrived in Bourton, she'd found herself comparing their relationship to the one that Agnes and Maud had shared, and she'd wondered if it could ever truly have been called love. It was more a convenient habit.

"I guess I should go, then," he said, standing up. "I wouldn't want to waste any more of your time."

"Dan—"

"No, no. I get it. I was just a way of passing the time until something better turned up. You know you weren't perfect either. I spent all those years with you moaning about your job yet doing nothing about changing it."

He was trying to hurt her now, she realised. And she knew she deserved it, but it didn't make it any the less painful.

"I think maybe you should go now, please," she said.

He pushed back the chair, scraping it against the floor as he went.

"I wasn't planning on staying where I'm not wanted. And I'll take that back now," he said, pointing to her hand.

"Oh, of course. Yes. Sorry."

She hadn't remembered that she was still wearing the ring and straight away went to remove it. It had felt loose when he'd put in on her finger, but for some annoying reason, it now caught on her knuckle.

She finally managed to pull it off and handed it back to him.

For a moment, neither of them spoke, as Dan looked at the ring lying in his palm. Then he closed his hand and put it in his pocket.

When he lifted his eyes back up, the anger of only a few moments before, had gone.

"I love you, Holly Berry," he said, touching her cheek gently. "I love you, and when you realise one day that you love me too, I hope it's not too late."

CHAPTER EIGHTEEN

*I*t had been nine days since the evening of the disastrous proposal, when Ben had seen Holly kiss Dan against a backdrop of a hundred candles. In all that time, he'd said exactly zero words to her. Gone were the morning walks to work together, not that she hadn't tried to engineer them. After the first day passed with no sign of him, she'd reset her alarm to ensure she'd be outside five minutes earlier than usual. On the following day, it was ten. By the time a week had passed, she was standing outside her front door thirty minutes earlier than she used to, hoping she might conveniently *bump into him*. Still no luck. Nor did she see him on the way home from the shop, either.

Given that the bank was also on the High Street, and passing the sweet shop was his most direct route home, she'd hoped that working late would give her the chance to run into him. But yet again, he somehow managed to evade her.

How it was possible to live next door to someone and see so little of them, just showed, to her mind at least, how much effort he must be going to, avoiding her. And it hurt.

She'd tried to keep herself busy. She'd headed back to the care home the following Monday after work and reprised the roll of bingo caller—although she still struggled to remember any more catch phrases than legs eleven and two little ducks. The entertainment there, in the form of Verity's attire and Sid's unscrupulous selling of contraband, was about the only thing that had cheered her up. But that was only distraction enough for one evening.

In another bid to take her mind off thoughts of her disastrous love life, she'd even gone to the lengths of finding information on the local running club. (She didn't actually join, that would have been a step too far, but with all the extra sweets and chocolates she'd been consuming since taking over the shop, she thought that maybe doing a bit more exercise was something she should look into.) In the end though, she'd decided, that as the nights were growing shorter and the rain more frequent, it would be something that would be better looked into in the spring when it was starting to get a bit warmer. Maybe Ben would be speaking to her again by then, she thought, although she didn't hold out much hope.

"He's been really busy at work," Jamie said that Thursday evening, as they shared a bottle of wine. It was a rare event to have her there for the entire evening with no parties or volunteering planned and while Holly knew how much she didn't want to get involved in their drama, she needed advice.

"I know you're speaking to him," Holly said. "And I know that you're lying."

"Well, technically," she replied, "he's always really busy at work, so I don't think it counts as a full lie, does it?"

"Can you just explain to him, please? Can you tell him I didn't know Dan was going to do that? That I didn't want him to do it."

"He knows. I've already said all that to him. I promise you I have. And, against my better judgement, I may also have told him that you're worried you've ruined things between you and that he really should hear you out."

"You have?" she couldn't hide the surprise in her voice. "I thought you didn't like the idea of us together. But then why's he still ignoring me?"

A silence followed, and she was certain Jamie was avoiding eye contact as she took a long sip from her glass, then stood up and moved to the fridge to fetch the bottle, despite the fact that both their glasses were still half full.

"You have to understand, Ben has baggage."

"Baggage?" Holly asked, pushing her glass forwards to get it topped up. It felt like she was going to need it. "What do you mean, exactly? Everyone our age has baggage, don't they?"

Jamie's hand hovered with the bottle. Her lips pressed together in a thin line.

"If he hasn't already mentioned it, I'm not sure I should be the one to tell you the story."

"You know he hasn't told me, and you can't say something like that and then clam up. What is it? What is this *baggage*?"

"It's his story to tell."

Holly gripped her wineglass.

"Well, he's not talking to me, and you are. And if you don't tell me, I'll just go to Caroline. So, you might as well spill the beans right now."

Another moment passed. Finally, Jamie let out a long sigh.

"Okay then," she said and sat back down. "Two years ago, he was engaged."

"He was?"

This was a surprise.

"Yes. Her name was Ella, and he'd been with her for years."

"So, what happened?"

Holly leant forward, as if she might miss something Jamie said, despite the fact that they were sitting right opposite each other. Jamie let out another sigh but carried on.

"She called it off. Two days before the wedding."

"Jeez."

"I know. Everything was paid for. The venue, caterers, honeymoon, the lot. And it was going to be a big do. Over a hundred guests. They'd been together since university. Met in their first week there, I believe. And just like that, she backs out."

No wonder he's so guarded, Holly thought.

"Why?" she asked. "What reason did she give for doing it?"

She was doing a quick calculation. If they'd been together since the start of uni, that must have made it around eight years. Even longer than she and Dan had been together. What was worse, she wondered, cancelling a wedding or cheating? Both sent pretty clear signals.

"She just said she wasn't ready to get married. That she still loved him and everything but wasn't ready for that kind of life. And Ben was really patient—you know him—said he understood, that he didn't want her to feel pressured into doing something she didn't want to. But that wasn't the worse bit."

"It wasn't?" Holly asked. Did she really need to know how it could have possibly got worse? Yes, she did, although she felt somewhat voyeuristic wanting to know all the juicy details of his failed relationship.

"They were still sort of together at this point although, understandably, he needed a bit of space to get over the disappointment. Well, they'd already wasted so much money, and the honeymoon was non-refundable, so he insisted she use it to go on holiday with one of her friends."

"And …"

"And when she was away—Mexico or Thailand? I can't remember. It was one or the other—she met a diving instructor."

A knot formed in Holly's stomach. She had a nasty feeling she knew how this was going to end but didn't want to interrupt, so stayed quiet and let Jamie finish her story.

"Well, within six months, the pair were married, and it turns out she was already pregnant. I'm actually still friends with her on Facebook, for stalking purposes only, you understand."

"In two years?"

That was a quick turnaround. No wonder he wouldn't want to rush into another relationship.

"The only good thing is, she's moved to the south of France, so there's no chance of him bumping into her. It was a really shitty time for him. I'm sure he'd absolutely hate me for telling you this, but you were the first date he'd been on since her. This was why I was so worried—for both of you."

"Crap."

"Exactly, and now I'm guessing this thing with you and Dan …"

"Has probably confirmed to him how fickle women are and put him off relationships for the rest of his life," Holly supplied.

The poor guy. In some ways, Dan pulling that engagement stunt had been quite flattering, whereas Ben had experienced the almost exact opposite.

"So, what do I do now? How can I convince him I'm not like this other girl?"

Jamie took another large swig of wine.

"I'm not sure you can. It's not just about you. It's about him. I know you didn't plan on hurting him and didn't know Dan was going to turn up like he did, but you can see why it was probably just too much for him to handle."

She certainly could. She completely understood. It had been a big step for her too, going on a proper date with Ben after everything with Dan and then Giles. Apparently, it had been the same for him.

"Although there's a definite plus side to this," Jamie said, breaking the gloom.

"There is?" Holly asked, struggling to see what that could possibly be.

"Yep. If you're not dating, you've got loads of free time in the evenings to help me at the care home."

"Great," she said, not cheered up one bit. "That's just great."

"Chin up. If you appear often enough, Verity might even give you a pair of her shoes. And they'll last way longer than any of your relationships have."

CHAPTER NINETEEN

*D*espite her apparent lack of enthusiasm, Holly had quickly grown to love the Weeping Willows Care Home and had even offered to do extra volunteering shifts, if they needed her. Jamie said that they were fine for the time being. It was for the bingo nights that they needed her. And so, that was what she continued to do.

"Garden gate, number eight!" she called, lifting the ball to show it off. "An eight," she repeated.

"What? We've already had the eight! I've already ticked it off!"

"That was eighteen, you old fool. You need to get new batteries for your hearing aids."

"There's nothing wrong with my hearing. It's people not speaking clearly that's the problem."

"If that's the case, then what are those things doing in your ears?"

"They're why there's nothing wrong with my hearing!"

Holly had learned that it was better to just let them get it out of their systems without trying to calm the waters. It appeared to be what some of them enjoyed the most about the sessions. And it was amusing. Luckily, there were no cash prizes involved, just the honour of winning, as she was fairly certain that at least fifty percent of them were cheating half the time.

She'd developed a soft spot for several of them. She suspected that's Sid's cigarette selling on the side had been going on since his early days. Even in his late eighties, though, a schoolboy charm remained, and it was difficult to tell him off.

Glennis, one of Sid's customers, took the game incredibly seriously, even when the others were larking about, and was constantly rolling her eyes and tutting under her breath.

Then, of course, there was Verity. The peacock-feather hat and flamboyant dress had not been a one-off, Holly discovered on her subsequent visits, nor was the late entrance. By her third trip, she was excited to see what the old lady would be wearing next. Thankfully, she didn't disappoint. Her dress was a tight-fitting, crotched ensemble with flared sleeves and tassels in silver and gold. To set if off, she'd chosen a long necklace with a vivid green stone that fell all the way down her breastbone and snakeskin-patterned heels that, once again, Holly was certain she'd break her own ankles in if she dared try just a few steps wearing them. Yet the old lady seemed to glide along as effortlessly as if she were barefoot. But it was her hair that was her most impressive feature. There was no hat this time, just perfectly curated, tight, pin waves. She wouldn't have looked out of place as an extra on the set of The Great Gatsby.

"How do you do that?" Holly asked her, as he handed out the bingo cards on that third Monday. "Do you have a hairdresser who comes in?"

"Do we? Ha! That fool can barely cut a straight line. No. This, my dear, is all self-taught. YouTube. Did you know you can find practically anything you might want to do there, nowadays?"

Yes, she did know. She'd used it to change a lock on the shop door when she'd first taken over *Just One More* and she'd done a pretty good job too, if she did say so herself. Unfortunately, a belligerent traffic warden and a badly timed gust of wind had meant that her handiwork was short-lived and the whole thing had to be replaced, professionally. Still, something mechanical was one thing. She couldn't ever imagine having the patience or skill to style her own hair, like Verity had hers.

She was about to say as much, when Jamie cleared her throat.

"All right, ladies and gentlemen! Time to get this show started!"

She pressed the button at the top of the cage and a ball ran down the metal track and into her waiting hand.

"And our first number tonight is … twenty-six … pick and mix. It's twenty-six. Our Holly should have called that one for us, shouldn't she?"

Everyone laughed and Holly thought it made a lot more sense than half a crown.

By the end of the evening, two slippers had been thrown, a hip flask of whisky had been confiscated, and one of the women had spent at least five solid minutes accusing one of the men of swapping their cards when she was in the toilet.

When the nurse finally came in to call it a night, Holly was wondering what on earth they were on to have so much energy and whether she could get some too.

"Holly, dear." Verity indicated with a lift of her chin that she wanted her to come over. "Can I borrow you for a moment?"

She looked at Jamie.

"You go for it," she said. "I've got to talk to Phil on reception to see if we can sort out name tags for the new volunteers. But a piece of advice: if she asks to practise makeup on you, find an excuse and run."

Across the room, Verity sniffed.

"Some people understand the power of a bold look," she said with a glare at Jamie. "No, I just need some help with the buttons on the back of my dress. Fiddly little buggers, they are. And I'm not quite so limber at reaching around the back as I used to be. I would ask one of the nurses, but Molly is on the night shift, and honestly, that girl. She's got all the delicacy of a stevedore. Lovely voice, mind, sings like a lark, but I'm damned if I'm going to let her near this fabric."

"You know, you could just wear a T-shirt and tracky bottoms, then you wouldn't have that problem," Jamie replied, with a smirk and caused Verity to grimace.

"Tracksuit bottoms? I always knew you were a plebeian. Why else would a woman choose to wear overalls to work? I mean, really."

Sensing that things were getting a bit too personal, Holly took Verity's elbow and guided her gently towards the door.

"It's no problem at all. I'll help you," she said, although she was worried that, come tomorrow morning, Verity would be speaking of her in the same tones as she had poor Molly.

Despite three visits, Holly's knowledge of the layout was still limited. She'd been into the kitchen last week, when one of the nurses had offered them a cup of tea and a ginger snap at the end of the evening, and she'd passed one of the large lounges, going to and from bingo, but she'd not been in any of the residents' own rooms before. In fact, she realised, she'd never been in a care-home bedroom at all.

Her grandparents had passed away when she was too young to remember them, but she'd seen enough television programmes to know what to expect: magnolia walls with faded prints of old watercolours, floral carpet, to disguise any stains, and bedlinen greyed from endless washing. So she was quite taken aback when Verity unlocked her door and switched on the light.

The first thing that struck her was the colour. Canary yellow on one wall, peacock blue on the others, not that you could see that much of them. They were almost completely hidden. There were large fans, abstract prints and at least half a dozen mirrors of varying shapes and sizes. But what really stood out were the photos. Hundreds of them. A lot were faded and some curled up at the edges. Several, of the Polaroid type, had names and dates scribbled on the white strip at the bottom. Most were in black and white, but there were a few more modern, digital printouts, too. And in almost every one of them, was Verity.

Holly's eyes were drawn to one in particular. The sepia tone was almost orange now at the edges and the light colours bleached to near white, but even the effects of time couldn't hide all the life in it. Verity was in the centre, a woman either side of her. Each was holding a drink. But it was the outfits, in particular the hats, that caught the eye. One lady was sporting a bowler hat and another in a deep-red top hat. Verity, however, stood out in the centre, with her crown of peacock feathers, the very same ones she'd worn on the first night Holly had come to the home.

"Oh, what a night that was!" Verity's exclaimed, noticing where Holly was looking and making her jump as she appeared next to her. "Felix Montagues' fiftieth, if I remember correctly. Yes, quite an occasion. Not that I can remember all the details. I'm just grateful that whoever snapped that photo took it from the knees up. He held the party in a bloody field, of all places. Can you imagine? In his defence, it was August, but August in

Scotland! It rained the whole evening. By the time we'd crossed to the marquee, my shoes had sunk all the way into the mud. Spent the rest of the night with them off. Whoever thinks wearing heels gives you blisters should try four hours dancing barefoot in a field. That'd make them grateful for their stilettos."

Holly was only half listening. Her attention had moved on to another photograph, this time a black and white one. A girl stood between an older man and woman. Was this a young Verity? she wondered. If so, she'd been absolutely stunning. Eyes glistened, and a perfect smile was aimed at the photographer. She was already taller than, Holly assumed, her parents.

She was about to ask, when she realised that Verity was no longer by her side but had crossed the room and was opening a pair of double-wardrobe doors. Her jaw dropped. Abandoning the photos, she walked over to get a closer look.

"You can't be serious?" she said.

CHAPTER TWENTY

*B*efore her was the most incredible selection of dresses Holly had ever seen in her life. It was as if she'd walked into the wardrobe department of a Hollywood film company. And this was not your average selection of dresses. Well, perhaps it would be for a cabaret singer. Sequins, feathers, lace, silks, velvets, every material in every colour imaginable, all inside this one wardrobe. Many dresses were full length, some so long that they concertinaed onto the floor. There were silk kimonos, coats, and furs that she was pretty sure were real, but didn't want to check. On the top shelf were boxes, probably containing equally flamboyant hats or shoes. She found herself mesmerised by the glamour and colour of it all.

Holly had never been much of a clothes person. Growing up poor, she'd had no chance to wear anything other than very basic items, and many of those second-hand. As a grown up, she'd always thought there were far better things to do with her money—such as saving for the perfect house—rather than splashing out on an outfit that she would only wear once or twice. But right now, staring at the array of colours and fabrics glinting and glistening, she could see how people could get the same rush from clothes as she did stepping into *Just One More* and seeing all the sweets on offer there.

"Where did they all come from?" she asked, finally finding her voice. "They let you keep all these here?"

"We're not incarcerated, you know," Verity said with a sniff. "Although I will admit it does sometimes feel that way. My nephew, Jonathon, had been wanting to put me away for years and I wasn't having any of it. Then there was a little incident with a chip pan. Well, I told him I wasn't going anywhere unless I could take my collection with me. That's why I chose this place. It wasn't perfect but it was the best of the bunch. I did have to downsize, but I know how to pack and I've got quite a lot in the space under the bed, too."

Holly found her fingers drawn to the fabrics. She was starting to empathise with the young children who couldn't keep their hands off her jars of sweets. This must be exactly how they felt.

"Where did you wear them?" she asked. "Have you worn them all?"

"Of course, I have. You only live once, and I always say it's too short to dress badly or drink bad wine. I was very fortunate. Did a stint in Monaco, working in one of the casinos. Then there were the three years when I was in Santorini, then Geneva and later Los Angeles. You can't keep wearing the same outfits in places like that, you know. Not the done thing at all. There were charity fundraisers, hunt balls, award ceremonies and the odd red-carpet event, too, and you need at least half a dozen dresses to go to Cannes."

"Cannes, as in the Film Festival?" Holly was unsure which was more unbelievable, finding a stash of haute couture in a building where lunch-time bibs were the norm, or the stories that Verity was telling her.

"My mother attended the first Festival, I'll have you know, in 1946. I had to wait a few years before I could go."

From her look of amusement, Holly presumed she must appear stunned.

"I was young once, you know," she said, with a sly smile. "Rather good-looking too, even if I do say so myself, and it didn't matter what your background was in those days, the men liked to have a nice bit of eye candy on their arms at big events. Of course, once I'd made a bit of a name for myself, I was more than happy to show up unaccompanied."

"So how did you end up in Bourton?" asked Holly, returning to the photos and looking at them through a different lens now. Some definitely seemed to have been taken on a red carpet. And one or two of the people standing next to Verity, looked rather familiar, like the man with a moustache and cane, and a beautiful woman with platinum-blonde hair and red, pouting lips.

"My sister lived here; God bless her soul. We adored each other but we were like the proverbial chalk and cheese. She preferred the quiet life and wasn't much of a traveller. Married young. Homely. I'm sure you know the type. I'd bought a little house here that I could stay in when I visited her. This was before she got ill, mind. When that happened, I moved back permanently. By the time she passed … well, I didn't feel like travelling quite so much myself anymore. And it wasn't a bad place to settle down. Nice walks in the country air. Besides, after a while, all the parties got to be the same. The same faces, same small talk, same backstabbing. But the dresses and the dancing …" Her eyes drifted away as if she'd suddenly been transported back in time. "I do miss all that. But I do still get to dress up occasionally, as you've seen, although it's hardly the same as being on a dance floor, the rhythm of a swing band melting away all your cares."

Holly watched her swaying, as if in time to music only she could hear. She had a wistful smile on her face and there was a look of peace, no *bliss*, in her eyes.

A party in a care home, Holly thought to herself. Surely that couldn't be too hard to pull off, could it?

CHAPTER TWENTY-ONE

*S*he'd been buzzing from the moment she'd left Verity's room, having finally helped her undo the back of her dress. They were probably the fiddliest buttons she'd ever had to deal with in her life, and it hadn't helped that her hands were shaking, she was so terrified she might damage the beautiful fabric.

"So, what do you think?" she asked Jamie on the walk back home. "She can't be the only one who feels that way. Do they ever have parties? I mean proper ones, with music and dancing."

"You realise half of them need a walker just to stand up?"

"So? Why does that matter? They could still enjoy the music and dressing nicely for the occasion and maybe having their hair done. And they could dance with their walkers."

"Wow, you're quite passionate about this, aren't you?"

"I think I might be."

Perhaps this was just the distraction she needed, or maybe it was because she felt if she were ever in that situation, she'd want someone to do the same for her. Besides, in less than two months, it would be Christmas and if you couldn't do something nice for people then, what did that say about you? She could see it all now: the lights, the decorations and the residents dressed up to the nines, dancing away to Frank Sinatra and Michael Bublé.

"Yes, I'm going to do it. I'm going to arrange a party for them."

She looked across at Jamie and could have sworn she saw a smirk cross her face.

"Well, if you're serious," her friend replied, "you'll have to get it past Nurse Donna, first."

"Who's that?"

"Nurse Donna? She's the Head Nurse. Nothing happens in that place without her say-so."

Holly shrugged. Okay, so she'd have to speak to this woman. Surely as one of the people in charge, she'd want what was best for the men and women in her care. How could she possibly say no?

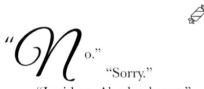

"$\mathscr{N}$o."

"Sorry."

"I said no. Absolutely not."

Holly had needed to make an appointment to meet with Donna and then wait until the Friday for her to be free. During which time, she'd been considering all the different ways to ensure that this was a party that Verity and the others would never forget.

Holly hadn't done much party planning before. Most of her friends had done the big one—their wedding—but obviously, she hadn't yet. There'd been a couple of good Halloween parties that she'd organised at university, with up-cycled costumes and reduced-price apples for bobbing. Several people said at the time that she had a flair for it, but there'd been nothing since then, certainly not when Dan had been on the scene. This was going to be her big chance to put all her creativity into action. Or at least that was what she thought was going to happen, until Nurse Donna gave her a very succinct answer to her request.

For a moment, Holly was too stunned to respond.

"Can I ask why?" she finally managed. "I mean, if it's something the residents would enjoy, then surely that would be a good thing?"

The woman frowned, creating large creases on her forehead. Impressively deep, actually, as if this were a well used expression.

"Mrs …"

"Ms Berry. Holly Berry," she said, despite the fact that she'd already introduced herself quite clearly when she came into the room, and she must have seen her name in her diary.

"*Ms* Berry, have you been volunteering here for long?"

"Not that long. I've just done my third bingo evening. I've only recently moved back to Bourton. I bought the sweet shop in the village. You probably know it? *Just One More.*"

Nurse Donna offered a tight-lipped smile that implied that even if she did know the sweet shop, she didn't give a monkey's who owned it and she certainly wasn't planning on spending her valuable time in idle chitchat.

"So, you're not exactly a long-term volunteer here. No disrespect intended."

"Like I said, I haven't been back in Bourton all that long, and this has been my first opportunity to get involved."

Holly had the definite feeling that whenever someone added

the qualifier, 'no disrespected intended' to what they were saying, then they absolutely meant it to be disrespectful. She just about managed to keep a smile in place as she waited to hear the rest of what this pompous woman had to say.

"Lots of new volunteers come in with grand ideas of what they want to do and how they want to *help*. If you'd had a little more experience, you would have recognised that there are lots of layers to everything we do here. It's not as simple as just *throwing a party*. Those bingo nights that you've attended. Did you think about where all the tables and chairs came from for the residents to use?"

"I assumed they were always there?" she replied, feeling like she'd time-warped back to her junior-school days and hadn't revised for a test she didn't know was going to happen.

"Well, you assumed incorrectly. Even for a small event like that, everything has to be set up in advance and then put away afterwards. And all the surfaces have to be wiped down and rooms aired after the residents have left. Painting, yoga, ukulele lessons. We run to a very tight schedule. Even a ten-minute delay can send some of my residents into a state."

"Well, if you're concerned about moving the furniture, I'm sure I can get plenty of others to help out."

"And what about food?"

"Food?"

"Would you be serving food and drink at this party of yours?"

"Uhmm … well … yes, I suppose I would, now you mention it," she said, trying to sound confident. "Nibbles and maybe some wine or sherry."

"And music, too, I assume?"

"Oh, definitely," she replied, with images of Verity dancing coming straight to mind.

"Okay." Nurse Donna sat back in her seat. "Then tell me, what do you do about the residents with food intolerances or who have difficulty swallowing or have to be spoon fed, or don't like the sound of other people eating close to them? And what about the ones who don't like music or loud noises or people waving their arms about in unexpected movements, like when you dance. Have you thought about that?"

Of course, she hadn't, as the smug woman had suspected.

"I'll admit, there are some fine details I need to look into," she said, crestfallen but not defeated. "If you give me a list of do's and don'ts, things that I should avoid, then I can take all those into consideration. I know it will involve quite a bit of work, but that shouldn't stop us from doing it, should it? Surely they deserve it?"

Once again, the nurse sighed, although this time there was a fraction less condescension in it.

"Holly—it is Holly, isn't it?—I do understand what you're trying to accomplish here. And it's admirable. It really is. But if it was something I thought was truly feasible, then we'd be doing it already. Damn it, I'd have a dance every week if I thought we could. But even if you could get enough help to set everything up, play music and even cater for all the idiosyncrasies of our residents, then there's still the very important fact that these things cost money. And I'm not just talking about for the food and drink and disco balls. Any event like this would involve more work for my team. We'd have to go through it all and ensure everything conforms to our health and safety regulations. We'd need extra staff on duty for the event itself and then, the next day, the residents would be more tired than normal and therefore might struggle with their day-to-day activities and need more help then, too.

"Right now, my budget is already stretched to the limit.

We've had to use our annual Christmas donation from the church to change the curtains on the second floor after a plumbing disaster, and we still can't afford to replace the carpets there. I'm sorry; there's just no way it's possible."

She stopped talking and offered the closest thing to a smile she'd managed since Holly had stepped foot in her office. But despite the nurse having poured cold water on her plans, as Holly considered all she'd said, something gave her reason to still be hopeful.

"So, you're saying that if I can raise enough money to cover all the expenses, including paying the extra staff costs you'd incur and provide satisfactory plans for how it could be run without upsetting any of the residents with … idiosyncrasies, then I can go ahead?"

"You would need an awful lot of money, more than you think, I suspect."

"But you'd agree?"

"Hypothetically."

A smile stretched across Holly's face.

"Okay, tell me exactly what I need to do, and leave it up to me."

CHAPTER TWENTY-TWO

The three women were sitting together in the pub. Caroline had just ordered a second bottle of wine.

"That's a pretty big number," she said, staring at the sheet of paper that Nurse Donna had given Holly before she left the care home. In the nurse's defence, she'd done a thorough job, spending a solid ten minutes listing all the extra costs that would need to be met if Holly were to hold her party for the residents. It was neatly organised, with sub-headings, such as staffing, cleaning, equipment hire and even an allocation to cover how much their electricity bill was likely to increase if they had a live band. Holly felt that was just a little pedantic, but she left it there, all the same.

"It's big, but it's doable, don't you think?" Holly said, still feeling optimistic that it could work. "I did a count earlier. Do you know that there are over thirty businesses on the High Street alone? If they all donated fifty pounds, we'd reach our target."

The women didn't look convinced.

"Fifty pounds isn't that much to ask, is it?" she said, hopefully.

"Well, it depends on how the businesses are doing and who runs them. I don't think that woman in the hardware store would give you the drippings of her nose."

"No, you're right there," Holly replied, remembering her own run-in with her.

"Think back to when you took over *Just One More*. Would you have given money to a cause that you weren't directly linked to, when you were struggling just to keep the business afloat?"

"But they are. The care home is in Bourton. They're in Bourton. Isn't that enough?"

"I think Jamie might be right on this one," Caroline said, tentatively. "A lot of them already support local charities. There's the St John Ambulance and Sue Ryder and the football clubs. Birdland and the Nature Reserve are both registered charities, too, and I know several people donate to the Cubs, the Scouts and Rainbows. Then there's the Badger Trust. Oh, and the Air Ambulance, and lots of the restaurants donate to the food bank in Cheltenham."

"But—"

"And Christmas is just around the corner. There'll be the Shoe Box Appeal and a big push for the homeless shelter."

"Okay, okay, I get it," Holly said, her good mood now very much deflated. "It's a stupid idea."

"We didn't say that," Jamie replied, topping up her glass.

"You pretty much did."

"No, we just said that it's a lot of money and you can't expect local businesses to just hand over cash when they have nothing to do with the care home. Particularly not with the problems they've experienced in the last couple of years. People have to be a lot more careful, that's all. That doesn't mean it's not possible. You're just going to have to work a little harder than you planned, that's all."

Work a little harder than you planned. The words reverberated around Holly's head. Wasn't that exactly what she'd been doing every day since she took over the sweet shop? Maybe not quite so much now as at the beginning, with the leaking roof, the lack of usable stock, the broken front door lock and glass, not to mention trying to reach the level of turnover the mortgage broker had required. Working harder than she planned had become second nature to her and she'd discovered she was actually rather good at it. With a spark of enthusiasm now returning, she lifted her glass.

"Well, here's to working hard, then," she said.

"*B*rainstorm. Go."

She stood behind the counter, pen poised over the new notepad, while Drey walked around the shop, straightening up the jars of sweets. The first part of the day had been as busy as Saturday mornings usually were, but lunchtime was surprisingly quiet, and Holly was making the most of it to pick her assistant's brains for charity-fundraising ideas. That was the advantage in having a teenager on the books; she was far more aware of what the fashionable, on-trend things were than she was. It was thanks to her brainwave that *Just One More* had started selling birthday-party sweet platters—twelve last month and fifteen on order for Halloween. Now she needed her to bring the same creativity to this challenge.

"What have you got so far?"

Holly looked down at the sorry state of her fundraising-ideas list. "Not much," she admitted.

At the pub, they'd started bouncing ideas around between them with good intentions, but the second bottle of wine had been their undoing. That and someone turning on the karaoke machine. She'd taken two pain killers the moment she woke up and thankfully that seemed to be keeping the headache at bay, although it did nothing to help with the current problem.

"A bake sale? A raffle? A sponsored silence?" she said, hopefully.

"A sponsored silence?" Drey's raised eyebrows said more than words ever could. "What are you, five? And how do you plan on doing a sponsored silence while you serve customers?"

"I was just thinking of things that we did at school?" she replied, rubbing her temples and wondered if perhaps the headache was about to kick in.

"Yeah, well, do you want to raise pocket money or proper money? Because there's no way that list will raise more than a hundred pounds, at most, and judging from those figures you showed me, you need a whole heap more."

Holly looked down at her list again and pouted, in much the same way as she probably would have done at five. That girl certainly didn't mince her words.

"Okay, what do you have in mind then?" she asked.

Drey took in a deep breath, straightened another jar and then stopped to consider.

"You could do a sponsored parachute jump. Although, to be honest, I think they're a little passé, and they cost a fortune to set up in the first place, which cuts into your sponsorship money. How about a sponsored marathon?"

"A marathon?"

"You could dress up as a sweet or something. Or, I don't know, an old person and push a Zimmer frame."

"An old person?"

"You're raising money for the elderly, aren't you?"

Holly couldn't help but wonder how many politically incorrect lines she would cross if she tried that. Then again, she would probably end up genuinely hobbling. She couldn't remember the last time she'd run—probably not since leaving school—and it certainly wasn't something she'd ever consider doing for fun. And how long would it take to train for it? Three months? Six? For someone at her level of fitness, it would probably be closer to a year. Not to be morbid or anything, but waiting until the following Christmas might be too late for some of the inmates. It had to be this year, which gave her little more than eight weeks. No, definitely not a marathon then.

"Okay, let's put that one on the back burner," she said. "A very slow back burner," she muttered to herself. "What else have you got?"

Drey took down another jar to screw the lid on properly, then moved to straighten the bags of fudge and sticks of rock.

"How about an auction of promises?" she said, turning around.

"A what?"

"An auction of promises. You know, you get people to agree to do things, like mow a lawn, or baby-sit or cook a dinner for four, and people bid on it."

"Does that work?"

She shrugged. "Rich people do them, I think. You could sell tickets, too, which would help, but you'd need to get plenty of people to come. You could hand out flyers to customers. Obviously, you also need people to offer to do things, too. Maybe some customers would be up for that."

Holly considered the idea. Maybe giving a bit of their time or bidding for others to do some service for them would be a better way to get people to part with their money than just handing over cash, and it would be far more entertaining. There must be plenty of things that would work. She was sure Caroline wouldn't mind volunteering a couple of hours babysitting and Jamie, well she could turn her hand to practically anything.

"But where could we hold it? We'd need a pretty big room."

"My mum's one of the leaders at Baden Powell Hall that they use for cubs and scouts. Bet we could get that for a couple of hours, if I ask her nicely."

"Really?"

"Sure, they're always hiring the place out."

"But we'd need it soon. Like, in a couple of weeks."

"I'm sure if you're flexible with the day, she'd be able to work something out."

Wow. Not only did Holly suddenly feel like she had a vague idea what she was doing, but the threatening headache was receding too. Although it wasn't quite enough to stop her glancing outside and wondering how and when Ben would actually start talking to her again.

"Great, so an auction of promises it will be," she said, focusing back on the task at hand. Now all she had to do was organise the whole thing.

CHAPTER TWENTY-THREE

"*I* think I may have bitten off more than I can chew," Holly said, with the pad of paper in front of her once more, this time on the kitchen table.

"Really?" Jamie said, with a smirk. "That sounds most unlike you. But don't they say, if you want something done, ask a busy person?"

Ignoring the dig, she continued to study her to-do list and wonder where on earth she should start.

It had already been a couple of weeks since Drey had come up with the fundraising idea and since then it had been full steam ahead. The hall had limited availability around all the Christmas fairs and choir practices that were already booked, and the only suitable date, a Thursday towards the end of the November, which was coming around quickly. As such, her nerves were jangling.

They had to start pushing the tickets, but she was worried they might not have enough offers to make the event worth people's time. Every spare moment, she'd been on the phone or popping into the other shops on the High Street or—her most common tactic—accosting her customers, to see if anyone had a hidden talents they were willing to donate for a good cause. They were selling the tickets at three pounds a head, which wasn't a lot, but it meant that they could make a small donation to the Scout Hall, which they were getting for free. On Drey's advice and to get around the licensing laws, it was going to be a BYOB night.

"Trust me, you want them drinking. They'll spend way may more money if they're tipsy and the whole evening will go with more of a swing," she'd said.

"Aren't you still below the legal drinking age?" Holly had pointed out.

"I am, but I have parents and older cousins, too. Trust me on this. People will be much happier bidding if they're too drunk to remember that they're already at their overdraft limit."

Holly had been a bit worried about the ethics of this somewhat cynical approach, but she decided not to wear her virtuous hat in the circumstances.

A digital reproduction company, out on the industrial estate, had agreed to do all the printing for free, in exchange for a prominent acknowledgment and one of their standard ads appearing in the programme.

The daughter of one of her customers worked at the Echo, and they ran a few column inches about the fund-raising sweet shop owner, complete with a picture that made her look like a startled hedgehog on a bad-hair day. But beggars can't be choosers, as her mother always said, and the publicity got them another forty ticket sales, meaning they were well on their way to filling the two-hundred-capacity hall.

"So tell me, what have you been offered so far?" Jamie asked, leaning over and breaking off a corner of white chocolate blondie. With all the stress of organising the auction, Holly had found herself over-baking again, and their conversation was taking place over a glass of bubbly and a choice of three different tray bakes. "What have people agreed to do? Besides Caroline babysitting, that is."

"And you with one hour of odd-jobs."

"Yes, besides me and Caroline."

"Okay, well one of Drey's friends is going to do a pet portrait—turns out he's pretty good actually—and Michael's agreed to do a two-hour dog walk or two one-hour ones."

"I didn't know he liked dogs?"

"I'm not sure he does, but Caroline and the kids really want one, and she signed him up, hoping it would warm him to the idea."

"Does she realise that it could completely backfire on her?"

"Well, it's her choice. Anyway, the Seven Hounds is offering a twenty-five-pound meal voucher, and the Brewery at Stow an ale-tasting visit."

"That sounds good."

"I know. The Swimming Pool has promised six free swimming lessons, adult or child, and the Riding Stables have offered a free lesson. The Bakery has come up with a free cake a week, for a year."

"Seriously? That's awesome."

"I know, I think that might end up being one of the most popular of the night. Although there are a couple of other good promises that could do rather well, like a monthly car valeting for a year and someone willing to do clothes alterations."

Holly continued to read through the list. She was starting to feel quite impressed with herself at how much she'd achieved in such a short time. And it was really encouraging how the community was coming together to support her project. Of course, she didn't know if she was going to make enough money from it, but at least she would have tried her best and that's all you can do—another of her mother's sayings.

Last week, when she'd helped Jamie at bingo, one of the residents had snuck in an old iPod and speaker and was playing Frank Sinatra, interspersed with a bit of One Direction. It had been rather nice, and one or two had got up between games and done a bit of impromptu bopping, although it ended abruptly when Nurse Donna came in and confiscated the equipment on the grounds that dancing without adequate supervision could result in falls and broken bones.

There would definitely be dancing at her party, she promised herself as she left. But there was still the job of selling the rest of the tickets and getting bums on seats for the event. That was this week's hurdle.

"So, what about you?" Jamie asked, bringing her out of her daydream. "What are you promising?"

"Me? I'm the one organising it."

"I know, but you still have to donate something. Yours will be the most important one of the night. You can't expect other people to shell out if you're not doing your bit."

Holly considered this. She'd already put in almost as many hours as the average full-time job, on top of running the shop. Even so, Jamie's words rang true. She needed to lead by example.

"I guess I'll do a bag of sweets a week for a year?" she said.

Jamie wrinkled her nose.

"What's wrong with that? That would be a decent thing for people to bid on. Everyone likes sweets."

"It's not very personal, though, is it?"

"Neither's someone valeting a car," she retorted, feeling rather put out. People paid good money for her sweets. That said, she would rather it wasn't one of her regulars who won—

she still had a mortgage to pay and needed all the profit she could make.

Jamie used her fork to cut off another slice of blondie. As she lifted it to her mouth, she froze.

"You should donate a baking lesson."

"What?"

"That's a perfect idea. Do a baking masterclass. You haven't got anyone signed up for that already, have you?"

Holly was pretty sure she hadn't but looked down her list just to make sure. There were several lessons on offer besides the swimming and the horse-riding ones, including an hour of guitar tuition, and a Ukulele class for up to four people but, no —she ran her finger back up again, just in case—nobody had volunteered to run a baking class.

"You really think that would be better than sweets?" she asked, still not convinced.

"Absolutely. Anybody can go to the shop and purchase sweets. People are going to pay more for something that you can't normally buy."

On reflection, it did make sense. If there wasn't much competition, someone bidding for sweets might end up paying less than they cost her to buy wholesale, which would seem a bit pointless.

"Okay," she agreed, picking up her pen. *One baking masterclass from Holly Berry*, she wrote and, strangely enough, felt rather excited about it.

*T*he next week, as she got ready to go to the care home, Holly was thinking about when she should break the news to them about the party. She obviously couldn't do it until they'd raised enough money from the auction and cleared everything with the Head Nurse. But she was feeling more and more confident it was going to happen. She would let Nurse Donna know that evening how well the ticket sales were going. Then, hopefully, she could pin her down on a date.

"Are you coming?" she called from the bottom of the stairs. They would have normally left by now. Jamie had been in the shower when she'd arrived home and still hadn't made an appearance. Nurse Donna was very particular about punctuality. Timing and structure were important to the residents and Jamie always made a concerted effort to start the bingo bang on time, but the way she was going tonight, they could end up being seriously late.

Jamie appeared on the landing, swathed in towels.

"I thought I told you. I can't do tonight."

"What? No, you didn't!"

"Are you sure? I have an Anne Summers party. Had to rearrange it from a couple of months ago. This was the only night they could do."

"Oh," she replied, surprised and suddenly incredibly nervous. She'd never run one of the nights on her own. Of course, she knew where everything was stored, and it wasn't exactly rocket science. But a bit of warning would have been nice. Had she known, she would have brushed up on the bingo calls.

"Don't worry, you won't be on your own," Jamie said, reading her expression.

"I won't?"

"No, I got a friend to step in, just for this evening. It'll be fine. They're going to go straight from work though, so they said they'd meet you there."

She glanced at her watch. It was ten to seven.

"You'll find them waiting outside for you," Jamie added. "They'll be the nervous-looking one, wondering if they're in the right place."

"Great, that'll make two of us," Holly replied, feeling tense.

It would be one thing making mistakes if she were the only one there, but now she'd have someone watching her and she'd have to look after them, too.

As she walked out of the house and up towards the care home, her mind quickly moved on from worrying about the evening, back to the Auction of Promises. What would happen if they didn't raise enough money? She could just donate what they did get to the home, she supposed, although from what Nurse Donna had said, it would probably end up going towards something mundane, like new carpets. Maybe they could hold onto it for another year and do a second fundraiser, then have the dance that Christmas. No. She shook her head. She needed to stop with the negativity.

She upped her pace past the Model Village and towards Birdland. Of course, they would make enough money. They would make more than enough, maybe even sufficient to be able to hold a summer party as well, she thought, before quickly reminding herself not to get too cocky.

The November air was chilly, but still warmer than this time last year. Not to mention drier. She could remember all too well coming out of the tube station back in London, to be hit by a wind so strong it blew back her umbrella before she'd even fully opened it.

Her legs were starting to ache from rushing, as she reached the gates of the nursing home. She turned in and saw someone standing in front of the door, silhouetted by the building's security lights. The square-shaped coat said that it was a man, even from behind. As Holly's footsteps crunched on the gravel drive, he turned around to face her.

"You?" Holly said. "You're volunteering with me tonight?"

Ben's cheeks coloured so dramatically that it was obvious, even in the gloom.

"Well, I don't have to stay if you don't want me."

CHAPTER TWENTY-FOUR

$\mathcal{I}$t had been almost a month since Dan's proposal and Ben's sudden exit from her life. She still found herself daydreaming about those moments by the water or in the car, when she'd been so certain they were about to kiss. Despite everything, each morning she hoped he might be waiting outside on the wall, like he once did, ready to walk into work together. And at five o'clock each evening, she'd find herself gazing out of the shop window, wondering if that would be the day he'd come in to walk home with her.

She had finally resigned herself to the fact that it just wasn't going to happen. He'd even stopped coming over to the house in the evenings, although Jamie assured her there were justifiable reasons—like him having to visit his nephew, or he was in Cheltenham for an important meeting. But she'd been certain these were all invented excuses.

Yet here he was, standing right there, with those dark eyes watching her. Had he always been this good looking? she wondered. Possibly not on their last date, when he'd ended up flapping about in the water, struggling to stay afloat, but apart from that, she supposed he must have been. His hair had grown a little. The extra length suited him.

Suddenly realising she had been standing there staring at him, Holly cleared her throat.

"Sorry, I just wasn't expecting to see you. How have you been?"

"I've been fine, thank you. Busy. And you?"

"Busy," she replied, inwardly groaning at the stilted conversation.

"Jamie mentioned you were doing a fundraiser."

"Yes."

"Sounds good."

"I hope so."

"I'd like to come."

"Well, there are limited tickets."

"Oh."

She saw his face fall and realised how ridiculous she must have just sounded. Why on earth had she said that? Why hadn't she told him she wanted him there? She hurriedly tried to back-track, hoping the lack of lighting would disguise just how fraught she must look. Her throat had gone dry all of a sudden. Where was a hard-boiled sweet when you needed one?

"I was going to reserve a table, actually. You know, for me and Jamie and Caroline and Michael. They'd be plenty of room for you, too, if you'd like to join us."

"That would be great, if you're sure there's enough space."

"There will be. There is. There will be six seats per table, I think. So, six minus four is two. Two empty chairs. Plenty of space for you. That would make five of us, you know." Oh God, so much babbling, it was actually making her lightheaded through lack of oxygen

"Okay. Well, if you let me know how much the tickets are."

"Don't be silly, I'll pay for you."

"I'd be more comfortable if I gave you the money. You know, keep things uncomplicated."

Uncomplicated. What a word to choose to describe their situation. They hadn't so much as kissed, so they should be. But they certainly weren't.

"Dan's gone," she blurted out before she knew what she was saying. "I mean, I told him to go. I didn't know he was going to do that. Propose, I mean. I never thought … I never expected."

He nodded slowly. Even in the dim light it was obvious that he was avoiding looking at her.

"Jamie did mention it," he said, then cleared his throat. "Shouldn't we think about getting in there? She said they like to start things promptly."

And that was it. She'd been put firmly in her place, again.

"You're right," she said. "We should probably get this over and done with."

And without a second glance, she marched past him, pushed the door open and strode inside.

"*O*h! Look at him! Look at him! Hasn't he got nice arms."

"What are you on about? You can't even see his arms under that jacket."

"You're quite right. Hey! You over there. Take your jacket off. Let's have a proper look at those arms."

"Arms, really? You've got a specimen like that in front of you and you want to look at his arms?"

It was hard to stay mad at Ben for long, if for no other reason than the verbal bombardment he'd been suffering since the moment he'd stepped foot in the Birch Room. It was as if the women had been caged up for the last thirty years and this was the first man under the age of seventy they'd seen.

"Please ladies, you're embarrassing yourselves. Try to show a little decorum." Verity called from the back of the room, where she was busy fanning herself, as if her temperature had risen a little, too. The fan in question comprised intricate white lace, layered on top of a deep-navy fabric. As Holly passed her, handing out the dabbers, she grabbed her lightly by the wrist.

"You know, in future, a little warning would be nice. I hate new people seeing me looking underdressed."

"Really?"

Holly raised an eyebrow as she stepped back to view the older woman's ensemble. Like the fan, the dress was of dark navy, with white beading along the neckline. It tapered into the waist, hugged the hips then flared back out dramatically, creating a fishtail effect.

"I'd pay good money to see what you look like in pyjamas and slippers."

"Not even on my deathbed, darling," the old woman said, with a wink.

Smiling to herself, she returned to the front of the room, where Ben had loaded up the balls, ready to mix them up.

"Shall I?" he offered.

"Be my guest," she replied.

With a crank of the handle, the cage turned, and a ball rolled down the metal chute and into the cradle at the end. He took it and held it up.

"Man alive, it's number five," he said, in the most perfect bingo-calling voice Holly could ever imagine. He then twisted around, displaying the ball to both sides of the room, before repeating, "Man alive, number five."

It was the first time she'd seen them so quiet, but given how she was equally stunned by this unexpected performance, she should hardly be surprised. Seeming not to notice—or perhaps assuming that bingo nights were always so focused—he turned the handle and picked up the next ball.

"Two little ducks, twenty-two," he said, then repeated it, to make sure everyone had heard.

Next came, "Life begins at forty. Number forty. Can you hear me at the back?"

"We can hear you," one of the women yelled back. "But it's not true. Eighty's the number you're looking for. Come back here and I'll show you."

Everyone laughed. Ben blushed, and Holly found herself grinning at him. Since she'd got to know him, she'd suspected he was the type of guy who had a hundred hidden talents he didn't like to brag about, but she'd never expected one of them to be bingo calling.

Well, she thought, pulling out a chair and grabbing a spare card and dabber for herself, this evening was turning out to be very different from what she'd expected.

CHAPTER TWENTY-FIVE

"*T*hat's it, I'm retiring," Holly said, as they packed the things back into the storage cupboard. "There's no way I can compete with that. You know they'll be gutted if I turn up on my own next week. Or even with Jamie. Where on earth did you learn to do that?"

"Oh, it's something you pick up, isn't it?"

"Is it?"

He shrugged. Everything was ship-shape and all that remained was for them to walk home. Holly was tempted to ask if he'd like to go for a drink, for no other reason than that was what she and Jamie always did. But they'd been getting on so well, and the last thing she wanted to do was end up ruining it all. So instead, she kept her mouth shut and held the door open for him to follow her out.

"Actually," he said, as they stepped outside. "I used to do this at the care home that my gran was in. Bingo calling that is."

"The one they pulled down and turned into flats?" she asked.

"That's the one. I haven't done it for years. Not since before

I left for university. I guess it's like riding a bike, something you never forget."

Riding a bike. When she'd first bumped into Ben—literally —he'd been riding a bike. Their first date was a bike ride, too. Not that she'd considered it a date. Back then it had just been a day out, with a local keeping her company, but now that she thought back on it, that non-date had been far more enjoyable than many of the actual ones she'd gone on with Dan, or anyone else, for that matter.

"I'm sorry I messed things up between us," she said, stopping at the pavement.

Ben had already walked ahead before realising she wasn't next to him any longer. He turned to look at her.

"What did you say?"

"I said I'm sorry I messed things up. But then I don't think I did, not really. I'm mean, I had no idea Dan was going to turn up, and I certainly didn't want him to. I'd just gone around to check on the lights, if you remember. Only it wasn't the lights, it was those damned candles. And we'd been having such fun together."

Her heart was pounding fit to burst. She should have kept her mouth shut, not ruined yet another evening. Then again, why should she? He was the one who'd ghosted her, like they were teenagers, or random strangers after an unsuccessful meeting arranged on the internet. Didn't she deserve an explanation?

"I think that maybe we're better off as friends," he said.

"Oh. Okay."

Friends. In all her short-sightedness, she must have failed to realise that he just wasn't as into her as she was into him. He took a step closer.

"I think you're amazing, Holly. You're fun and spontaneous, and you're the life and soul of the party."

But she wasn't girlfriend material. At least, not to him.

"But I'm not like that," he continued, looking down at his feet, "and I think it would be best to leave it at being friends, before either of us gets hurt."

Her head seemed to be nodding of its own accord. Well, she'd wanted an answer and now she'd got one. This was the time to stop talking. To call in quits and cut her losses. And yet her mouth was starting to move, and she knew she couldn't stop it.

"Are we, though?" she asked.

"Sorry?"

"Are we friends? It's just that when we were before, we used to do things together, you know, walk to work, cycle rides, that kind of thing. That all seems to have stopped."

"I'm here now, aren't I?" he replied, then sighed and shook his head. "You're right, that's on me, and I'm sorry. I promise, from now on, we'll go back to normal. Friends. Just like before."

"Promise?"

He looked at her with those eyes that still made her heart flutter.

"Scout's honour. Speaking of which, how can I help with this auction? I assume you've bitten off more than you can chew, as usual."

"Why do people immediately think that about me?"

"I have no idea."

*T*he week leading up to the event was chaotic, even by Holly's normal standards. The unseasonably perfect weather had meant the shop had been rammed all week. Normally, she was grateful for every bit of sunshine, particularly in the winter months when the number of tourists always took a nosedive, but this had been unprecedented. So much for thinking she'd be able to sort things out while she worked.

In the end, she'd no choice but to get Caroline in for another two mornings, so that she could run back and forth to the Scout Hall. Ticket sales had really picked up and she was now worrying if they'd be able to fit everyone in. Just keeping track of who was attending was involving a lot of extra work. Requests for tickets were coming in via email, by telephone and from people catching her on the street as she walked to and from work. Most collected their tickets from the shop—which often meant extra sales, too, which was nice—but it was tough going.

The florist was donating centrepieces for the tables and they would have to be collected and taken to the hall. They would go to the home afterwards, which was a bonus. She seemed to be updating her spreadsheet of promises every two minutes. This was all good but took so much time.

Thankfully, Drey had adopted her normal leadership role, enlisting fellow students to help run the evening, so that Holly would be free to enjoy that part of it after all the hard work.

"It's fine," she'd said. "I've got loads of friends who need stuff to put on their personal statements for their uni applications. Everyone's desperate for any type of volunteering work to make themselves look good. We were meant to have all these enrichment hours but hardly anyone got them. This'll tick a box or two."

Free help was nice, although the motive behind it didn't exactly inspire Holly with confidence. Drey noticed her uncertain look.

"They'll be fine. I'll supervise them. Remember, I did practically run the shop before you arrived on the scene."

That was true. While Maud had been mourning her partner, Agnes, it had been Drey, the Saturday girl who'd kept things going, dealing with suppliers and keeping the shelves stocked. And if that wasn't impressive enough, she'd done it all without getting paid. Yup, Holly had good people about her. People she could trust. She just needed to get through to the night, so she could actually enjoy it.

Ben, true to his word, had been almost back to normal, in the sense that he came past the shop on the way home each evening, ready to walk Holly home. Unlike before, however, she was normally sending him on various errands instead.

"There's a woman living on Roman Way who I said I'd deliver tickets to. Any chance you could drop them off and collect the money?"

It wasn't something she'd normally do, but the lady had come into the shop on crutches, found she'd forgotten her purse and then got completely flustered, refusing outright to take the tickets without paying, despite the fact that she was a regular.

"You know Roman Way is in the opposite direction to where we live."

"Well, I could do it myself, but I've still got to ring around everyone on the promise list, just to make sure I've got all the details exactly right. If there are any changes needed, I'll have to get hold of Drey straight away for her to alter the programme before it goes off to the printers."

"I get it," he said, holding out a hand. "I'll drop them off."

As he opened the door to leave, she called him back.

"Here," she said, picking up a chocolate hedgehog from the counter and throwing it across to him. "As a thank you."

He caught it and grinned.

"You know you'll never be rich if you keep giving away all your profits."

"You're right. Can I have it back, please?" she teased.

"No chance," he laughed, unwrapping it as went.

They were friends again, she thought, as he disappeared out of view. And being friends was definitely better than not having him in her life at all. Who knew, maybe she'd meet the man of her dreams at the auction.

CHAPTER TWENTY-SIX

"*I* feel sick. I'm going to be sick." Holly could feel the nausea threating to overwhelm her. "I think you might have to go without me. I'll give you twenty quid. You can bid on something for me."

"You're not sick. You're a drama queen," Jamie said, unsympathetically. "And I have no idea why. It's all done. You've organised everything to the nth degree. Young Drey's doing the compering and hosting, so all you have to do is sit back and enjoy yourself."

"And worry if people are having a good time and if we're raising enough money."

"Seriously, chill out. Here, have a go at this."

Jamie pushed a long-stemmed champagne flute across the table to her. Was it really a good idea drinking now? she wondered, staring at the glass. Then again, like Jamie said, her bit was done. It was over to the students and their extra enrichment hours. She picked up the bubbly, opened her mouth and necked half of it in one go. A second later, a burning sensation hit the back of her throat.

"What the hell was that?" she asked, coughing and spitting while simultaneously trying to cover her mouth and stop the searing liquid from spilling out of her nostrils. "I thought it was Prosecco?"

"It's moonshine. Harry gave me a bottle of his homemade stuff when I was up at the farm last week. I thought you knew that's what it was."

"Why the hell did you pour it into champagne glasses then?" she replied. The taste was somewhere between aniseed and paint stripper, with a definite aftertaste of something floral.

"They're pretty glasses. I thought I'd go for classy. This is a special occasion."

Holly's eyes were now watering, and her throat was still stinging, although her nose seemed to have stopped running.

"Nothing could make that classy. Trust me."

"Honestly," Jamie said, topping up their glasses, as if Holly's reaction was a sign that she wanted more of the horrific stuff.

Given that her throat had already been seared by the concoction, possibly never to recover, it did seem silly to leave it there. She took a smaller sip this time and was slightly better prepared as it hit her tonsils. She wouldn't go so far as to say it was pleasant, but she'd learned from experience with these home-brews, that if you drank enough, almost anything could taste reasonable eventually.

"I've put another bottle in the fridge for us to take tonight. Do you know who the other person on our table is?"

She shook her head. "I think someone who's coming on their own will be put with us. Drey's got the table plan."

"Is there anything that girl doesn't do?"

"I'm pretty sure she's going to be the CEO of a FTSE company when she leaves school. Either that, or she'll be working for me forever."

Holly's mind went back to the table arrangement. She would try to seat herself away from Ben, perhaps between Caroline and Jamie, or next to whoever this extra person was. The last thing she wanted was to be sitting next to him all evening, mourning a relationship that had never even got off the ground.

"Right, what are you wearing?" Jamie asked, thankfully taking the empty glasses away this time rather than refilling them. "We've got to leave in an hour, so you'd better get dressed, pronto."

"I am dressed." Holly said, looking confused. Okay, she was still in the outfit she'd worn to the shop that day, but they were some of her nicest work clothes. The dress was knee-length in a jersey fabric with a polka-dot pattern that grew more intense the closer to the hem it went. And the plain black cardigan was, well, a plain black cardigan. She didn't think she could improve much on that. Catching her reflection in the glass of the cabinet door, she realised her hair could perhaps do with a brush, but other than that, she thought she looked pretty good.

"You want people to spend money, don't you?" Jamie said. "So, *you* need to look like you have money. Money attracts money. Think of those idiots like Giles Caverty."

"What about him?" she asked.

Thinking about that man was something she didn't like doing at the best of times, and she was surprised Jamie would bring him up, given how much she hated him, too.

"Think of how much money that type of guy spends. You know, I heard he once paid a hundred-and-fifty pounds for a pair of socks. Can you believe that?"

"That cannot be true."

"I'd bet it is. Anyway, that doesn't matter. The point is, you want people to think they're at a high-class do and then show off, outbidding each other. You've got to look the part, too.

Holly looked down at her dress again, feeling she'd probably been insulted. It was true there was a bit of bobbling in places, and she'd had to repair a seam of the cardigan that had become unstitched, but she thought she'd done a pretty good job of it. No one—except perhaps her mother—would be able to tell. She suddenly wished there was another glass of the moonshine handy.

"I don't know what else I have, that would be better," she said. "I mean, I've got my nice jeans. And a couple of other dresses I wear for work."

The sound that Jamie made in response could have come from Holly's mother or aunt or any elderly person, for that matter.

"Okay, here we go. I guess it's about time I showed you this, anyway."

"Showed me what?"

"You'll see. Come on. Upstairs. Now. And not a word to Nurse Donna."

Now Holly was really confused.

What she was looking at made no sense. No sense at all. She couldn't take her eyes from what was now in front her. It was like one of those optical-illusion images that you need to be a certain distance away from for it to become clear. But even after blinking and rubbing her eyes, she couldn't fathom it.

"I don't understand," she said, frankly.

One thing she'd always admired about Jamie was her

chameleon-like ability to adapt to any situation. Not just in terms of her occupation—handy woman here, Ann Summers party host there—but also physically. She never looked out of place. She looked equally at home in overalls, fixing the roof of a sweet shop, as she did in a smart dress in a nice restaurant, or in jeans and a vest top, playing pool in the pub. But this. This took things to a whole new level. It wasn't just that they were dresses—she had seen her in those plenty of times—it was the *dressiness* of the dresses. Silks, satins, sequins, everything shimmered. And she'd never once seen her in sequins. About a quarter of her built-in wardrobe was taken up with the extravagant garments.

"These are just like Verity would wear," she said, barely able to stifle a gasp. "It's like a miniature version of her collection."

"Where do you think they all came from?" Jamie asked, with a smile.

"Verity?"

"The one and only."

"But how?"

Jamie raised an eyebrow. "Honestly, if you think she's got a lot of clothes now, you should have seen how much she had when she arrived at the home. Cases and cases and even a massive packing box. So many, they had their own van and you could hardly see the floor or the bed for them all. There was no way she could keep all of them. Not a chance. She threw a strop, as you can imagine, a rather dramatic one. Said she'd refuse to leave her room if she had to get rid of any of them. In the end, Nurse Donna let her use a spare room and gave her two weeks to sort herself out. Most of the nurses have at least one vintage Christian Dior in their wardrobe at home now. I brought a box here for her, with the understanding that if she ever needed a particular item from it, I'd return it to her."

"And have you ever done that?" Holly asked, still stunned that her housemate had a stash of haute couture she hadn't known about.

"No, of course not. I don't think she even remembers they still exist."

Holly's hand had alighted on a beautiful silk number. It was the colour that drew her in, a bright royal blue. It had black beads decorating the collar and cuffs. Understated, but exquisite. The type of thing an A-list celebrity, who didn't need to show off to stand out, would wear to a film premiere. Tastefully demure.

"You can't think I should wear one of these?" she said.

"Why not?"

"Should I not at least ask Verity, first?"

"You think she's going to say no?"

She didn't think that at all. In fact, she believed the lovely old lady would be delighted one of her dresses was getting another outing, even if it was just to the local Scout Hall.

"I don't know if any of them will fit," she said, feeling a surge of excitement at the prospect.

"Only one way to find out," Jamie grinned back.

The blue dress looked incredible. But so incredible that Holly knew there was no way she could wear it. To start with, it would need her highest heels, to make sure that the hem didn't trail on the ground and there was no way she could cope with those all night. She wanted to feel comfortable and at ease, and she'd rather wear her spotty work dress than feel self-conscious.

"What about this one?" Jamie said, picking out another. It

was a slinky number, no beading or lace, just silver all the way from the neck to the floor, where it pooled like a puddle of molten metal.

"It's a little too flashy as well, don't you think."

"You think that the care home is flashy? Verity would wear this to bingo in a heartbeat"

That was a good point. It was still a mystery to Holly, how a woman could dress so inappropriately and yet never look out of place. It was definitely a lot to do with confidence. There were always those people—more so in London than here—who looked completely at home and at ease, no matter what they were wearing. Maybe she needed to channel a bit of Verity's faith in herself to go with her dress.

"Okay, then. Let's give it a try."

She took it from Jamie and slipped it over her head. The fabric was cool and almost weightless, as if she were wearing silver leaf rather than material. She pulled her shoulders back. You could only get away with a number like this if your posture was perfect.

"Wow." Jamie let out a low whistle. "Don't let this got to your head or anything, but you could be a Bond girl."

She studied her reflection in the mirror. It did look stunning. It clung to her in all the right places, managing to accentuate her waist, whilst sweeping over her hips in a very flattering way. Maybe she wasn't quite a Bond girl, but this was certainly the best she'd looked in a very long time, perhaps ever. Now she'd have to do something special with her make up, too. This morning's slap just wasn't going to cut it. She'd have to get a wiggle on.

"Okay," she nodded, turning from side to side, making sure there wasn't something wrong with it they'd somehow missed. "That's me sorted. Which one are you going to wear?"

"Me? I'm just going to wear something from my standard get up."

"No way," Holly protested. "Either we're both wearing one of these, or neither of us is. In fact, I'd better ring Caroline. We're all in this together, and I'd hate for her to feel under-dressed."

CHAPTER TWENTY-SEVEN

*F*orty minutes later, they were all set. Holly felt as if they were about to go to a school prom. This was definitely the most dressed-up she'd been ever.

"Drey's just texted," she said. "She's already there and says everything's good to go. She's got two of her school friends on the door collecting tickets, and the place is starting to fill up. I guess one of us should knock for Ben."

Jamie looked at her, with a raised eyebrow and a knowing smile twisting on her lips.

"I don't know why you're looking at me like that?" she said, indignantly. "There's nothing going on anymore. Not that there was before, but he's made it perfectly clear he only wants to be friends. Besides, you didn't even want us to date."

"*I did,*" Caroline protested. "I think you're perfect together."

"And I may have been a little hasty," Jamie admitted. "He has seemed rather down since, well … you know."

"Don't blame me."

"Honestly, I sometimes want to hit that man," Caroline muttered under her breath.

"I guess that, as his *friend*, you should be the one to call for him, then?" Jamie said. "I'll just get my bag and keys and see you outside.

Holly didn't bother arguing. She had too much going on in her mind right now, like how she was going to manage in the shoes Jamie had lent her. They were at least a size too big and they'd had to pad out the toes with tissue paper. She picked up her own handbag and headed out.

While there was no arguing that the silver dress was a defi-nite showstopper, there's was also no denying that the polka-dot one would have been a darned sight warmer. Maybe she should pop back and grab her black cardigan. She was about to yell for Caroline to pick it up for her, when Ben's front door swung open.

"Ready to g——" he stopped mid-word, in shock. "Wow."

She looked down and dug her toes into the gravel, unable to meet his eyes.

"I think I might have missed the email about the dress code," he said.

Holly raised her eyes and looked him up and down. He was dressed the same way he always did, wherever they went, regardless of where. Jeans and a shirt. Nothing flamboyant. He still looked good, though.

"Jamie said we need to look like we have lots of money, to encourage other people to bid against us."

"I don't think you'll get anyone bidding against you looking like that. They'll let you have whatever you want."

Her cheeks had started to burn. She wanted to say some-thing in return. Thank you, would have been appropriate, but she was now struggling with overheating issues.

"Right? Are we all ready?" Jamie asked, appearing in the doorway, car keys dangling from her hand.

"You know it's only a five-minute walk," he said.

"Do you know how long a five-minute walk would take in heels this size?" Jamie asked, lifting the hem of her dress slightly. "Come to think of it, I'm not sure I can actually drive in them, either. Here——" She threw the keys to Ben, who snatched them out of the air with one hand.

"I guess that means I'm the chauffeur, then," he said.

Holly had spent a year in Brownies when she was in Year 4 or 5. It was just before one of her dad's many redundancies. Her mum had managed to find a uniform, complete with sash, in a second-hand shop, which had swung it for her. She had then picked off all the badges that the previous owner had achieved, and tidied it up, until the whole thing looked almost as good as new. This had the added benefit that they wouldn't need to pay for badges when Holly earned them herself.

Unfortunately, it wasn't long before her dad lost his job yet again, so that even the small weekly subscription was beyond their means and the uniform went to the back of her wardrobe, awaiting better times. But when that day came around, she was already far too big for it not to mention too old for Brownies. Holly had herself unpicked the few badges she'd managed to get and donated it back to the local charity shop, so that someone else would be able to make use of it—hopefully for longer than she had.

The Scout Hall was close to the Primary School. She'd been there quite often as a child, usually dragged there by her mum to second-hand and bric-a-brac sales. Organising this event had been the first time she'd set foot in the place since well before her move to London.

They parked on the opposite side of the road, next to the shop that used to sell fruit and vegetables. During the daytime you wouldn't have a hope in hell of getting a space there, but tonight, it was practically empty.

"Okay, so Drey's friends are checking the tickets on the door; Drey will do the comparing; and two of her friends, supervised by Florence from the Post Office, are going to note down the winning bids and collect the money and people's details at the end of the auction. I think I should be on standby to help out, just in case things get too hectic."

"What, with writing down telephone numbers? Holly, you're allowed to relax. You've done the bulk of this. You found the venue, sourced all the prizes and got everyone together. Enjoy yourself now, okay? I want none of your paranoia tonight."

She pouted at this, but her friend's straight talking was probably just what she needed. Then again, Jamie was always so laid back, she was practically horizontal most of the time.

"It's going to be great," Ben said, taking her hand and giving it a squeeze. "Three of my better-heeled clients at the bank said they were coming."

Holly stifled a gasp, as a flutter of excitement ran through her. This was caused by his touch, not the news. His hand snapped back. Had he felt it too, she wondered? Was that even possible? And why was she still getting these ridiculous feelings, when he'd made it plain that he only wanted to be friends? Never in her life had she wasted so much time on a man who wasn't interested in her. And there were other, much more important, things to think about now.

"So, these customers of yours," she said, clearing her throat and pressing her hands against her dress, to avoid any accidental contact, "did they say if they were going to bid on anything in particular?"

"They did. One of them is interested in the dog-training lessons and the grooming voucher. Another likes the look of the gel manicure. And the third is hoping to win the golf tuition."

"Okay, that's good, that's very good, in fact," she said.

"Yes, let's hope there are others who are interested in them, too, and will bid against them and push the price up."

"That would be nice."

They were edging dangerously close to that awful, single-sentence, question-and-answer territory they'd got themselves into before. She glanced over her shoulder and caught Caroline and Jamie exchanging wry looks, although what the hell that was all about, she had no idea. Maybe she shouldn't have told Ben there was room for him on their table, after all. Sitting with two strangers might have been preferable.

Moving together, they crossed the road to the hall, the three women holding their dresses up carefully to avoid their hems trailing on the ground. In the entrance was a trestle table, manned by two teenagers with coloured streaks in their hair and wearing thick, black eyeliner. Holly smiled to herself. These were definitely Drey's people.

"Tickets please," one of them announced as they approached. Holly looked behind to the others.

"Don't you have them?" Jamie queried.

"I thought someone else picked them up."

"What? From the shop that you own?"

She immediately realised the flaw in her argument.

"It's fine," she muttered. "Could you check with Drey, please?" she said, turning back to the youngsters. "She knows us. Can you tell her Holly's here?"

The boy tilted his head.

"Holly as in *Holly* Holly? Sweet-shop Holly?"

"Yes," she said, feeling even more conspicuous in her floor-length silver gown.

"You can go straight through," he said, eyes lit up for some reason. "Drey will show you to your table."

So saying, he bowed his head slightly and swept his hand towards the inner door, indicating that they could now pass into the hall. He was looking at her as if she were some kind of celebrity.

"Wow," Caroline said, as they went in. "This looks good."

It did, indeed. When Holly had popped by on her way home from work, it had still been very much a work-in-progress. The flowers had arrived, but the table cloths hadn't, meaning that nothing could be set out. Drey and her friends had done a great job smartening up the space since then and making it look a little less like the multipurpose community space it was and a bit more like a low-to-medium-price wedding venue. Glasses sparkled on the tables. Each one had a wine cooler and bottle opener, bearing the logo of the local off-licence, meaning that, even if they were pilfered at the end of the evening—which was quite on the cards—the shop might still benefit from the advertising on them.

A couple of businesses had put up advertising banners at the far end by the stage, including the golf school in Wyck and the riding school in Naunton.

"Can we sit anywhere?" Caroline asked.

Holly shook her head. "No, quite a few people wanted to book entire tables, so we've had to make a seating plan to ensure they don't get split up."

This one says it's reserved for Stubbs," Caroline read from the label.

"And this one here says it's for the Farquhars," Jamie said, reading another. "Do you think that's *the* Farquhars? You know, the ones with the manor house outside Burford."

"I don't know," Holly replied. "Are they rich?"

"Crazily."

"Then let's hope so."

She was about to move across to the next table, when Drey bounced across to them. She had always been one for looking quirky, with a regular change of hair colour, but tonight, it was slicked back with lots of gel, wet-look fashion, in a high pony-tail. She was dressed in a fitted, tux-style black suit, with a white shirt and black bow tie. Her black eyeliner, rather than appearing goth, was flicked delicately, almost cat like at the corners. Although only seventeen, Holly would have said her Saturday girl could easily pass for mid-twenties.

"You look amazing," she said, giving her a hug. "Absolutely amazing."

"You don't look too shabby yourself. We've got a bit of a problem, though. The microphone's been playing up, so I might have to shout at you all night."

"Let me have a quick look," Jamie said.

Drey's shoulders relaxed in relief.

"It would be so great if you could sort it. Thank you." She turned back to Holly. "You guys are on table one. Seemed like the right place to put you."

Jamie passed two canvas bags filled with booze to Holly and Caroline.

"Why don't you guys take this over and get pouring. I'll join you when I've got the PA system working."

"If you can get it working," Drey said, her pessimism returning.

"*When,*" Jamie stressed.

And for reasons Holly couldn't explain, her level of concern took a massive surge upwards.

CHAPTER TWENTY-EIGHT

*W*ith Drey and Jamie heading off together, Holly, Caroline and Ben moved forwards to find their table. Drey wasn't joking when she said they'd got the best seats in the house. It was directly at the front. She'd also found herself a podium out back, from where to conduct the auction. Not only that, but the resourceful girl had also rigged up a projector. At the moment there was just a bright-blue square showing on the back wall, but no sooner had Holly's attention landed there, than it changed to a picturesque image of Bourton—one of the bridges with the green in the foreground. Written across it, in pale-blue curly lettering, was, Weeping Willows Care Home Fundraiser.

"People are starting to arrive," Caroline said, nodding towards the back of the hall, where a group shuffling through the doorway. The man leading the party was dressed entirely in red: red trousers, red gilet, red cravat. He even had red glasses and shoes. Only his shirt was not solid red, but a very faint check. It would have been wrong to overdo it, Holly thought.

"Wow, is that Harrison Dentry?" Caroline said. "How did you get him here? That family is loaded."

"I think his wife comes into the shop," Holly replied, scanning through the people. "Yes, there she is."

"Let's hope they spend a decent amount tonight."

For the next five minutes, Caroline gave Holly the lowdown on everyone arriving.

"Veterinary nurse. Just got married to a Moroccan entrepreneur. Probably wants to flash his money tonight. Local solicitor—don't go to him if you need help, though, dodgy as hell. Head of the Allotment Association." And so on.

Along with almost every name, she had a matching story. Occasionally, there were people Holly recognised herself, although her anecdotes were a bit different to Caroline's.

"Mr Barns, sour apple fan. Mr and Mrs Jenkins, liquorice fanatics."

Ben remained silent. Was he bored? Holly wondered. To be fair, he was usually the quietest of the four of them when they went out, until he'd had a couple of drinks that was, and right now the girls were several ahead of him.

"Here," Caroline said, unscrewing the top on a bottle of wine she'd brought, "Who's for a glass?"

Holly lifted hers. She was definitely leaving the moonshine in her bag, for the time being.

"Ben?"

"I shouldn't. I am the nominated driver, after all. Don't worry, I've got some water here," he said, lifting a plastic bottle as if they might not know what it looked like.

"You can't be serious?" Caroline said. "It's a five-minute walk back."

"I don't know if Jamie would want to leave her car here overnight."

"Her car that is less than half a mile away from where she leaves it every single night. If you're that bothered, then you should drive it home now and return on foot, because there's no way I'm letting you sit there with your sober, sour face all night."

"I do not have a sober, sour face."

"Not normally you don't, but today you definitely do," Caroline persisted. On the one hand, Holly felt for Ben. He was clearly being peer pressured into drinking. But at the same time, she was grateful. A couple of drinks might help loosen things up between the two of them. Get them talking again. Maybe get him thinking about her as more than a friend. She bit her lip. Why was she still so hung up on him? Weren't there people here who were supposed to be rich, generous too, as they were at a charity event. Maybe she could find someone else to distract her.

"Fine," he said, pushing his glass over to Caroline. "But just a small one for now, in case Jamie does want me to move the car."

She'd already started filling it, so it was already well over the halfway mark.

"You can always leave some," she said, helpfully.

He pressed his lips together in annoyance, but thankfully, he picked it up and started sipping.

The room was buzzing now. Obviously, a lot of people here knew each other, apart from those they were sharing a table with. There was endless air kissing, and hair flicking and *Darling, you look simply marvellous*, along with chatter about the night itself, what they were planning to bid on, what they'd donated and who hadn't given anything at all.

While Holly knew everything that was on offer—and had the spreadsheets to prove it—she still found herself glancing through the programme. There were a couple of things that had caught her eye. A tree surgeon had offered his services. There were several candidates for surgery in her parents' garden, but she had no idea how much something like that would go for. The past year had been financially challenging for her, and the last thing she wanted to do was set her heart on something she wouldn't have enough for. She'd try a couple of bids. Maybe she'd get lucky.

She was still browsing the list and wondering what might be within her budget, when a phone started ringing loudly on the floor beside her. Her immediate thought was that it was hers, even though it wasn't her ring tone. Caroline picked up her handbag and started rifling around inside it.

"It'll be Michael. I bet he gave her extra milk when I told him not to, and now he needs to know where the bed sheets are. I knew he'd be late for this. Excuse me while I go and yell at my husband."

And just like that, Holly and Ben were on their own.

The empty space Caroline's exit had left between them seemed a metaphor for their relationship. Thinking that Jamie should be back by now, she looked around the room, only to be disappointed when she discovered her lying on her back, head beneath a piece of equipment, spanner in hand. She wouldn't be coming to her rescue any time soon.

Still, Caroline wouldn't be too long, she told herself. Besides, there was only another ten minutes until the whole thing was due to begin and there was still that sixth person to join their table, too. She hoped it would be someone more sociable than the pair of them were right now.

"So …" Holly started, without the slightest idea of what she was going to say next.

'More wine?' Ben asked, picking up the bottle.

"I still haven't drunk this," she replied, indicating her full glass.

"No, of course you haven't. Right. Well, you know you've done a great job here tonight."

"It was Drey, really. I sometimes think she's trying to usurp me. One day I'll probably arrive at the shop and find her name above it as proprietor, not mine."

He laughed. It was slightly strained, but he was making an effort.

"Well, I'm sure you're going to raise the money you need for the Christmas dance. And after managing to organise this, that should seem quite easy."

"I've been so busy, I haven't given it much thought. I could do with a rest, actually.

"You, Holly Berry, are a woman who I don't think even knows the meaning of the word."

"I'm not sure that's a compliment."

"It is. Trust me, it is."

She could feel a tingling sensation running through her, partly from frustration. He was giving out so many mixed messages. Why would he be so flattering, so flirty, when he'd made it abundantly clear that he didn't want them to be anything more than friends? And flirting wasn't him anyway. He struggled to speak to people outside of work.

Not knowing how to respond, she picked up her drink, took a long sip and looked around the room again. Jamie was on her feet now, and Drey was tapping the microphone on the podium. This seemed like a positive sign. Caroline would undoubtedly return soon, she thought and turned her attention back to the door.

Over half the tables were full now, and it looked like the rest of the guests were arriving en masse just before the scheduled start time. Holly wondered if she should go and see if Drey's volunteers needed any help. But as a couple waved to their friends on a nearby table and moved away from the door to join them, the man behind them became visible. A tall man, with overly polished shoes. Holly felt her stomach drop and she blinked, repeatedly. She couldn't believe what she was seeing.

"What is it, Holly?" Ben asked, noting her reaction.

She'd gone from hot to cold and back again. In fact, she was now burning with anger.

It was Dan, again.

CHAPTER TWENTY-NINE

*H*olly couldn't move. She hadn't drunk too much. Her perfect silver dress wasn't caught on anything. Nothing was physically stopping her. But right now, she was frozen to the spot, her throat tightening and threatening to prevent any more air reaching her lungs.

"Holly, are you okay?" Ben asked, sliding across onto Caroline's empty chair and taking her hands in his. "Holly?"

"What's he doing here?" She gasped. "I told him it was over. I haven't spoken to him since he left. I don't understand."

He turned to follow her gaze and his jaw locked. For a moment, Holly thought this was directed at her. Perhaps he thought she'd invited him. Maybe, even, that it was the reason she'd got all dressed up. But then, no. He knew her better than that. She'd made it clear to him that she didn't want Dan in her life. How she'd been upset that he'd turned up at all.

And she'd told Dan in no uncertain terms that he needed to move on with his life—without her. So, what the hell was he doing here?

She was hit by a wave of nausea and reached for her glass.

"Here, have some water," Ben said, putting the bottle in her hand, instead. "I'll deal with this."

She took a sip, not realising what he'd just said until he pushed back his chair and stood up. She grabbed his arm.

"No, I don't want scene. Please, just let it go. There has to be another reason for him being here. Maybe someone else he knows invited him."

Ben was visibly grinding his teeth.

"This isn't right, Holly."

"No, I know it's not, but Drey's about to kick things off. It'll be fine. We'll just pretend we haven't seen him."

"I don't know if that's going to work."

She was about to disagree. She was very good at ignoring people she wanted to avoid. Unfortunately, it was becoming clear what he meant.

Breaking into a wide smile, Dan was walking straight towards them.

"Wow, isn't this fantastic?" he said, as he reached their table.

"What are you doing here, Dan?" Holly asked, no hint of warmth in her voice.

Jamie had said she thought everything about him turning up out of the blue and the whole proposal thing had been weird, even joking that maybe Holly should take out a restraining order on him if that sort of behaviour continued. Now Holly she was thinking she'd been right on the money.

"What do you mean?" he said. "I've come to support you. I saw the article about the fundraiser online and thought, what a great idea. And I was up here, anyway. You know that Cheltenham transfer is still on the cards. Might be too good to turn down."

She was trembling now, all the way down to her toes. Ben had sat back down and his hand was on her leg, squeezing it just above her knee in an *I've got you. Tell me what you need me to do* way.

Don't move, was what she wished she could transmit back to him. *Just stay by my side.*

Okay, so Dan was here, and that was less than ideal, but she wasn't going to let it ruin her night. She was with her friends and she was going to enjoy something she'd worked so hard for.

"Well, thank you for your support," she said, offering him a forced smile. "I guess you should find your seat. I think Drey's about to start. Have a good evening," she added, with a touch of finality.

She was surprised to see his stupid smirk grow even more pronounced.

"Oh, I have. I'm on this table," he replied, plonking himself down next to her.

The room was suddenly very hot and her head was starting to spin.

"Would you excuse us for a second?" Ben said, standing and taking her hand to pull her up, too.

"Sorry, excuse me. Sorry," Holly said, as she accidentally elbowed one person coming the other way and then another.

She'd be fine. She just needed to get outside. As they reached the door, there was a round of applause from behind them, as the PA system burst into life.

Cold air finally hit her skin, and she gulped in one breath and then another. It was heaven. With jagged, juddering breaths, she leaned back against the wall, before remembering the delicacy of the borrowed dress she was wearing. She moved away and rested her hands on her knees.

"How can I help, Holly?"

Ben was crouching in front of her, so that he could look her in the eye.

"I could get him removed or just put on another table. I can sort something out, anyway. Tell me what you'd like me to do and give me five minutes."

She was getting her breathing under control now, although tears were still trickling down her cheeks, which was bloody annoying. This had probably been the most trouble she'd ever taken over her makeup.

"What the hell does he think he's doing?" she said, eventually. "It's not normal, turning up like this, is it?"

"No, it's not," he agreed. "I think he's angry, Holly. You've hurt his pride and he's trying to get back at you. He's doing it because you rejected him."

God, her head was spinning. Where was that bottle of water? She pushed down on her knees and tried to steady her thoughts.

"He was never cruel like this before, though," she said.

"Then maybe he has just come to support you."

She lifted her head just enough to show him a raised eyebrow.

"You need to decide what you want to do."

She took a deep breath. It misted the air as she let it back out again.

"I want to enjoy my night. I want to forget all about him being here."

"So, you want me to get rid of him?"

It sounded remarkably like he was offering to put a hit out

on Dan, which at that moment, was moderately tempting. She shook her head.

"No, that way, he sees he's rattled me and gets to win. No, we go back in there. We have a good night, and we completely ignore him."

"Are you sure you can do that?"

"I thought you once said I could do anything I put my mind to."

His smile in reply was small, yet it sent a welcome warmth through her.

"Ben …"

"That man, I swear he's an idiot. I mean, I love him and everything, but that doesn't stop me from sometimes wanting to lock him in a cellar with a massive box of common sense."

Caroline stopped her mini rant and cocked her head.

"Michael's going to be another thirty minutes. What are you two doing out here? Are you all right, Holly?"

"Dan turned up," Holly said.

"What? You mean *Dan* Dan? London Dan? Your Dan?"

"Yep, that Dan," Ben replied.

"Crap."

"I know. And not just that. He's on our table"

"So, what are you going to do?"

For the first time since they'd come outside, Holly felt she had the strength to stand upright again. She lifted her hands off her knees, straightened her back and took a deep breath.

"We're going to have a good night and pretend he's not here."

"Can you do that?"

"That's what I asked," Ben said.

Holly offered them her most withering look.

"Yes, I can do that. And now we need to go back in. I don't want to miss Drey's opening speech."

And with that, she strode towards the entrance. There were only two people handing in their tickets now, and she marched straight past them and into the hall, where she stopped so abruptly that Caroline bumped into the back of her.

"What is it?" she asked, before seeing for herself. "Is that Jamie talking to him? Laughing with him?"

"She's never met him before."

"Well, I never. I'm going to give that man a piece of my mind."

"No, you're not. A quiet night, remember?"

Caroline scowled.

"Ben. You can't think that's a plan. Go tell him to do one."

"It's not up to me. It's up to Holly."

It felt good, having Ben side with her like that. Caroline grimaced, sucking in an angry breath.

"Well, if he thinks he's drinking my wine, he's got another think coming."

She pushed past Holly and headed towards their table. Holly felt Ben slip into place next to her.

"I'd forgotten she could be like that," she said with a smile, recalling their school days. Caroline would be the first to the aid of someone she thought needed defending, willing to stand up to anyone, even boys in higher years, for doing something out of order, like kissing another girl behind the back of one of her mates or being a bully. It terms of friendship, she was pretty awesome.

"Come on, I hate to say this, but I think we should get over there before she does him some real damage. Besides, Drey's about to start."

"As long as you're sure," he said. "And if you feel uncomfortable, at any time, and you want to leave, just get up and go. You don't have to worry about any of us. Or, although I've never done it before, if you want me to tell him to *do one*, I'll give it a go."

Holly smiled sadly. Why-oh-why couldn't he go back to being the miserable know-it-all she thought he was when they'd first met? That would make this *just friends* nonsense so much easier to bear.

CHAPTER THIRTY

*T*here was no right place to choose. Obviously, taking a seat next to Dan was a definite no-no, but the tables only sat six, meaning that the furthest she could get from him was two away, but that would put her directly opposite him. Which was worse? Holly wondered, as she approached their table, having him within reaching distance, or seeing that smug face every time she looked up? Definitely the second, she decided. This was something her friends seemed to have already worked out, as Caroline staunchly refused to be intimidated and sat down next to him, whilst pulling the wine bottle away and out of his reach.

"I'll take that, thank you," she said.

Jamie glared at her from across the table, at which point Caroline glared back, equally forcefully.

"Jamie, a quick word outside, please," she said, standing back up only a moment after she'd just sat down.

"But it's about to start."

"Outside. Now."

Getting that this was obviously something that couldn't wait,

Jamie, both confused and reluctant, rose to her feet, leaving Holly there with Ben and Dan. They sat in silence for a while.

"So, looks like there are lots of good things to bid on," Dan said, eventually. "Not sure what I like the look of the most. Anything you fancy, Hols?"

Her breath was quivering in her lungs as she steeled herself against reacting. Fortunately, she was saved by Jamie and Caroline's quick return, any hint of Jamie's previously friendly demeanour towards Dan now totally absent, as Caroline took a seat on one side of him and she took the other, next to Holly.

"Just say the word," she muttered to Holly, through gritted teeth.

Once again, it sounded as if one of her friends was contemplating hiring a hit man. She wondered if it would be possible to find such a person up here, amongst these picturesque country villages. She had the feeling that if there were any to be had, Jamie would know how to get one here, pronto.

A sudden rapping on the microphone caused the volume of chatter in the hall to drop, as everyone's attention turned to the stage, and for the moment, Holly forgot all about Dan. Drey stood there, mic in hand, a smile on her face. She probably appeared confident to most of them, but Holly knew the young girl well and could see her nerves in the slight tapping of her foot. When Drey's eyes fell on her, Holly offered her the widest smile she could, along with a double thumbs-up. She was so glad Drey had agreed to do this. The last place Holly would ever want to find herself, would be up on a stage like that, with all these people looking at her.

"Ladies and gentlemen, first of all, I'd like to offer a massive welcome and thank you for coming and joining us here tonight. I can see lots of bottles on the tables and lots of happy faces.

Hopefully, by the end of the evening, the smiles will be even bigger, and your wallets will be empty."

A chuckle went around the room.

"So, as you are probably aware from the programmes on the table and the fliers that we sent around, we're here this evening to raise money to put on a Christmas Dance for the residents of the Weeping Willows Care Home. I think we can all agree that we're lucky to have such a wonderful establishment in our community, and I'd like to start by thanking Head Nurse Donna, who is sitting at the table in the corner over there."

Drey pointed to the back of the room, and Holly did a double take. The person she was indicating looked nothing like Nurse Donna. Gone was the customary blue uniform, and her hair was loose, in a style that complemented her carefully applied makeup and attractive outfit. She quickly threw a smile in her direction, not sure if she would notice, given the applause she was currently responding to. She'd try to catch up with her at the end, hopefully with the promise of a big fat cheque.

"There are lots of other people we also need to thank," Drey said when the appreciation for Nurse Donna had subsided. "And I hope to get through them all during the course of the evening, but since we're here primarily to raise money for a dance, I think it's only fitting that we kick off the night with our first lot, which is three private ballroom-dancing lessons for a couple. Perfect for a first wedding dance, or anyone with a Strictly Come Dancing addiction. Now, can we start at forty pounds?"

It didn't take long for the bidding to get under way and the classes finally went for a fantastic one-hundred-and-twenty pounds. After that came the dog walking sessions, and then twelve cupcakes, to be ordered and decorated in the theme of your choice. These brought in another fifty pounds between them.

"How are you doing?" Ben asked, leaning towards Holly. "If you want to get some air at any point, you just let me know."

"I'm doing good," Holly replied, keeping her eyes on the stage. "Besides, Caroline's babysitting offer is up soon, and I want to be here to support that."

"Okay, well remember we're all here for you."

It was tougher than she thought not to look at Dan, even though she tried her best not to. She wanted to block him out entirely and focus only on Drey and her friends and the bidding war that was now taking place over a luxury manicure, complete with a full set of patterned acrylic nails. But it was hard. And whenever she accidentally glanced in his direction, she'd find that his eyes were on her. It was unnerving.

They were a little over halfway through the programme, when she needed to go for a toilet break. She'd put off the inevitable, willing her bladder to hold on for as long as possible, knowing that leaving her seat would be the perfect time for Dan to accost her, but she needn't have worried. The moment she got to her feet, Jamie and Caroline leapt to theirs.

"I'll come with you," they said, in unison, and her heart flooded with gratitude that she had such perfect friends, something she'd never experienced all the time she'd been in London. Everything there had conspired to make her unsociable. This new Holly was the one she was meant to be.

They'd only just returned from their bathroom break and were sitting back down when Drey's commentary went in an unexpected direction.

"Okay ladies and gents, right now we're arrived at a very important lot in tonight's proceedings."

Holly glanced down at her programme, wondering if they'd reached the ride in a Maserati.

"Holly Berry," Drey announced, "I wonder if you would come up here for a moment."

A cold chill flooded through her when she realised what was about to happen, and all the blood was draining from her face, as she felt Jamie's hands trying to hoist her up from her seat.

"What … no. No," she mumbled, but her friend didn't seem to be aware of her protestations.

"Come on up, don't be shy," Drey said, an evil glint in her eyes that Holly reciprocated with the sourest glare she could manage. But there was no way around it. It wasn't just Dan's scrutiny she had to worry about now. Everyone in the room was looking at her.

"Go on!" Caroline encouraged. "You can do it."

The silver dress suddenly felt too low cut and dangerously long. She wasn't sure whether to be more worried about falling out of the top of it or tripping on the bottom.

As she reached the stage, she gritted her teeth and angled her head away from the microphone.

"I'm going to dock your wages for this," she growled.

"Trust me. You want to raise money, don't you?"

Drey turned back to the audience, beaming.

"Ladies and gentlemen, we're here tonight because of this lady. Holly Berry. Now some of you may already know Holly, but for those of you who don't, earlier this year, she became the new owner of *Just One More*, the brilliant little sweet shop on the High Street here in Bourton-on-the-Water. And she's done an amazing job there—and I can say that, as she's my boss, although I'm hoping she's had enough to drink tonight to not remember the compliment tomorrow. I don't want her getting big-headed."

Laughter followed. All Holly could think about were her burning cheeks.

"Now, what you might not know about Holly is that, as well as being a fantastic boss and the amazing person who arranged this event tonight, she's also a sensational cake maker. Which is why she's supporting this cause herself by offering a two-hour baking masterclass, during which she will teach you how to create whatever your heart desires. Now, from someone who has been lucky enough to try her Baked Alaska … trust me, this is something that you don't want to miss. Now, can I start the bidding at twenty pounds?"

And just like that, his hand shot up into the air.

"Twenty pounds," Dan shouted.

CHAPTER THIRTY-ONE

*T*his couldn't be a nightmare, Holly reasoned, because never in her life had she had one this bad. She'd never been one to suffer the whole turning-up-to-work-naked scenarios, but even if she had, this was a thousand times worse. Her horrible ex-boyfriend was bidding for a two-hour cooking lesson with her. Was he for real? If he ever set foot in her kitchen again, she was going to throw a cake at him, not make one with him.

"Great, we have our starting bid," Drey said with her characteristic enthusiasm. "You have to believe how good this woman's baking is, guys. Now, do I hear twenty-five?"

From somewhere at the back of the room, someone called out, "Twenty-five," but the words had barely been uttered when Dan was straight back on it.

"Thirty," he said.

"Thirty-f—"

"Forty."

Each time the woman made an offer, he was right there with

the next figure. Even when she reached seventy-five pounds, he was still there with eighty.

Holly's stomach had twisted in knots. He couldn't be serious, could he? Bid by bid, the amount went up and her throat grew drier. The woman was persistent but she was slowing down, taking longer to come back each time.

Praying that if telepathy were an actual thing, she was about to be granted the power, she looked pleadingly across to the woman. She shook her head. Determined as she was, she'd reached her limit. And so that was it. Holly was about to be sold to Dan for eighty pounds. It was probably the most he'd ever spent on her during their entire relationship. But they weren't in a relationship anymore. A fact he didn't seem to have grasped.

"The current bid stands at eighty pounds," Drey said, with a sideways glance at Holly and then a double take as she saw the appalled look on her face. The penny had dropped, and she realised there was more to this than met the eye. Better late than never, Holly thought. Although maybe not, if there was no one left to bid for her.

"Can I get eighty-five pounds?" Drey asked, looking out at the crowd. "Trust me, if you want to try your hand at something new, this woman can teach you. Souffles? French pastries? You won't get another chance like this, ladies and gents. Let's not stop yet. Eighty-five pounds is what I'm looking for. Who's going to give me eighty-five pounds?"

Holly's heart was thumping. Please. Someone had to save her from this. Dan's eyes were already glinting with satisfaction and a grin was spreading across his face. And then, just like that, a new hand went up. And another male voice came in with a number.

"One hundred pounds," it said.

Everyone in the room gasped. Everyone, that is, apart from Dan, who was ready with his next bid.

"One hundred and twenty-five."

"One fifty."

"Two hundred."

"Two fifty."

Each time Dan got his bid in, Ben was there with his next, although unlike Dan's, Ben's face was the epitome of calm, his eyes locked on Holly.

"Two hundred … and … sixty," Dan said, slowing his pace for the first time since the bidding had begun. His fingers were holding the stem of his wineglass so tightly that his knuckles had gone white. But Ben's smile only broadened, as he countered with two hundred and seventy-five.

If she thought she'd been nervous when she'd first been dragged up on stage, it was nothing to the terror that gripped her now. She could see by the look in Dan's eyes that it had gone past purely embarrassing her. Ben seemed equally determined, with his sights fixed firmly on vengeance.

"Two hundred and eighty," Dan practically spat.

"Three hundred," said Ben, as calmly as if he were ordering a croissant at the bakery.

Shit! Three hundred pounds! If he won, she was going to have to repay him. And it only seemed like yesterday that she'd finally got back in control of her finances. Perhaps she could do it in instalments. Hopefully, it wouldn't go up anymore.

There was tension in the room. There'd been bidding wars earlier in the evening. One for a taster clay pigeon shoot up on Clapton Hill and another for a hot stone massage at a hotel in the village, but nothing like this. It felt as if everyone were holding their breath, waiting for the outcome.

"Three hundred and five," Dan came back.

He'd hated it when she'd splurged out on ingredients, liked freeze-dried raspberries or whole vanilla pods. She couldn't imagine how much it was hurting him to contemplate shelling out this kind of money on her cookery. Hopefully, he wouldn't have to. It would only take a couple more bids to knock him out of the race entirely. She was certain of it. Just as long as Ben didn't give up.

Now with just the slightest flicker of a smile on his lips, he raised his hand again.

"Four hundred pounds," he said.

A second, collective gasp went up, even louder than the first. Dan's jaw dropped open. He seemed momentarily dumbfounded by the sudden leap. Thankfully, Drey was straight on it.

"Sold!" she said, bringing her hammer down with a bang. "Four hundred pounds for a baking masterclass with the wonderful Holly Berry. Well, thank goodness there's only a few lots left. I don't know about you, but I don't think my heart could stand much more excitement like that right now."

No, Holly thought, the pounding in her chest only just starting to lessen. Neither could she.

CHAPTER THIRTY-TWO

*S*he went straight from the stage over to the computer, where the auction winners had to fill in their details and hand over their cash to Maureen from the Post Office.

Ben was already there.

"Thank you," she said. "Thank you so much for doing that."

"It wasn't fair for you to be put in that situation."

"I'm so grateful. I honestly don't know what I would have done if he'd won. I think I'd have had to withdraw, and that would have looked terrible."

She now realised that he was holding his wallet in his hand, and that one of Drey's assistants was writing him a thank-you card, in lieu of a receipt. (This had been one of Caroline's ideas, and Holly had thought it was a nice touch.)

"You haven't just paid for it, have you?" she asked.

"Of course, I did. I won."

"But … but …" *But I need time to figure out where the hell I'm going to get four hundred pounds from*, was what Holly wanted to say, but she was having difficulty forming the words. The truth was that, as her bank manager, he probably knew more about her financial situation than even her accountant. He would have known before he even starting bidding that she'd have trouble paying him back.

"Here," she said, opening her bag and pulling out her purse. "Let me see what I can give you now towards it."

Her face sank as she saw the one crumpled five-pound note there and she remembered she'd forgotten to bring more, in all the excitement of getting ready. She could feel the heat of embarrassment returning to her cheeks.

"I hadn't ever considered you paying me back," Ben said, stepping away. "I would never have bid on it if I hadn't planned on paying."

"You've just handed over four hundred pounds? You can't give that amount away."

"Well, I actually just parted with fifty and an IOU. I don't generally carry that amount around with me on an evening out. Anyway, I didn't give it away. I paid for a *baking masterclass*."

She shook her head. The aftereffects of all the adrenaline were making her feel a little woozy.

"You're sure you want to do it?" she asked.

"Do you have a problem with that?"

It was the first time that evening that he'd looked put out. On the stage, Drey was already onto the next lot. Hands were going up again, the drama of Holly's promise forgotten. She was having trouble processing what was going on. It was embarrassing enough that Ben had swooped in to save her, but then pretending that he actually wanted to learn how to bake was a step too far, even for him. Apparently, he read her expression.

"It's a running joke in the family that baking is the one thing I can't do, besides swimming, that is," he said. "I can cook pretty well, but for whatever reason, my cakes always sink or burn or have soggy bottoms. It would give me great satisfaction to take something to a Sunday lunch which I had successfully made myself."

She scanned his face, wondering if he was just trying to make her feel better. That wasn't his style, but she knew he wouldn't be enjoying owning up to being bad at something. She'd been witness to that at the lake.

"Okay, one baking lesson," she said, thinking she'd have to make this the best that there had ever been.

"Great," he replied. "We should probably go back and sit down. I think there are still a couple of lots left to go."

He smiled at her. It was a small smile that barely lifted the corners of his lips, but his eyes held hers. Before she could blink twice, he'd moved away and was returning to his seat.

Jamie was sitting with her elbows resting on the table. Michael had now appeared, over an hour and a half late and was desperately apologising to Caroline. But it was Dan who drew Holly's attention, for no other reason than how distracted he looked. When she took her seat, he shifted his gaze away from her.

"Everything all right?" she asked, speaking generally and hoping that someone other than Dan would answer.

"Everything here is excellent," Jamie answered. "I was just telling Daniel here about how I had to get a restraining order put on an ex-boyfriend and all the trouble it caused him. Employers don't look too kindly on that sort of thing. Not surprising really, stalking is a very serious crime. That's why people go to prison for it and if you ever need a Basic Disclosure Certificate for a job, you're definitely stuffed."

Dan's cheeks had gone beyond crimson and were now bordering on puce. He reminded Holly of the Victoria plums that grew on the trees at the back of her parents' garden. She didn't want to look at him directly, but at the same time, she knew that was exactly what she had to do.

"Jamie's right," she said, looking him as square in the eye as she could manage, considering he was avoiding making eye contact. "If you come back again, if you ever come near the shop—screw it, if I even hear that you're in Bourton—I will call the police. Do you understand?"

How could it have come to this? she wondered, from being someone who she'd imagined spending the rest of her life with, to someone who made her skin crawl simply being in the same room as her. She felt her knees start to tremble again, along with the desperate urge to flee. But she stood her ground.

Finally, his eyes met hers.

"You're a fool, you know that don't you?"

Then, pushing back his chair, he glowered at Ben.

"She's not worth it and her baking's shit. I lost count of the number of times she gave me food poisoning."

"Is that right?" Ben replied, in a calm voice. "Thank you for the warning. But perhaps, next time, you shouldn't bid so fervently on something you think is going to make you ill. Now, I think it's time you left, don't you? I can show you out if you can't remember the way."

CHAPTER THIRTY-THREE

$\mathcal{I}$n all her life, Holly Berry had never been so busy. Not at university, when she worked two jobs between lectures. Not when she'd started back at the sweet shop and had a to-do list longer than her arm. Not even on that day in the summer when she'd had to sell an obscene amount of sweets to reach the turnover target of the mortgage broker and had customers filing in and out from the moment they'd opened to well beyond what would have normally been closing time.

Right now, she was trying to keep on top of things at the shop on the busy run up to Christmas, organise the dance at the Care Home and make her normal Monday-night bingo-session appearances there. Plus, for some reason that she couldn't fathom, she'd also decided that all the sweets she was consuming weren't doing her health any good and she should really get more exercise, as well as eat better. As such, before the auction, she'd agreed to go for an after-work run with Caroline the next evening, which had been a huge mistake and had left her legs feeling like they'd been replaced by iron girders the following day. When the weekend rush hit the shop, she was practically limping between the shelves as she served the customers.

"Wonderful auction, Holly."

"We had such a fantastic night."

"I heard you raised enough money for the dance. That's great news."

The compliments about the Auction of Promises came in thick and fast. The person who'd won the cake a week from the bakery had already claimed his first and the group ukulele lesson had been booked.

"You know I told you that my friends all had loads of fun at the auction," Drey said when she came in on the Monday. "They could actually do with a few more hours volunteering. Any chance you could get us in on the dance, too?" she asked, popping a Pontefract cake into her mouth.

They weren't one of Holly's favourite sweets, but the little black discs of sticky liquorice still looked good. Annoyingly, she'd determined to go at least one full day without eating any of her stock. Given that it was only ten o'clock, she wasn't convinced she was going to make it. Maybe if she just got to lunchtime, that would be a good place to start. Or perhaps she could eat only the fruit-flavoured sweets. They had to have some goodness in them, didn't they?

"I don't see why not. I think it's a case of the more people, the merrier."

"Fantastic, I'll let them know. Have you fixed a date for it yet?"

"No, I'm going to see Nurse Donna tonight and get it in the diary."

"And what about the other thing? Have you set a date for that?"

Holly didn't need to ask what the *other thing* she was referring to was. It had been a full four days since the auction and Ben's chivalrous purchase of her promise, but they hadn't seen each other long enough to discuss when it should happen. A four-hundred-pound baking lesson was going to have to be longer than just the two hours she'd originally envisaged. They would be spending at least a half day together, if not a whole one, and she wasn't sure how he'd feel about that.

"I'm going to talk to him about it at the bingo tonight," she replied, in a manner that indicated that the topic was not up for discussion. To underline this, she picked up a broom and went to the shop entrance. November meant an endless supply of damp leaves trodden in and she seemed to spend half her day sweeping them back out again. Still, she suspected it was better than the sleet-and-snow slush she expected with the arrival of winter.

"Everyone thought it was well romantic," Drey continued. "Having two guys fighting over you like that."

"They weren't fighting over me, they were fighting over my baking lesson."

"Yeah, right. Your cakes are good, but not *that* good."

Holly stopped sweeping and leant on the broom.

"What are you doing here anyway? It's a Monday. Aren't you supposed to be at college?"

"Enrichment hours."

"Enrichment hours? Here?"

"You know we're meant to spend two hours a week developing skills outside the classroom. Like sewing or jogging or volunteering. Things that make us more employable."

"Yes, I know all that, obviously, but you're already employed here. Surely you ought to find some other way of spending your time."

"Probably, but it's far more fun winding you up about Ben.

Are you looking forward to your bingo date tonight? Can't wait to hear all about it from Caroline. You know she thinks he's into you, don't you? He's just got *issues*, she said, indicating speech marks with her fingers. "Why do people always think it's women who have those? He's a clear example that men are just as bad. I think it's really tough how we're supposed to be the only ones who are emotional vulnerable."

"Go," Holly said, lifting her broom and pointing to the door with it. "There are no customers and I have important managerial jobs to do that you're distracting me from."

"Managerial jobs?" she scoffed. "Yeah, right. I know the minute I leave, you'll be back to staring out that window and daydreaming about your bank manager. But you shouldn't give up on that one, you know. There's definitely mileage there."

Holly glowered at her or did the closest thing to a glower she could manage when it came to her young assistant. There was something about Drey—like an annoying little sister or cousin—that made it impossible for her to stay mad at her. And there was also the fact that, without her, the shop would have gone to developers before Holly had even come back to Bourton.

"Fine, I'm going. I've got an essay to write for English, anyway. Though I need to pick up some barley sugars for my mum first and some peppermint creams for me."

"Fine, weigh them out and disappear."

She bagged up her choice of sweets, typed the prices into the till—less staff discount—and put the money inside.

"Okay, I'll see you Saturday. I can't wait to hear how the bingo date goes."

"It's not a bingo date!" Holly yelled after her, although the fluttering in her stomach told a different story, no matter how much she tried to pretend it didn't.

CHAPTER THIRTY-FOUR

"*R*ise and shine, it's twenty-nine!" Ben said, holding up the ball so everyone could check it before hastily scanning their cards and stabbing them with their coloured dabbers. "Remember, ladies and gents, it's all to play for now with the full house. And someone keep an eye on Pauline there. I think she might be getting an extra card out of her pocket. Am I right, Pauline?"

Holly was a hundred percent surplus to requirements, but she didn't mind in the least. There was something about watching him, the way his face lit up as he called out each number. She'd seen this focus and energy before, when he'd helped with her finances. There was obviously something about numbers that brought out the inner child in him, although why on earth that would be the case was beyond her.

Her mind wandered to Ben's fiancée, or more precisely, to the diving instructor she'd met on the non-honeymoon. What must he have been like? Pretty amazing, if he was worth throwing away what she'd had with Ben. She couldn't imagine what more anyone could want in a partner.

Then again, maybe some people would say that about Dan, especially considering his latest antics. And he had a good job and had apparently turned over a new leaf. But no, their situation was entirely different. Dan, she had learnt, was manipulative. Now that she looked back, she wondered if the way he'd immediately shut her down whenever she'd suggested something, like a cheap holiday, was because he'd wanted them to save or because he wanted to have complete control over her and everything they did. And where had all her friends gone? She'd been so sociable at university. She'd had a solid group of mates there. Of course, they'd moved on to different places, but now she wondered if their total disappearance from her life had more than a little to do with Dan's appearance in it. Ben wasn't anything like that.

"House!" someone called from the middle of the room. "I've got it, see? Right there. I've got it. Full house! Full house!"

"All right Pauline, calm down will you? Don't get your knickers in a twist," the man next to her huffed and crumpled up his own card.

Ben looked at Holly with a suppressed smile, before turning back to his adoring fans.

"Well ladies and gents, that's it. I'm afraid our time is up for tonight. Now, if you will all please get you dabbers ready, my beautiful assistant, Holly, will come and collect them back in again. And we're counting tonight. Don't think we don't know about the graffiti in the upstairs toilet. Drawn in little circles, apparently. We'll get banned from coming, if you do that again. Really, at your age. I'd have thought you'd have known better."

Holly could have sworn she saw a little smirk on Sid's face, and she wondered exactly what the subject of the graffiti was. Then again, maybe it was better not to ask.

She walked up to Verity, who was today wearing a gown

with navy sleeves, which perfectly showed off her many silver bangles.The elderly woman caught her arm with a hand that was heavily adorned with glittering rings, then looked towards Ben and winked.

"No offence, but I think he may be a little young for you," Holly said, with a smile. "Although, then again, you might have more luck than me."

She wasn't sure why she'd said that and immediately wished that she could take her words back, but it was too late. She saw a flash in Verity's eyes.

"So, you do like him. I knew it."

"No," she replied, in a voice that made her sound more like a schoolteacher reprimanding a student than a volunteer at a care home. "I mean, yes, I like him but not like that. Everyone likes Ben. He's nice. He's got lots of nice features."

"Is that so? Which of those features is it that you admire the most?"

Her perfectly shaped eyebrows lifted and her immaculately painted lips pursed, knowingly.

"Now stop it," Holly said. "If you don't, I won't let you know about the surprise we're organising."

Verity's lips tightened. "A surprise, you say. For me?"

"For everyone."

She'd got permission from Nurse Donna that very evening, before she'd come in to start the bingo. The dance would be three hours long, from five to eight pm, early enough that they shouldn't disturb their neighbours or disrupt the residents who preferred an early bedtime. The money they'd raised from the auction would be enough to cover the extra nurses they'd need on duty to supervise the dancing and ensure the guests weren't helping themselves to anything they weren't allowed. It would also pay for new decorations and a live band. Above all else, Holly was looking forward to seeing the residents dance.

Perhaps this would be the ideal time to tell everyone. After all, part of the enjoyment would be in the anticipation. Drawing in a long breath, she raised her voice to include the rest of the room.

"Excuse me, everyone. Can I have your attention for a second? Sid, that means you, too, if you can give Margaret her drink back and sit down. I think you'll all quite like to hear what I've got to say."

She cast her eyes across to Ben. For some reason, she was suddenly nervous. What if they didn't want it? Maybe she should have consulted them first, before raising the money. What if this was a huge mistake?

"Are you going to tell us or not?" someone called out. "You can't hang around if you've got something to say to people our age. You don't know if we'll make it to the end."

"Speak for yourself, my heart's in perfectly good order."

"Just your liver that's ruined then, is it?"

Holly held up a hand, achieving near silence.

"So, a couple of weeks ago, I had a talk with Nurse Donna—"

A few hisses went up at this. She hurriedly shushed them.

"No, we don't want any of that. Particularly not when you hear what she's agreed to."

She now had their full attention, and all eyes were on her.

"We had a bit of a charity fundraiser last week, for this place."

"Which Holly organised," Ben cut in.

She took the compliment with a shrug.

"Which I and a lot of other people organised. And we did it

because a couple of you have mentioned how much you miss dancing."

"Are you going to hire a bus and take us all to a recording of Strictly?" one of the women asked.

"No," she chucked. "I'm afraid it's not quite as exciting as that. But I have arranged for you to have your own dance. Here. Complete with … a live band."

Eyes, that only moments before had been creased in concentration, opened wide in surprise.

"No. You don't mean it."

"I do."

"What type of band? Not a rock band, I hope. Not that modern stuff."

"We haven't decided on the band yet, but I promise they will play the sort of music that you can dance to. And …" She turned now to Verity. "It will definitely be the type of event to get dressed up for."

The whoops of delight were enough to lift Holly's spirits to an all-time high. She was relieved and thrilled in equal measure.

"Excuse me," Verity called, over the buzz of excitement. "Am I to take it that this is a formal dance?"

"As formal as you wish to make it," she replied.

"Well then, you should probably find yourself a date, shouldn't you? You don't want to get stuck with one of these old coffin dodgers."

"I'll have you know I won second place in the under-four-teen male tap-dancing contest on Southend seafront back in '57," Sid protested.

"How many boys entered? Two?" someone called back.

Holly could sense that it was time to end her little speech. The women were already discussing their hair and several were making a beeline for Verity, obviously thinking about her extensive wardrobe and hoping they could borrow something for the occasion.

"I'll give you more details when I know them myself," she said, leaving them to their chatter, as the nurses arrived to usher them to bed. "For now, I guess you should start thinking about who you want your first dance to be with."

And before she could stop herself, she found herself looking towards Ben and was surprised to find that he was looking at her, too. He quickly turned away and started busying himself packing away the rest of the bingo gear.

It was the coldest night of the year so far, without doubt. Holly dug her hands deep into her pockets, making a mental note that gloves were now a necessity for any evening trips out. And possibly daytime ones.

"So, I think they were pleased with the news," Ben said as they took the path down past the maze.

"You think so?"

"Absolutely. What type of band were you thinking of?"

"Oh, I don't know yet, but I'll have to get onto it soon. Maybe swing music?"

"Oh, okay."

They continued walking. His eyes remained fixed on the pavement in front of them.

"What?" she said, after almost a minute had passed in silence. "Just spit it out."

"Spit what out?"

"Whatever it is you don't want to say to me."

She offered him her most pointed look, and he let out a long sigh.

"I just think you might have jumped the gun somewhat, telling them there'd be a live band, when you haven't booked one yet."

"I've got the money," she said defensively, feeling somewhat put out by his negativity, especially after he'd been bigging-up her efforts that evening.

"It's not that," he said, patiently. "There aren't many good bands available locally, let alone one that has a solid swing repertoire. And with the dance being just the week before Christmas, I wonder if any will be free. I needed a DJ for the bank Christmas party, and I had to book him months ago."

She sighed. She'd been so fixated on raising the money for the event, she hadn't thought about the logistics. There was a good chance she might have the same problem when it came to the catering, too. She'd have to start emailing around when she got home.

"So," she said, in an attempt to dispel the gloom that was threatening to settle on them. "Any idea when you'd like to do this baking lesson? Or what you want to make? It could be an evening after work, or I'm sure I could get Caroline in for a couple of extra hours, if you'd rather we do it on a weekend."

"How about Saturday?" he replied, with barely a moment's thought. "Or is that too soon? The sooner I learn, the sooner I can get some practice in for Christmas."

"Saturday? As in this Saturday?" she asked.

That was only five days away, which wouldn't be much notice for Caroline to cover her, but there'd not been a single time she'd asked her that she'd said no. And she had mentioned wanting to pick up as many extra shifts as possible, to help with the expense of Christmas.

"I don't think that will be a problem," she said. "I'll just need to check with Caroline."

"Well, if that works, just send me a message. And I don't mind what we make. Some basic, beginner go-to recipes, perhaps. In fact, I look forward to seeing what you choose."

CHAPTER THIRTY-FIVE

*E*ight thirty on Saturday morning and Holly was wondering why it was so difficult to find an outfit to bake in. Tracksuit bottoms or pyjamas were what she would normally wear. But that didn't feel appropriate when Ben had paid such a huge amount for a one-on-one lesson. Especially as her current cat pyjamas had a couple of holes in them. The tracksuit bottoms were better, in that they were plain and sans-holes, but they weren't exactly flattering, and she wanted to look good. Of course, she would have wanted to look good regard-less of who she was teaching, she told herself as she applied another lick of mascara, but she couldn't cook in restrictive clothing. She had to been relaxed to enjoy baking and tight jeans would make it hard to concentrate on the job at hand. Like they were warning you of the possibility of becoming obese.

"Sod it," she thought, picking up the grey tracksuit bottoms from her bed. Weren't these the sort of things chefs wore, anyway? Besides, she'd have an apron on over the top. And what was the point in wearing nice clothes if she was just going to get them covered in flour?

Dressed and downstairs she checked she had all the necessary ingredients. In truth, she probably had a lot more than she'd need. Beginners' baking turned out to be a minefield to plan a lesson around. There were so many recipes she considered basic. There were breads, Victoria sponges, scones—everyone needed to know how to make those—not to mention shortbread. But then there were also more fun things, like chocolate brownies, and chocolate chip cookies, that were the real treats. And, of course, pie crust. Could someone really say they could bake if they couldn't make an apple pie?

As she'd expected, Caroline had been more than happy to take on the extra work, although she'd insisted that she'd rather do the whole day, than a half, as Michael's parents were over and any excuse to be out the house for as long as possible would be appreciated. Holly had accepted in a flash. There'd be a lot of clearing up and washing up to do after the lesson—not to mention the fact that baking inevitably took longer than she planned. Besides, an afternoon away from Saturday shop madness would make a very nice treat. She might even head over to Cheltenham or Bath and look around the shops for a bit. She hadn't even started her Christmas shopping. The closer it got to December the busier the shop would get and the harder it would be to take time off. She didn't somehow think a large box of chocolates would cut it with her parents this year.

Jamie—somewhat unusually—had a date and was spending the day up in a microlight. She'd been gone since seven, leaving Holly hours to fuss over whether she'd got everything she needed.

At bang on nine, the doorbell rang. Even though she'd been

expecting it—or rather, anticipating it—she still jumped. Her mouth went dry. *It's just a baking lesson,* she reminded herself as her pulse spiked. *Just a baking lesson.* She took a deep breath and headed to the front door, smoothing down her apron as she went.

Inexplicably, seeing Ben in jeans and a T-shirt, always made her smile. It had done since before she'd realised she might have a crush on him. He looked so out of character, trying to appear casual. When they went to run the bingo, he came straight from work and merely loosened his tie as a sign that he was off duty. But seeing him like this felt a bit like when you were a child and came across a teacher out of school.

"I'm not late, am I?" he asked.

"No, not at all. Come in. Come in. I've just been setting up the kitchen."

It all seemed very formal, Holly holding the door open for him to enter and then closing it behind him, then leading him to the kitchen. He stopped in his tracks, eyeing the mass of ingredients laid out.

"We're going to use all this?"

"Hopefully. I thought we'd work in tandem. I'll make something, and you follow along next to me. I borrowed some bowls and things from my mum, so we should have plenty of equipment. Here," she said, picking up a piece of folded fabric and handing it to him. "You can't bake without an apron on. Now, where would you like to start? I was thinking perhaps with bread, so we can leave it to prove and come back to it later, but it's up to you."

"I trust your judgement entirely," he said.

"Then bread it shall be. So, first we need to activate the yeast."

Good, she thought. Straight to the point. No messing around. Just focused baking. The time would fly by if they carried on like this and there would be no opportunity for her mind to wander to other things.

It didn't take long for them to find a rhythm. She should have guessed that he'd be the most ideal student, following each of her instructions to the letter. Unfortunately, that included when she wasn't paying proper attention. Having left their dough on the windowsill to prove, they'd moved on to pastry.

"Did I tell you to add all the water to the flour?" she asked,

"You did," he replied, staring at the gooey mess coating his fingers. "Was that wrong?"

"It was, but I'm sure we can work it out. Shouldn't be too much of a problem."

Using a spatula, she scraped the overly moist mixture off him and back into his bowl, grabbed the bag of flour and poured more over it, then dug her hands in and started kneading it all back together.

"That should do it," she said, gesturing for him to take over. But he simply stared at her.

"What?"

"You've got some …" He pointed to her face.

Getting covered in flour was a given when Holly baked, but she'd never had to worry about other people seeing her like that before. She lifted a hand to rub it away, only to realise it was still covered in sticky pastry mix and she would only make matters worse.

"Here," he said, lifting a cloth from the counter. He took a corner and gently brushed away the streak of white. His eyes locked on hers. He was so close she could smell the citrus of his soap and see his pupils expanding. Why was her stomach doing flips like this? And why wasn't he moving? He'd finished wiping her face and yet remained stock still.

"Holly …" His voice was breathy, her name a whisper. She

too was rooted to the spot. Unable to move. He'd dropped his hand yet didn't move away. Her eyes closed as she waited for whatever was going to come next, her pulse now pounding so hard, she was certain he'd be able to hear it.

"Hol—"

A high-pitched beeping sliced through the air and they jerked away from each other. The intrusive timer had ruptured the most wonderful dream, and continued to sound, insistently. But it hadn't been a dream. It took Holly a moment to realise what the noise was.

Clearing her throat, she stepped away and turned off the device.

"The dough's ready for knocking back," she said, moving to the windowsill and grabbing their bowls. She put them down on the table and removed the tea towels.

"Of course," he said, blinking, then dropped the cloth back on the worktop. "Now, show me exactly what we need to do here."

For a while, tension caused Holly to make mistakes, mis-weighing ingredients and then setting the wrong temperature on the oven. Luckily, she caught both errors before disaster struck, and by the time they were rolling out the shortbread dough, awkwardness had been replaced by busyness.

"I may have been a bit ambitious, thinking we could bake so many different things," she admitted. "How long have we got until the apple pies are ready?"

"Another twenty minutes," he replied, glancing over at the timer.

"All right. Then we need to get the scones out, too. Which should make enough room for the brownies."

"And the choc chip cookies?"

"They'll have to wait until the brownies are done. But they cool much quicker."

"Fair enough," he replied, surveying the table.

There was, she was ready to admit, an awful lot already there: two Victoria sponges, two large apple pies, a mountain of wholemeal bread rolls and enough shortbread to feed a small army.

"What are you going to do with all this?" he asked.

"Me? It's your lesson. It's all yours."

"You are aware I live on my own? It would take me a month to get through half of it."

"Can't you take some into the bank? It'll keep until Monday."

He didn't look convinced.

"But surely it would taste better fresh? It seems a waste to leave it sitting in the fridge all weekend."

She opened her mouth, about to say that he really shouldn't put the rolls in the fridge or they would just harden, when his eyes lit up.

"That's it. I don't know why we didn't think of it before."

"Think of what?"

"I know where we can take all this. How many cake boxes have you got?"

CHAPTER THIRTY-SIX

*I*t took a bit of effort finding enough containers big enough to fit everything in. Ben had grabbed a couple from his place, and Holly found an impressive selection right at the back of the cupboard under the oven, that she hadn't even known about. Once everything had cooled sufficiently they packed it all up—leaving behind one apple pie and a dozen brownies—and then came the task of fitting it all into her car without risking anything toppling over.

"You're going to have to carry the sponges on your lap," she said, as she opened the passenger door for him. "Will you be okay with that?"

"Piece of cake," he replied, winking. "See what I did there? Piece of cake? You know, because I'm holding the cake?"

She groaned. "I think I like you better without a sense of humour," she replied, with her most unimpressed look. "Let's just hope they let us take it all in. I know Nurse Donna gets funny about food—you know, allergies, that type of thing."

"Well, at least we didn't use nuts. Worst case scenario, the staff get a nice treat."

"That's true. Right, are you all buckled in?"

Holly always walked up to the Weeping Willows on a Monday night, so she was surprised how quickly they got there by car. She felt she'd barely left her front door when they were parking up on the gravel driveway. Switching off the engine, she went around to open the door for Ben, before grabbing the cookies, bread rolls and brownies from the boot. They made their way carefully to the entrance, where she was forced to use her nose on the buzzer.

"Hi," she said to the receptionist, a blast of warm air hitting them as they stepped into the foyer. "We brought some cakes and stuff for the residents."

The narrow-faced woman had thick, dark hair and streaks of shimmery bronzer on her cheeks. She wasn't someone Holly had seen there before, but as she normally volunteered on just one evening a week, that wasn't surprising. However, when the woman's scrutinizing glare fell on the boxes they were holding, she felt somewhat intimidated.

"Or they could be for you? For the staff, that is. We brought them for the residents, but—"

"Did you ring?"

Holly cleared her throat. "Ring? You mean to say we were coming? No. But we're not staying. Just came to drop these off."

"We don't allow unscheduled visits."

Holly could feel her cheeks aching from the smile she was trying to hold in place.

"I do know that. I volunteer here, you see. But we're not visiting. Like I said, we're just dropping these off. Cakes and brownies. See?"

She lifted one of the boxes a little higher, as if that helped the explanation. The woman would have had to be blind to have missed them. She looked unmoved.

"They really are very good," Ben added although, judging by her glower, they could have been by royal appointment and it wouldn't have made the blindest bit of difference.

"I do some volunteering here," Holly said again, thinking that maybe the woman hadn't heard her the first time, and it was the fact that she was a stranger that was causing the difficulties. "I'm the bingo caller. We both are, actually."

As she turned and motioned to Ben with her chin, the boxes wobbled dangerously in her hands.

"We're the Monday-night bingo callers. Ben more than me, if I'm honest. He's better at the rhyming slang."

"Tonight's not a Monday."

It was only the third sentence she'd deigned to utter. Holly felt as if they had been judged and been found wanting.

"No, I'm aware it's not Monday *now*. But we did the baking today. If we waited until then, it wouldn't be fresh."

Still, the woman didn't move. Her lips clamped tighter together. Whatever she was earning here, Holly thought she should give it up and become one of those living statues you saw in Convent Garden. She'd earn a fortune, if she could manage other faces as well as this grumpy one.

"You can ask Nurse Donna. She knows us both."

"Nurse Donna is away for the weekend."

"Oh."

Holly was feeling more than a little deflated. This had felt like such a good idea, bringing the cakes up to the care home so that they could all have a bit of a treat, but this woman didn't seem to care in the slightest, and now her arms were aching.

"I'm Holly. Holly Berry?" she said, hopefully. The woman continued looking at them as if they were as distasteful as a smudge on her computer screen. Holly could feel her teeth grinding now.

"Maybe if we ring up tomorrow, we could bring them in then," Ben tried. "They'd still be all right, wouldn't they?" He looked at Holly for an answer.

Yes, they would be, but she couldn't bring herself to say that. She was too busy glaring back at the receptionist. Why would someone want to stop you from doing a kindness? she wanted to know. She realised the place had rules and regulations that they had to abide by, but really, being made to feel like a criminal for wanting to drop off cakes, had to be taking things a step too far. Bowing her head in defeat, she was turning back towards the door, when a crisp voice called out.

"Holly? Ben? What are you doing here? I haven't gone complete doolally already, have I? I thought it was Saturday."

As always, Holly's eyes were drawn straight to the outfit. The short dress Verity currently sported was just as glamorous as the evening gowns she wore to bingo. In graduating shades of purple, it had an asymmetrical hem and sleeves that tapered to the elbow, only to flare out again to the wrists. She had accessorized it with a thick purple choker and an impressive array of amethyst rings. Jamie had been right; this woman's wardrobe was endless.

"We did a bit of baking," Holly said, dipping her chin to indicate the boxes in her arms.

She didn't dare move them again. Her muscles were already starting to spasm from the weight, despite all the running up and down stairs carrying great bags of sweets that she did at the shop, which she thought must have turned her into some kind of body builder. That was obviously not the case.

"We didn't book a visit though, so we're going to try and come back tomorrow."

"Pfft!"

Verity waved a hand in the air, creating a shimmer in the fabric of the sleeve.

"When you've gone to all this trouble? I don't think so. Now what's this nonsense about, Julia? This is Holly and Ben, and they're welcome here at any time. Even more so if they have baked goods."

The woman, who Holly now knew was called Julia, sucked in a deep breath that flattened her nostrils.

"You know it's not that simple, Verity. There are rules that have to be followed."

"Is that so? And did those rules apply when you borrowed my Chanel handbag last week? Or my shoes, for that matter? In fact, you haven't returned them yet, have you?"

The receptionist's cheeks coloured and her glower lessened a fraction. By contrast, Verity's grew more intense. Her glare was unwavering. Julia finally dropped her head, with a sigh.

"Fine, but it all has to go into the kitchen. You can't take them into the lounge. That's more than my job's worth. Do you understand?"

"Every word," Verity said, with a mock bow, followed by a wink at Holly. "We shall take them straight there now. Come on you two, what are you standing there for? You heard what the woman said."

CHAPTER THIRTY-SEVEN

$\mathcal{T}$hey were being led through parts of the care home they didn't know existed. The place was like a rabbit warren, one full of double doors, reproduction prints and pastel carpets.

"So, you two are spending your weekends together now, are you?" Verity asked. "I knew I was right. I've always been good at spotting the perfect match. Except when it comes to me, that is. Fourteen marriages I've set up in my time, and all of them lasted. And yet mine ... well, the less said about that, the better."

"Ben and I were just doing some baking," Holly tried to explain, avoiding looking at him as she spoke.

"Baking? Oh yes, that would be a good way of starting, then maybe gardening, and soon you'll be frolicking naked together at the Summer Solstice, rubbing lavender oils into each other's skin and discussing what you're going to name your first child."

"I don't think it's going to go that way, actually," Holly said. Her throat felt like sandpaper and she wasn't sure which thought would be more horrifying to Ben. The oil rubbing or the child naming.

"We'll see. Now, here's the kitchen," Verity said, pushing open a large wooden door, before stopping and eyeing the boxes in Holly's hand.

"Would one of those contain chocolate brownies?"

"Yes, how did you know that?" she replied.

"Aaaaah," Verity replied, tapping the side of her nose. "I told you I can sense things."

"Would you like one now?" Holly asked, feeling decidedly uncomfortable.

The old woman's eyes glittered.

"Maybe I could just take a couple? You know most of these won't make it as far as us. The staff here are gannets. You'd think they didn't have anything to eat in their own homes. I've got some plates in my room. Why don't we take the brownies and leave Ben to pop the rest through to the counter in there? You don't mind doing that, do you, Ben dear?"

If Ben did mind, he had no time to answer. Before Verity had even finished speaking, she'd taken the first box from Holly and was placing it on top of his already precarious pile. As soon as that one was in place, she added another and yet another, until all that remained in Holly's hands was, mysteriously, the one with the brownies.

"I think we should probably help him a bit," Holly said, now barely able to see the top of his head. She was mainly concerned that the fruits of their labours were going to end up in a giant, gooey heap.

"Don't worry, they'll be someone along to help him any second now." Verity pushed open another door and called, "Woo-hoo! Pauline! Can you give this young gentleman a hand? Fantastic. There we go. She'll be right out."

Holly didn't get to see if Pauline did come to Ben's rescue, let alone as quickly as Verity had implied she would. No sooner had the old lady called through the door, than she pirouetted around, looped her arm through Holly's and swept her away back down the corridor.

Somehow, in the late afternoon light, Verity's room seemed a little sadder than before. The floral wallpaper was peeling near the window and it was all-too obvious how faded her photographs were. But the wardrobe doors were open and the row of clothes looked just as impressive as they had on her first visit. She could also now see the boxes beneath the bed, that Jamie had spoken about, stuffed to bursting.

"Shall I put this down here?" she asked, gesturing to the dressing table.

"Yes, yes. Just a second. Let me find some plates. I've got some under the sink in the bathroom."

When Verity reappeared, Holly realised she should have known better than to expect the standard institutional white tea plates she'd seen elsewhere in the building. Instead, she produced two fine bone china ones, with a pink-and-lilac floral edging. She suspected there would be cups and saucers to match.

"Now, take a seat in that chair and tell me all about what's going on with you two."

"You mean me and Jamie?" Holly asked evasively, suddenly feeling she'd walked into a cleverly prepared trap.

"No, of course I don't mean you and Jamie. Although you should know that girl has a whole selection of my dresses and I bet she never wears them. She seems to spend all her time in those dreadful overalls. You can help yourself to any that take your fancy, my dear, if you have a nice occasion to go to. Just tell her I said so. And if she hasn't got anything that suits you, then just come to me and we'll find something nice here. Now, back to what I was saying. You and the lovely Benjamin, how's it all going?"

"Actually, his name is Benedict, not Benjamin."

"Really, well yes, I guess that makes sense. He doesn't look like a Benjamin, does he? Now tell me, are you in the throes of young love?"

Holly rolled her eyes.

"I don't think we can be counted as young," she said. Verity raised an eyebrow and she quickly added, "and even if we could, we're definitely not in love."

"Now, don't give me that. I've seen the way the pair of you look at each other."

Now it was Holly's turn to raise an eyebrow.

"Maybe this isn't the right time to discuss my failed love life," she said.

The old woman shifted in her seat.

"Darling, have you noticed where I am? I have one relative left. My arrogant nephew visits me twice a year, just before his birthday and then at Christmas, hoping I'll write him a cheque. This dance that you've planned is the biggest thing to have happened to me since I arrived in this bloody place so, please, let me live vicariously. And you never know, I might be able to help," she said, expectantly.

Holly looked again at the faded photos on the wall. They were no recent ones. None showing Verity's current style of hair, and none obviously taken in Bourton, let alone here at the home. When she turned back, her look of expectation had deepened to one of almost desperation, and she felt a tug of emotion in her chest. Picking up her plate, she settled back into the chair.

"There's really nothing to tell. I wish there was."

"So, you are sweet on him?"

"Possibly."

This was as far as she could commit.

"Darling, you can't tell me he's not interested in you. Anyone with eyes can see that boy is smitten."

"I thought so for a while, but apparently not."

Verity straightened her back and took a deep breath.

"Perhaps it's time to treat him mean and keep him keen. Maybe try taking a turn on the dance floor with another man."

Holly wasn't sure she'd ever taken a *turn on the dance floor.* Still, the image it evoked made her smile.

"I think another man may have very well been the issue. I think it may have scared him off. Made him think I wasn't interested."

"But you are?"

Holly felt that familiar sinking feeling. Was talking to Verity about this really a good idea? It could hardly change things. And would it alter the dynamics of the bingo evenings, if Verity knew she was pining over the man calling out legs eleven?

"Honestly, there's no point even discussing it," she said, with an air of defeat.

"I think you're wrong. I think you should tell him. Put your heart on your sleeve. He'd be lucky to have a strong, successful woman like you."

The snort that provoked sounded somewhat discourteous.

"Alas, I tried that. It was a big, strong no from him then, too."

"Oh …" Verity closed her mouth, as if she'd run out of things to say. Which was fair enough. So had Holly.

"I think maybe it would be better to just cut my losses on this one," she finally said.

Verity wrinkled her nose, creasing her perfectly applied foundation and blusher.

"I'm not so sure. I mean, as I said, I usually have a good instinct about these things and you two …" She paused. "Then again, maybe I'm losing my touch. It's been a very long time since I've had anything to do with young people. Oh, there are the girls here. And they're lovely enough, but it's their job to be kind. It's not as if we're friends. Not really. And I used to have so many."

Holly watched as sadness seemed to envelop her. She'd never seen her like this before. She couldn't help thinking that maybe all this business of getting dressed up each day, picking out clothes and putting on makeup, was just a ruse to give herself less time to dwell on how lonely she actually was.

Her mind drifted back to Maud. It had been nearly a year now since she'd seen her, when she'd handed over the keys to the sweet shop and finally cut her last tie to her beloved wife, Agnes. She'd been surprised how much her old friend had changed in the years since the funeral, how careworn she'd become. Judging from the photos, the same could be said for Verity.

"You have me," she said, breaking the silence.

"Sorry, dear?"

"You have me. I'm your friend. I'm not here because I'm paid to be. I'm here because I want to be."

"It's nice of you to say that, dear," Verity replied, with a watery smile, but in a manner that indicated Holly was saying it because she thought it was what Verity wanted to hear. And maybe it was, but that didn't make it any the less true. She had never got over the feeling that she should have been there more for Maud, when Agnes died. She should have given her old friend the love and support she needed. And while she couldn't change the past, she could definitely do something about the future, for Verity at least.

And she would.

CHAPTER THIRTY-EIGHT

The following day, Holly dropped by the florist's on her lunch break. The woman who ran the place, Irina, looked more like an artist, with hair falling out of a loose bun and a paint-splattered apron. They'd got to know each other quite well, when she'd agreed to donate the table decorations for the Auction of Promises.

"Don't worry, I'm not after another freebie. I'd like something colourful," she told her.

"If you want flowers that are in season, the colours are a bit muted this time of year, but personally, I love it. The whites and greens make me feel Christmas is just around the corner."

"That sounds lovely," Holly said, then watched as she moved around the shop, selecting one long pale stem, then another and gradually building up an impressive bouquet in her hand.

"How does this look?" she asked.

"Beautiful. I love the way you've put them together," Holly replied.

"Are they for someone special?" Irina asked, taking them to the counter.

"Actually, they are," she said, a smile coming to her face as she thought about Verity. "It's a lady I see up at the Weeping Willows Care Home. I thought this might add a bit of cheer to her day. She gets almost no visitors. I think it gets quite tough for her at times."

Tougher than she wants to admit, she thought to herself, although she didn't say as much. The florist nodded, as she tied the final bow around the cellophane wrapper.

"It's such a different world now," she said. "Everyone is so far apart. Do you know Gregory, who runs the antique shop on Victoria Street?"

Holly screwed up her eyes as she tried to put a face to the name. She was certain that she must have met him, but she couldn't for the life of her think what he looked like.

"Vaguely," she answered.

"He's a lovely man," Irina said. "He's had that place for over thirty years, now. One of his children lives in Thailand and another is in Australia. He and his wife get out to see them when they can, but that's got to be hard, hasn't it? Having your family so far away."

"It must be," Holly said, not wanting to say she didn't think Verity had any family—besides the nephew that she'd spoken of —to come and visit her.

Instead, she smiled and asked her to make up a second bouquet, for her mum this time. After she'd been into the home, she'd pop up and see her parents.

*A*fter the fiasco with the cakes, Holly had rung in advance to tell them she'd be coming. Thankfully, it was a different woman on duty in reception, one who came into the sweet shop for a weekly fix of acid drops and coconut mushrooms.

"Verity's in her room," she said, then added kindly, "Would you like me to show you the way?"

"It's fine. I think I can remember," she replied, feeling slightly nervous for some reason. She'd visited Weeping Willows countless times before, but never on her own and never to see just one person.

After one wrong turn—which was pretty good, really—she knocked on the laminated door displaying Verity's name. She suddenly panicked, wondering if she had any allergies and viewing the bouquet in her hand in a different light. Surely the receptionist would have said if she wasn't allowed any flowers.

Now distinctly flustered, she was still second guessing herself and wondering if she should hide them around the corner, when the door swung open.

"Holly, what are you doing here? Is everything all right?"

For the first time she could recall, Verity was wearing trousers, which flared in flowing swathes of emerald silk and were paired with a kimono-style top, that was patterned with white cranes and pale pink lilies.

"Everything is fine. I came to see you, that's all."

Verity tipped her head to one side, as if she couldn't quite believe that was true.

"Oh, and these are for you," she said, offering her the bouquet.

"For me? Are you sure?"

"Of course, I am."

A sheen of tears appeared in her eyes, as she stepped back from the door and beckoned her in.

It took her a moment to find her voice again, and Holly wasn't sure whether it was because she was overwhelmed by the gift or simply wasn't used to people invading her space, without her prior approval.

"Do you know, the last time someone gave me flowers was in 1999," she eventually said.

"I can't believe that," Holly replied, following her in.

"Trust me, it's true. I remember because it was New Year's Eve. You know, the big one, when everyone thought that all the computers were going to crash, and the world was going to implode. I could have told them that the new millennium wouldn't actually start for another year. Anyway, I was in my sixties and already felt rather old. My neighbour bought me a bunch of flowers because, she said, whatever happened to the computers, the flowers would be just fine."

Her eyes drifted away wistfully.

"She sounds like lovely a person."

"Oh, she was. She really was. Sad though. She didn't make it to the next New Year's Eve. She was older than me by quite a bit, I'd like to add. Then her poor husband ended up in a place like this. He wouldn't be around anymore. There aren't many folks even my age still kicking about."

"Verity, you're not that old," Holly said firmly, making her laugh.

"Oh, don't let all this fool you," she said, pointing to her face. "If I wasn't wearing my makeup, you'd be running down the hall, thinking you'd seen a ghost."

"I don't believe that's true at all."

"Well, that's never going to happen, so it's not something

you have to worry about," she chuckled. "Now, tell me about the party. Only three weeks to go."

Holly gulped. She knew it was creeping up on them, but she'd been counting in days, and twenty-one sounded like she had far more time. And she hadn't even sorted out a band yet. She'd messaged several places, but so far, they'd either not got back to her or had, only to tell her they were already booked. She was having a sinking feeling that Ben might have been right. Her only back-up option was Drey's school rock band, which she didn't think would go down well with Nurse Donna or the residents, except perhaps Sid.

"Have you picked out something to wear yet?" Verity continued. "And have you asked that nice young man of yours to be your date?"

"What are you talking about? I'm not dressing up. It's not my party, it's yours. I'll be there in an official capacity only, as chaperone."

"What tosh. You'll be the belle of the ball. And don't think I haven't noticed you avoiding the other part of my question."

Holly forced herself to smile. Spending time with Verity was going to be a trial, if she didn't know when to drop a subject. Still, she knew how to distract her.

"Enough about me, what about you?" she said. "Have you decided on what to wear? I take it there will be a costume change involved?"

The old woman's eyes twinkled.

"Oh, my darling, I have something very special planned. Trust me."

"And will I be allowed a sneak preview?"

"That would ruin the night, wouldn't it?"

They spent another half hour discussing parties that Verity had been to, countries she had visited and which of the film stars she'd met in person who had disappointed. Holly then announced that she ought to get going and, despite saying she never received flowers, she of course produced a beautiful cut-glass vase. Holly went to her bathroom and filled it with water, then arranged the flowers and put them on the windowsill. It was dark now, but she thought they'd look stunning in the morning light.

"Right, I really must go now," she said. "But I'll see you tomorrow for bingo?"

"You can bank on it. And don't give up on that boy. When you've been around as long as I have, you can spot a good thing, and he and you are that. I feel it in my bones."

"I think you might need to give up on that one," Holly said, as kindly as she could.

"Me, give up? I wouldn't know how."

Holly suspected that was true.

CHAPTER THIRTY-NINE

ecember arrived, and overnight, the temperature plummeted. Each morning, she woke to find the gardens and cars frosted white. It was difficult to put out of her mind exactly how close the party was, now that they were in the same month.

Most items on her to-do list had a tick against them. Drey had recruited all the volunteers they would need, and Nurse Donna had rostered the extra members of staff. Holly herself had booked the catering with one of the local cafés. She'd been extremely lucky that they'd taken on the job at such short notice. They were as busy this time of year, with their delicious hot chocolate, cakes and warm crumbles, as they were in the summer, selling ice cream and cold drinks. What had swung it, had been that the owner's mother was actually a resident of Weeping Willows, and he'd promised Holly the best deal possible.

Only one thing was still eluding her, and it happened to be what the residents were looking forward to the most. The thrill of dancing to a live band was always referred to whenever she met up with Verity, which she'd done three more times in the last week.

On the first visit, the old lady had insisted on teaching her how to play bridge. In return, Holly had taught her how to play Shit Head, the only card game she could ever remember the rules to, without someone there to jog her memory.

On the next visit, Verity took her through some of her favourite photos.

"This one is David Attenborough. I know he doesn't look like that now. None of us do, but he was really quite dashing. I met him in Mauritius. He was there filming something to do with bats, and I was there with some man or another. I forget which one now."

Something in her eyes made Holly think that wasn't quite the case, but Verity didn't seem to like to give too much away about her own love life. Holly could quite understand that. Then they'd talked about trivial, light-hearted topics, like furniture or favourite meals and, of course, outfits.

But by far the best get-together had been when Holly got permission to take Verity out for an hour on the Saturday, to see the Christmas lights being switched on in the village centre. For once, she'd dressed almost sensibly, in a huge fur coat—that Holly hoped wasn't real, but suspected was—fur-lined boots, a white muff and a matching fur hat.

It was the first time since moving away from Bourton that Holly had seen the Christmas lights and they were just as beautiful as she remembered. Choirs, from both the primary and secondary schools, were singing carols. There was a hot soup stand and another selling hot chocolate and Father Christmas came out to give all the little ones lollipops, courtesy of *Just One More*. Then there was the main event: the switching on of the lights, which this year was being performed by a local dignitary.

The High Street had already been displaying lights for a few weeks. They were draped along shop fronts, between lampposts, around trees and across the bridges. Small spruces decorated the gables, but it was the main Christmas tree that really mattered. Twenty-feet high, smack in the middle of river, with a large gold star at the top. Even Holly, at nearly thirty, felt a flutter of excitement as the moment approached.

Jamie was supervising the small stage she'd erected for the event, from which a local councillor was just finishing his address to the expectant crowd, which included Caroline and Michael, who'd brought their children along. Over on his own, nursing a cup of soup, was Ben. Having just spotted him, Holly was about to wave and beckon him over, when the countdown began.

"Three, two, one!"

A huge cheer went up.

"It's beautiful," Verity gasped, as the tree lit up.

"It is, isn't it?"

This year, they'd gone for blue and white lights, hundreds of them, now mirrored in the river below and making it look as though the stars and fallen into the water.

"You know, I should get you back," Holly said, as people started moving away. "I promised Nurse Donna we'd be no later than six-thirty and it's already twenty-to-seven."

"Just one more minute," Verity whispered, the lights reflecting in her eyes. "Just one more minute."

When they reached the nursing home, one of the carers came and helped the old lady from the car and Holly noticed how awkward her movements were. It was no wonder, really. Every year she found her own joints growing a little stiffer in the cold, and her mother often said the same. But there was something about the way Verity seemed to be finding the short distance from the car to the entrance difficult, that made Holly wonder if taking her out in the cold had been a good idea.

"Thank you again, Holly darling," Verity called from the door. "If you could get me a picture of that, it would be worthy of my wall. And we'll put it right next to one of us dancing at this party of yours," she added.

Holly suspected that was the highest praise Verity could give.

⁂

The following Monday evening, Holly marched down the High Street towards Rissington Road, gloved hands deep in her pockets, scarf wrapped around her neck and wearing the thickest socks she owned inside her furry boots. Ben was waiting outside the bank for her, and she offered him a quick nod of acknowledgement as he fell into step beside her.

"Good day?" he asked.

"I guess."

Holly continued on without breaking her stride.

"Busy?"

"Pardon?"

"Was the shop busy?"

"Oh, I suppose. Yes. Quite busy."

She dug her hands deeper into her pockets.

"What is it?" he finally asked, as they reached the junction by the Post Office. "Have I done something to upset you?"

"What?" she replied, seeming to pay no attention to what he was saying.

"I said, have I done something to upset you? You've barely spoken two words to me. If you want to do the bingo on your own tonight, I can go back."

"On my own?"

She shook her head, finally making sense of what he was saying. She let out a long sigh, which caused a cloud of water vapour to appear in front of her.

"It's the bloody music situation. I know they're going to bring it up again tonight. The other day, when I saw Verity, she started telling me about the big bands she'd danced to when she visited New York and another time, at The Blackpool Tower Ballroom, where she'd been dancing with someone from the West End. She's going to be so gutted when all I produce is an iPhone and a Bluetooth speaker. They all are. Even Sid's being trying to get requests in."

She sighed again, producing yet more condensation in the air around them. She'd run out of ideas. She'd contacted every local band that she could find online and then tried even further afield, offering to cover transport costs. She'd put up a poster in the sweet shop window and even joined a couple more Facebook groups, so she could put a shout-out there. No one was available. Even Drey's school rock band now had a gig.

"How professional does it need to be?" he asked.

"How professional? I got out a ukulele last night to see if I could manage a tune," she joked, mirthlessly.

He let out a contemplative hum that she immediately pounced on. "What is it? Do you know someone? You do, don't you?"

He shrugged.

"You could try asking Michael."

"Caroline's Michael?"

"We were in a band together at school. I don't know if he carried on or not, but he was pretty good back then. For a fifteen-year-old, that is."

She stopped in her tracks. "Hang on a minute. You're telling me you were in a band. How did I not know about that?"

"Because it's not something I choose to share. I was terrible."

"I don't believe that. You're good at everything. Well, except swimming."

"Swimming and the double bass. Trust me. But Michael was the one who held us all together. I suspect he does still play. He might have a couple of friends he could call on and put together a two- or three-piece band. But that's only guesswork. I mean, if Caroline hasn't already mentioned him to you …"

Holly was walking faster now, a spring in her step. No, Caroline hadn't mentioned it, but maybe she just hadn't considered it because she'd been looking for professional musicians. As they reached the gates of the Care Home, she halted.

"Would you mind going in and setting up on your own? I'm going to ring her straight away. If it's a hard no, then I need to keep thinking, but maybe …"

"No problem," he said. "I'm not sure you're that much help setting up, anyway."

This felt good, this felt positive. She was becoming increasingly confident. It was going to work. She could feel it in her bones.

Deciding it would be better to have the conversation inside the grounds than out on the road, she started walking again, and they turned together onto the gravel driveway. A heartbeat later, they stopped. An ambulance was parked by the entrance, its back doors open and several people, including Nurse Donna, standing around, looking worried.

A lump was forming in Holly's throat. Ben took her hand and led her forwards.

"Let's go inside. You can come back out and ring Michael when they've gone."

She found herself nodding mutely, unsure why the sight of the ambulance was having such an impact. It was a care home, after all. The clue was in the name. There were bound to be times when someone would need to go to hospital. Yet something about it was worrying her.

As they passed the vehicle, she glanced in. The end of the stretcher was visible, as were the feet of the person lying on it. On one was a beautiful teal stiletto shoe. And there was only one person here who would wear something like that.

CHAPTER FORTY

"What happened?" Holly said, rushing over to Nurse Donna, who was engrossed in conversation with one of the paramedics.

"Holly."

"It's Verity, isn't it? What happened to her?"

"What are you doing here?" she asked, before her expression cleared. "Of course, it's bingo night, isn't it? Why don't you go inside and set up? We'll see to everything out here."

"But it *is* Verity, isn't it?"

"Are you a family member?" the paramedic asked.

Holly shook her head.

"No. But I'm a friend. A good friend."

The paramedic looked at Nurse Donna, who inhaled deeply before offering a quick nod.

"Your friend has had a fall. We don't think it's too bad, just a bump, but we're taking her to the hospital to get her checked out."

"Then why are you still here? Shouldn't you be going?"

"We're short-staffed tonight, Holly," said the nurse. "We're just trying to sort out someone to go with her."

"I'll go," she immediately replied. "Please, let's go now. We shouldn't delay if she needs to be at the hospital."

The paramedic and Nurse Donna exchanged another look.

"All right. Yes, that would be very helpful, Holly. Thank you. You have my number. Keep me updated, please."

"Yes, of course," she said.

She was about to step up into the ambulance, when she suddenly remembered Ben, still standing by the front door.

"Crap," she said and darted across to him. "I need to go with her."

"I know. It's fine. I've got this."

"Are you sure? You can cancel the session, if you prefer. I'm sure everyone would understand."

"Holly, don't worry about me. I'm more than capable of running a bingo night on my own. Go be with Verity."

"Thank you," she said and then, in a reflex action, pushed up on her toes and kissed him on the cheek, before disappearing back to the ambulance.

Verity was now propped up on pillows. A minor bump, the paramedic had said. It certainly didn't look like that. It was the first time that she'd seen her looking anything less than immaculate, and it wasn't just the swollen ankle and scuffed shoe. A bruise was blooming across her hairline and down the bridge of her nose, where there was a cut. Soon, Holly suspected, there would be two black eyes to match.

"Holly dear," she croaked, then winced. Just talking was enough to cause her pain. "What are you doing here?"

"Oh, you know, apparently someone was being overly dramatic, and they asked if I'd like to take a trip in an ambulance. I've never been in one before, so I thought, why not?"

"No? I've got a great ambulance story."

"Of course, you have."

The old woman tried to smile but fell into a fit of coughing. The paramedic who'd been speaking to Nurse Donna hopped effortlessly into the back, unclipped an oxygen mask from a side panel and placed it over Verity's nose and mouth.

"Best if you don't try to speak for now," she said. "We won't be long."

⊱

*H*olly had, fortunately, spent very little time in hospitals. She'd visited her dad when he was getting kidney stones removed, but that was pretty much it. A fact that she was now even more grateful for than she had been before.

Despite it being nearly ten o'clock at night, the corridors were full of people rushing back and forth. Nurses, looking exhausted, were talking on the move to doctors, who looked equally tired.

As she sat there on the hard plastic chair, she wondered if she was the only fit person in the entire hospital who wasn't doing something useful. She felt she was just taking up space, as she sat waiting for news of her friend. But she couldn't leave, not until she'd seen Verity again.

By the time the ambulance had arrived in Cheltenham, the old lady was struggling to keep her eyes open.

"It's most probably the shock," the paramedic had said to Holly as they'd left the ambulance, and she'd dropped the trolley's wheels to the ground. "Her vitals are good, but they may give her a CT scan, to check there's no concussion, although it doesn't always show that up. Go in through the front door and tell them at the desk who you're with. Someone will come and update you when there's any news."

That had been two hours ago. Once, she'd asked a passing doctor—giving him Verity's name and where she'd come from, but he didn't know anything about her, so she apologised and went and sat down again. He already looked stressed enough without her adding to it. She'd leant her head back against the wall and carried on waiting.

She took out her phone and idly flicked through it. The battery was down to fifteen percent. Normally this wouldn't have worried her, but she was going to have to get home at some point and though she knew Cheltenham quite well, she wasn't sure how to get from the hospital to the bus station without her map app. Although, in fact, she'd likely missed the last bus.

And so, she just sat.

Was there actually any point in her being there? she wondered, later. Yes. Verity knew she'd been in the ambulance and might hope she'd stayed. They were bound to let her in to see her, eventually.

Her stomach growled. She'd planned on grabbing chips on the way back from bingo. Her last meal had been a quick sandwich lunch and she'd not had time for anything since. A fact she now massively regretted.

Delving into her bag, she found half a packet of coconut ice and a bag of cherry lips. It was either these or pay an astronomical price for a cold pasty from the vending machine. She chewed down on the coconut ice. The packet empty, she regretted her decision. Not only did she feel exhausted, useless and in the way, but also sick.

Still concerned about the state of her battery, she glanced at her phone again. Nothing. No message from Ben or Jamie. Her housemate was doing one of her parties that night and could easily be running late. She'd left Ben to not only cope with the bingo session on his own but probably also having to reassure the old people, after one of their number had departed in such dramatic fashion. He'd probably headed straight home and collapsed. She went to put her phone back in her bag, then hesitated. She should message him and thank him for taking over.

She swiped her phone open again and typed, *Thanks for today. No news yet.* That was all she had the energy to write. She pressed send but then immediately heard the ping of a message coming in. She frowned—that had been impossibly quick—then realised it hadn't come from her phone after all but from one belonging to the person standing directly in front of her, holding out a cup of steaming tea and, if the smell of vinegar was anything to go by, a bag of chips.

"I thought you might like some company," Ben said.

CHAPTER FORTY-ONE

*H*olly didn't realise she'd fallen asleep, until she woke to find her head on Ben's shoulder and a line of drool connecting it to the corner of her mouth.

She hurriedly sat up and drew the back of her hand across her mouth, wondering whether wiping his shirt, too, would just draw more attention to the fact that she'd dribbled all over him.

She blinked repeatedly, waiting for her eyes to adjust. The nurses looked refreshed, quite possibly because they weren't the original ones, she realised. And it was much brighter than before she'd nodded off. The white corridors were almost glistening in the morning sunlight.

"What time is it?" she asked, bouncing to her feet then fumbling in her bag for her phone. It wasn't there. Where the hell was her phone?

"Is that what you're looking for?" Ben said, pointing to the seat next to her, where her phone sat with a charging cable connecting it to a nearby socket.

"Oh, that's brilliant. Thank you," she said, picking it up and noticing that the battery was now at 100%.

But her relief was short-lived.

"Crap. It's eight-thirty. I should be at the shop. And you should be a work, too," she said, panic rising through her.

He yawned and stretched his arms out wide above his head. Why wasn't he moving?

"It's fine, I rang in sick."

"You did what?"

"I said I was in hospital, which I am, so technically I didn't lie. But also, I am the boss, remember, which does have its advantages."

That might be all very well for him but wasn't of much comfort to Holly. She was her own boss, but people would still be waiting for her to open up shop. What day was it? Tuesday? She'd completely lost track of time. Yes, it was Tuesday. She breathed a sigh of relief and dropped back onto her chair.

"It's fine," he said, putting a hand on her arm. "I rang Caroline to ask if she could open up for you. I forgot she normally works Tuesdays anyway, but she's fine to cover tomorrow, too, if you need her."

"You rang Caroline? You did that for me?"

"Well, you were pretty wiped out when I got here, almost didn't finish your chips, in fact. And I hope you don't mind, but while I had her on the phone, I asked Michael about the band."

"You did?"

"He said he might be a bit rusty, but he's sure he can rustle up a crew to do a few songs. But they'll need to get the music and practise, so let him know what you're after, as soon as possible."

"You sorted that out, too?"

She was dumfounded. The hustle and bustle of the busy hospital faded into the background. All she was aware of was his smiling face.

"Why are you doing all this?" she asked.

"Like I said. You didn't look like you were in a fit state to do much yourself."

She sat up straighter now, any concern about the dribble stain on his shirt forgotten.

"No, I don't mean that, particularly. I mean all this sweeping in and rescuing me."

"You don't need rescuing, Holly. Of that I'm absolutely certain."

His gentle smile would usually cause her stomach to swarm with butterflies but not this time. This time it was making her mad.

"Why are you doing … *this*?" she said, her hand going backwards and forwards between the two of them. "I told you how I felt and what I wanted, and you made it perfectly clear that anything other than friendship was off the cards for us. So why are you still here? And why are you doing all these things for me?"

He was perplexed. The smile had been replaced by a look of bafflement.

"We agreed to be friends."

"This isn't being friends. Me falling asleep on your shoulder. You bringing me chips and sorting out the band. You paying *four hundred pounds* to rescue me from Dan, for crying out loud."

"Holly I—"

"I can't do it, Ben. I can't have you here. Because this doesn't feel like nothing. It feels like *something*, every time I'm with you. I know this is on me. I was obviously far more into you than you were to me, but I can't do this. If the only option for us right now is to be friends, then I can't do it. I don't want to be *friends* with you, Ben."

There were both standing, although when that had

happened, she didn't know. Her blood was pumping, her throat felt parched and her eyes were stinging, as tears now threatened. She would not cry, she told herself.

"You should go now," she said, quietly.

He didn't move.

"Will you be okay to get home?" he whispered.

"I don't need you saving me!" she shouted.

"Miss Holly Berry?"

"What!" she yelled, spinning around, only to cringe in embarrassment at the sight of a nurse standing there. The woman backed away half a step. "Holly Berry? You're here with Ms Eddy, aren't you?"

"Verity?"

"Yes, Verity Eddy. You can come through and see her now, if you'd like to."

Holly swallowed, trying to regain some of the composure she'd just lost so spectacularly.

"Yes. Thank you. I'll come straight away."

She reached over and picked her bag, then unplugged her phone from his charger.

"Holly." Ben reached out and touched her hand, only to quickly withdraw it again. "Holly," he repeated, as if those two syllables could somehow convey something meaningful on their own.

"You need to go now, Ben. I'll be fine from here. I am fine."

"Please, if we could—"

"And maybe it would be better if I ran the bingo on my own, next week. It's the last one before the dance and then Christmas. I'm sure Jamie will be able to find a permanent replacement for me after that, if you want to continue."

His expression clouded with a look of hurt that sliced right through her. But what had she got to feel bad about? He was the one who'd been stringing her along. No, this was the right thing to do, for him and for her. Either they were all in or they were all out. And he wasn't in, so that's all there was to it.

In a side room, Verity was propped up on a pillow, with one ankle slightly raised. The swelling had increased since they'd been in the ambulance, and the bruising was very much worse, in multiple shades of blue and purple that spread down her foot. Her face, however, was not as bad as Holly had expected, and her vibrant red lipstick somehow worked to offset the blues there.

"Holly, darling, they tell me you've been waiting all night. Why on earth? You didn't have to do that."

"I wanted to make sure you were all right. It must have been a nasty fall. What did you do? Did you trip?"

Her lips twisted coyly.

"Possibly."

"What she did was fall over on these ridiculous heels," the nurse said, picking them up from under the bed. "Honestly, these things would be a death trap for anyone, let alone someone of her age."

Holly prepared for a barrage of insults to be aimed at the nurse. Verity hated it when anyone mentioned her age, medical professional or not.

"I will have you know that my balance in these is as good as it was in my twenties. If not better."

"Even if that were true," the nurse said, "your bones are not. It's not nice to hear, I know, but you're much frailer now. How you didn't fracture anything is a minor miracle. But, next time, you might not be so lucky."

"So, what now?" Holly asked. "Can she go back to the home?"

The nurse checked the chart at the end of the bed.

"The doctor wants her to stay another night for observation. Her scan seemed clear, but it's just to be on the safe side. And when she does go back, there's to be no weight bearing on that foot. And *definitely* no high heels. Soft flat shoes and a walking stick are what she needs."

Verity pretended to gag at this, so comically that Holly had to laugh.

"Don't worry, I'm sure we can find you some practical shoes that are perfectly attractive."

"You'd better," she said, "because I'm not setting foot outside my room if you put me in a pair of those dreadful alligator shoes. Ghastly things."

"I think you mean crocs, but I get the message." Holly grinned. "I guess I'd better go shopping, then."

CHAPTER FORTY-TWO

*A*s she was already in Cheltenham, Holly decided she could spare an hour or two wandering around the town to see if she could pick up something that Verity would consider acceptable in terms of alternative footwear. With her limited knowledge of shoes and her restricted budget, she wasn't holding out much hope, but after an hour, she was back at the bus station, carrying two bags. One contained a pair of jewelled faux-fur slippers, that she hoped would be on the right side of garish for Verity to allow. In the other was a pair of flat pumps that she'd picked up from a hippy shop on the street where the cinema used to be. They were made of a black fabric that had been embroidered with brightly coloured stars and moons, quite unlike anything she'd seen anyone wearing at the home, which she thought could be a winning factor.

She climbed onto the bus and took a seat near the front, dropping down heavily and resting her head against the window. As she stared zombie-like at the back of the seat in front of her, her mind wandered from Verity to Ben. Had she been too harsh? He'd only come to help her. Chances were, he'd have done the exact same thing for Jamie or Caroline. But they'd never been on dates with him, thinking that they were more than just friends. And no matter how kind he thought he was being, he was stopping her from moving on, and she had to do that. She couldn't live at Jamie's house forever and neither did she want to. She wanted a home of her own. A family of her own. And to do that, she would need to start putting herself out there, which was going to be incredibly difficult if Ben was always hovering in the back of her mind. The perfect gentleman who just wanted her as a friend.

As the bus rumbled away, she closed her eyes. They'd been far from friends when she'd first arrived at Bourton. It shouldn't be that difficult.

The two weeks leading up to the dance were as manic in the shop as any time Holly could remember.

"Do you have any more of the small, dark-chocolate Santas? We bought some last week," the woman said.

"Sorry, we're all out. We have milk chocolate reindeer, though. And white-chocolate Santas, if they would be any good," Holly replied.

"No, we need dark chocolate. She's lactose intolerant. Couldn't you just check in your stockroom? Perhaps you have some tucked away that you've forgotten about?"

"I can promise you, I don't."

"Perhaps if you could just check?"

Holly gritted her teeth and smiled. Even the nice customers were stretching her patience to the limit.

"Hello, I need a huge mixed selection of sweets, say a

quarter each of twenty-five different types. It doesn't matter which ones."

"Twenty-five?"

"Can you do that? They all have to be different, mind. Can't have any duplicates."

"Sure, no problem."

"And my bus leaves in ten minutes."

Each evening, she felt like she'd run a marathon. She'd probably walked one, what with flitting between the shelves and rushing up and down the stairs. After a brief reprieve, the cold weather had come back again in full force. No snow yet, but there was a hard frost every single morning and the Council trucks were out early and late, salting the roads.

Cold, like a sudden, unexpected downpour in the summer, brought people into the shop and the week before the dance, she'd needed Caroline in each morning, just so she could get the shelves restocked before the midday rush began. It worked very well with the two of them working together. There was a rhythm to it, much the same as she and Drey had. Drey, herself, was busy organising the volunteers for the dance and had three college assignments that she needed to get in before the end of term. So, for the first time ever, she was saying no to picking up extra shifts.

Still, the till was the busiest it had been since the height of summer, and her bank balance was comfortably enough in the black, that she felt she might be able to splash out a little on her family's presents.

"How's Michael getting along with the songs?" Holly asked Caroline as she came downstairs with a plateful of sandwiches, the day before the dance.

It had been chaos all morning, with customers requesting everything from a dozen gift-wrapped boxes of Belgian chocolates for work, to a hundred sugar mice that were going to be tied by their tails to a Christmas tree. This was the first time they'd had a non-work conversation.

"Sid put the list together," she continued. "I'm wondering if Michael's heard even half of them before. I certainly hadn't. I'm not even sure if they're all actual songs. I wouldn't put it past the folk up there to try and wind me up."

"They were practising last night," Caroline replied. "I'm probably biased, but I think he and the guys are pretty good. That reminds me. Are you speaking to Ben yet?"

Holly wasn't entirely sure how Caroline had made the leap from Michael's band to Ben, but she wasn't surprised. It seemed that half the time she spoke to anyone, he somehow filtered into the conversation—and she was definitely not the one to bring him up. She'd already had *the talk* from Jamie several times, none of which had ended well.

"I told you it was a bad idea from the very start," she'd said over dinner one evening, not long after Holly's outburst at the hospital.

"Yes, I know," she'd replied.

"Now I have to choose who I can invite to the pub. I liked it when we were a happy foursome."

"So did I. You were right. Is that what you wanted to hear? You were right. It was a bad idea. But you don't have to worry. I'll make a perfectly good recluse. I'll just stay at home and drink all your good wine, while you're out with him."

Jamie had responded with a half laugh, but was well aware that she meant what she said. Holly did feel guilty, though. Jamie had done so much for her since she'd moved back to Bourton. In addition to fixing the roof of her shop and giving her a place to live, she'd made it feel like it was home, that she was welcome there. And she'd repaid her by messing up their friendship group.

"You were a perfectly happy little trio, before I turned up," Holly reminded her, trying to ease the sadness a little. "You'll be fine."

"It's not about whether I'll be fine or not. It's about the fact that I'm cross. And not just at you, I hasten to add. I'm mad at him, too. Maybe even more so. If you two could just stand to be in the same room as each other."

"Of course we can, Jamie. You're making out like I can't be within three feet of the man without going into anaphylactic shock. I just don't want him to pretend there's some great friendship there, when there's not. That's all."

Caroline, however, had been much more compassionate when discussing the situation, a quality she continued to show as she took her first bite of the sandwiches on offer.

"It's just so annoying" she said, slumping against the counter. "You were perfect together. You are. And I know what Jamie says, but she's only frustrated, too. You know about what happened with Ben and his ex, don't you?"

"Yes," Holly replied, feeling guilt starting to gnaw again.

"And it was awful. Really awful. And you know he hadn't dated anyone, not one single person until you. Which was why I was so sure it was going to work. Is there no way you can just sit down and talk this through? You two were perfect together," she repeated.

"There's nothing to talk through," Holly insisted. "We were never together, remember? We went on two dates, that was all. And we were only friends in the first place because I'm friends with you and Jamie. I was just flattered that someone would ask me out and he … well, I don't know what he was thinking. In different situations, we'd likely never even look twice at each other."

"That's not true."

"Yes, it is. Now, don't you need to get off soon? I thought you said you'd got to take Ellis for one of his jabs after lunch."

Caroline glanced at her watch before scrunching up her nose.

"You're right. I'll take this with me, if that's okay?" she said lifting another sandwich.

"And you can come all day tomorrow? I want to go to the Care Home early. I've got a surprise for the residents. I hope they're going to like it. Turns out we had a bit of money left over. Oh, and that reminds me. I can pay Michael and the others a bit more. I'm really grateful how they stepped in at the last minute to save the day."

"In that case, I'll get him to keep practicing after Christmas. Who knows, there might be a second career for him in it, playing at care home parties. Goodness knows we could do with the extra money." Caroline smiled, then turned serious again. "Holly, about Ben—"

"No. We're done talking about him. Now I'm focusing entirely on the dance. Who knows, maybe one of the old guys will see me in my finery and decide I'm the woman of his dreams."

Caroline muttered something that she didn't quite catch and was about to ask her to repeat, when she swept up her handbag from behind the counter and threw the strap over her shoulder.

"Okay, see you tomorrow. Good luck with everything."

CHAPTER FORTY-THREE

*T*he surprise that Holly had spoken to Caroline about came thanks to one of the local hair salons, which had a training academy attached to it. During a conversation with her stylist when she'd popped in to get her hair cut—for the first time since moving back to Bourton—she mentioned the party she was organising at the care home.

Following a few days of numerous text messages, Holly found herself standing outside the Weeping Willows at one p.m. on the day of the party, accompanied by twelve young men and women, each carrying a large bag filled with heated rollers, styling products and makeup.

"You're setting up in the Oak Room and the Elder Lounge," Holly found herself directing them. "The largest room is being prepared for the party. The Oak's the second biggest, but the Elder is a fair bit smaller. We need to make sure that everyone's got enough space to work. Perhaps the ladies should use the Oak and the gentlemen, the Elder. Does that sound about right?"

They all nodded their agreement.

"Great. Now, I'm afraid we've only got regular chairs, so they're going to be a bit lower than you used to. We've arranged a timetable, giving each person forty minutes. If you think you're going to need more than that, let me know. Perhaps if those of you looking after the men finish first—which seems likely—you could take up the slack with some of the ladies."

She was starting to enjoy this. It still felt a little odd, ordering people around, especially the care home workers and the residents, given their experience and age, but it was all coming together rather nicely.

In the Birch Room, Drey and her team were working on decorating the ceiling. Large silver snowflakes glinted and spun slowly, suspended on invisible threads. Holly was so busy staring at them that she didn't notice the teenager crouched on the floor, holding a camera with a huge lens on the front, until she almost tripped over him.

"Can you mind where you're stepping, please?" he said, clutching the equipment protectively to his chest.

"Sorry," she said, regaining her balance as Drey hopped down from a stepladder.

"Holly, this is Justin. He's the one who made all the decorations."

"I just need to get some photos for my portfolio," he said, now climbing on the vacant stepladder to try and get a better angle. Having snapped a couple of shots, he came back down. "It's awesome. I can use this for my art project and then the volunteering will count as enrichment hours, too. Basically, I've just halved the amount of work I need to do next term. Now I'll have plenty of time to practise with my Fortnite crew."

"It's a video game thing," Drey explained to a blank-faced Holly.

She wasn't entirely sure that making extra time to play video games was the best reason to help and volunteer, but the snowflakes did look amazing. They'd also found some silver fabric, which they'd draped over the pictures and the curtains. There was still a lot of peach showing, but hopefully, when it was darker and the fairy lights they'd strung around the walls were on, it would look altogether Christmassy.

"Thank you so much, Justin," she enthused. "You've done a wonderful job here. I'm very grateful."

"Hey Holly, where do you want us?"

The voice came from the doorway and she turned to see Michael standing there with an impressively large amp in his hand.

"I thought you weren't coming until three?" she called over to him.

"It is three. Ten past, actually."

"It is?"

She glanced at her watch and felt her stomach lurch. How the hell had the time gone so quickly? The party started at six. That meant they had less than three hours to get the room finished and the band set up, not to mention the fact that she needed to go home and change. Verity had been most insistent about that.

"Okay, right," she said, refocusing. "So, if you can set up in the bay window over there, where there are plenty of plug sockets nearby."

She looked at the amp again and shuddered.

"That thing does have a low volume setting, I hope? I've promised the Head Nurse it won't be too loud."

"Don't worry, I'll set it just loud enough that we can hear the keyboard over the double bass and drums."

Drums. Of course, there'd be drums. Her nerves ratcheted up. The last thing they needed was to get a noise complaint from one of their neighbours. She'd never be forgiven. Probably never be allowed back on the property again, either.

"Don't worry," he said, apparently able to read her expression. "We've kept it light. Just a snare, a high hat and a small bass drum, that's all."

"Okay, well, I hope the space will be big enough for you," she said.

He looked at the other man with him, who was holding a wooden box, which she guessed might be his stool. He nodded.

"I thought there were going to be three of you."

"He'll be up after work. Couldn't get off early like the rest of us," Michael explained.

"But he is reliable? He's not going to let us down?"

The drummer went to say something, but Michael shot a look in his direction that Holly couldn't interpret.

"Don't worry, he's perfectly reliable. Now, we're all good here, I'm sure you have lots to be getting on with."

Did she, though? The food had arrived earlier that day. Everything was to be served cold, so there was no need for any reheating, and most of it was fine without refrigeration, too. The room was looking amazing, and the first volunteers for the dance would be arriving at five thirty.

Holly chuckled sadly to herself. She'd always thought that at some point she'd be part of the PTA. That when her kids started school, she'd get involved. She'd anticipated taking her child to a school disco and helping with a hundred excited teenagers. Maybe this was going to be her lot, instead, chaperoning geriatrics. She cheered herself up thinking, if this went well, there was no reason it couldn't become an annual event.

"Okay then, I'll go check on the residents and see how they're doing," she said. "If you need anything, you can send Drey to find me. You know Drey from the shop, right?"

From the other side of the room, Drey lifted a hand and waved at them.

"Don't worry. We've got this," she called.

In the Elder Room, Holly discovered that all the men had already been spruced up and several ladies were admiring their new coiffure and comparing their rather elaborate nail art. It was possible the trainees had got a little carried away, but they looked delighted.

"I'm glad I didn't go for plain blue nails," she overhead one of them say. "Jean looks like she's got frostbite, if you ask me."

"That's putting it nicely."

She chuckled to herself and moved on to the Oak Room, where she found who she'd been looking for.

In the fluffy slippers that she'd bought her, Verity was sitting wearing an equally fluffy dressing gown of the exact same colour. Her hair was up in rollers and her nails were currently being painted a deep burgundy.

"How's the guest of honour doing?" Holly asked.

"Me? The guest of honour? Pfft!" she said, dismissively. You're the one who made all this happen. You should be the guest of honour."

"Ahh, but I wouldn't have done it if you hadn't been so insistent that you needed a chance to dance, remember?"

Verity tipped her head to one side. "Yes, I suppose you're right. We can be joint guests of honour, then. And you should be aware what a privilege that is, you know. I don't normally share centre stage with anyone."

"Then I accept the distinction with gracious appreciation," Holly laughed, bowing low. "How are you doing though, seriously?" she asked. "You are taking it easy, aren't you?"

Verity rolled her eyes at this comment, just as Holly should have expected.

"Do you really think I'd be wearing these things on my feet, if I weren't taking it easy?"

Holly laughed again, although Verity scowled.

"I'm glad you're finding it funny."

"Well, I'm sure whatever you wear tonight, you'll look brilliant."

The scowl dropped.

"Well, of course I will. But that's not what I'm interested in at the moment. Have you decided what *you're* going to wear? You're welcome to have a rummage through my wardrobe, if you can't find anything in the selection I gave that friend of yours."

"Don't worry," she replied. "I know exactly what I'm wearing, and I think you're going to approve."

"Now this I am looking forward to seeing."

CHAPTER FORTY-FOUR

"Wow, you look like a movie star," the young man had exclaimed as he'd finished doing her hair, earlier.

Holly had felt a little guilty about approaching one of the stylists, but they'd already finished with the residents and it wasn't as if she was asking for much. Just something sleek and simple. That was what she'd said to guy; and that was exactly what she'd got. In all her life, she couldn't remember her hair ever looking so shiny or smooth. The frizzy wisps that plagued her day-to-day existence were plastered down with enough spray to create a new hole in the ozone layer, while the back had been tied into a small chignon at the base of her neck.

Now back home and all dressed up, she looked at her reflection in the mirror and had to admit she felt like a million dollars. It wasn't just the plunging neckline, but the whole look. The curves. She would never have worn anything like this when she'd been with Dan. Not just because she would never have been able to afford it, but because she'd always felt the need to blend in. But now, she didn't feel that anymore. This was her.

She was Holly. Holly Berry, proud owner of the *Just One More* sweet shop. Holly Berry who arranged charity auctions and organised dances. She was proud of who she'd become, and she didn't need a man on her arm to make her feel she was good enough. She *was* good enough. She had confidence.

"Right, that's enough admiring yourself," Jamie said, bringing her out of her reverie. "We need to get going. It's already five forty-five."

"What? I was meant to be there by now."

"Really? I thought you'd want to make a dramatically late entrance."

"Why on earth would you think that?" she asked.

Yes, she loved the dress and how it made her feel, but she still had no desire to be the centre of attention.

At Holly's insistence, Jamie had dressed up too, and she looked like a completely different person. Given the combination of the swanky clothes, the high-heeled shoes and the temperature, not to mention how late they now were, they were driving up to Weeping Willows. As Jamie had arrived home after her and blocked her car in, the quickest option was to take her van. She threw towels over the front seats to protect their dresses.

"It's not that bad, but you know what oil is like. Bloody stuff gets everywhere."

For the entire journey, Holly braced herself against the dashboard, praying that some grease-covered spanner wouldn't come flying up from the footwell and mark her dress. She wasn't sure how many movie stars arrived at celebrity events in a white van with towels on the seats and a ladder strapped to the roof.

Thankfully, they made it there without any incidents and as she stepped out onto the gravel, all her concerns faded.

"Do you hear that?" she asked, tilting her head.

Jamie stopped and listened, too. The music wasn't loud, certainly not loud enough for the neighbours to complain. At least she hoped not. There was something so exciting about a live band. The soft tinkle of the piano contrasted against the earthy thump of the double bass, while the percussionist kept the tempo nice and up-beat. Then, as they struck up *Fly Me To The Moon*, she knew, before even stepping inside, that they were in for a very special night.

"Holly."

Nurse Donna was there at the front door, almost as if she'd been waiting to greet her. The woman still somehow managed to make her nervous.

"Nurse Donna."

"That's quite some transformation you've given our Birch Room."

"In a good way, I hope," she said, tentatively.

"I believe so."

Holly stared at her, hoping that her expression might give some indication as to whether she was pleased with how the night had panned out, but it was as rigid as stone. From the first day she'd met her, it had never looked anything other than severe, but her reaction tonight left Holly feeling disappointed. She was hoping that maybe, after doing all this, she would have been a little friendlier towards her. That she might see that Holly wasn't just the newbie volunteer wanting to change everything without understanding anything, as she'd once commented. If anything, she looked sad.

"I'm going on in. Check the band is okay," Jamie said, slipping past the pair and off down the corridor.

At Jamie's departure, the nurse's unease seemed even more tangible.

"Is everything all right?" Holly asked.

The nurse pressed her lips together

"Is the band too loud? I can ask them to tone it down."

"There's no easy way to say this," she replied, dipping her chin.

"What? Has someone complained?"

"No, no. It's nothing like that. In fact, I commend you for all you've achieved. The residents will have a wonderful time, I'm sure. The staff, too."

"Then what?"

This was becoming more and more odd. She racked her brains for some explanation of what could possibly be wrong.

"Holly, I'm so sorry to have to tell you this and tonight of all nights. I know how fond of her you'd grown. We were all so fond of her."

Realisation hit her like a physical blow.

"No."

"It was very sudden. We don't believe she can have felt any pain."

"No! It can't be true! I was speaking to her just this afternoon. She was telling me about her dress. About going barefoot."

"Holly, the time you've spent with her and the interest you've shown in her over the last few weeks meant the absolute world to her. She was brighter than I'd seen her in a long, long time."

"No!"

She could feel her eyes stinging with tears. She didn't know why she was shouting, but she couldn't help herself.

"No! You have to be wrong. I saw her. I spoke to her. This was all for her. She wanted to dance again. She wanted to dance."

"I know. I know."

"No. I don't believe you. I don't. I need to see her. I need to speak to her. There's been some kind of dreadful mistake."

Holly felt a hand on her elbow and saw Nurse Donna's lips moving, but she couldn't hear her words. She could barely even stand.

CHAPTER FORTY-FIVE

*T*he nurse took Holly to Verity's room, gently guiding her by the shoulders, if she was about to take a wrong turn. Every step of the way, she was hoping it wasn't true and at any moment her friend would appear around the next corner.

As they pushed open the door and stepped inside her room, the gloom swept over her. The main light had been switched off and just her bedside light was on, next to another vase of flowers that she'd brought her.

Verity was lying on the bed, as if just taking a little nap. She had changed and was wearing a deep maroon gown, the same colour as her nails, but the fluffy slippers were still on her feet.

Kneeling down next to her, Holly took one of her hands. It seemed almost weightless. The knuckles were white, and the translucent skin exposed a network of lifeless blue capillaries beneath. Had they always been so frail? she wondered.

"She was fine," Holly said, again.

"I don't know if it will be of any comfort to you, but she wasn't. She was very poorly. These last few weeks she'd really perked up again, with you visiting her so often, but I'm afraid that this was inevitable. The end was always very near. She knew that."

Holly sniffed and wiped her eyes, her freshly applied makeup forgotten.

"Why didn't she say anything? If she knew, then why didn't she tell me?"

"I suspect she thought you'd treat her differently. You were like a breath of fresh air to her. She needed that."

"I needed it, too," she whispered.

She should have realised, seen the signs herself, she thought. Thinking back, when the carer had come and helped Verity from her car, after they'd watched the Christmas lights being switched on together, she had just assumed that it was quite normal to help residents like that, but now she knew there had been more to it.

"Come with me," the nurse said, squeezing Holly's hand. "I know this is sad and you'll need time to process it, but not now. Tonight, there are others here who want to see you, to thank you. And I might have even promised to join in a dance myself, and I would hate for you to miss that."

Holly didn't move, Verity's cold hand still in hers. She was wearing all her lovely rings, but it was only now that she saw how loose they were and how they hung between her knuckles with no flesh on the bones to keep them securely in place. Her grandparents had passed away when she was very young, and she had no real memory of them. Certainly not enough to miss them. Agnes had been the only person she'd ever lost, who she'd been close to, and at the time, she'd been living in London, which had somehow made it easier to detach herself from it. To compartmentalise the sadness, almost as if, being so far away, she could imagine nothing had changed.

"Maybe I'll just stay for a short while longer," she said.

"It's not something you ever get used to," Nurse Donna said. "You'd think that being in the job as long as I have, it would be different, but every time one of them moves on, it hurts. But you must focus on the lives they'd enjoyed—and boy did Verity live hers to the full—and what they gave you while they were a part of your world, however fleetingly, not what's missing now that they're gone. If you do that, everything seems to have a purpose and it's not so hard to bear."

What had Verity given her? A reason to smile. Belief in herself. She'd given her strength, too, she now realised. She made her see that it was okay to be herself. To not conform. It was the same strength she'd learnt from her parents and from Maud and Agnes, too, but lost somewhere along the way. Verity had somehow reignited it. She would be fine. Whatever she faced, she was going to be all right.

"You'll let me know about the funeral arrangements," she said, rising to her feet.

"Of course, I will. Now, how about you come and see your handiwork?"

She could hear the music, even from this side of the building. As they got closer, she recognised the up-beat refrains of Glen Miller's *In The Mood*. The band really was very good.

"How do I look?" Holly asked, wiping under eyes, in case her mascara had strayed. Nurse Donna drew a thumb across her cheek.

"Like you're going to give one or two of my old fellas a heart attack," she said, with a smile.

Holly tried to reciprocate, but in the circumstances, she wasn't in quite the right place for dark humour.

"You look lovely. Now, don't go mad, but I made a big bowl of non-alcoholic punch. Why don't you get yourself a glass?"

This time, Holly did manage a smile.

Nurse Donna pushed open the door to the Birch Room.

If Holly had been able to give the art student a grade for his work, it would have been an A***. Never had she seen such an incredible transformation in a room. In fact, had she not known where she was, she would have sworn they'd all been teleported to some fancy wedding venue.

The stars dangling from the ceiling had increased twofold since she'd left, and the fairy lights would have certainly given Dan's proposal a run for its money.

"Holly, you're here!" Drey swept in from the side. "I was about to message you to find out what had happened."

"It looks incredible, Drey" she managed as she put her arm around the girl. "Thank you so much."

"We had to up the lighting level, unfortunately. They told us it was a health and safety issue. Guess we wouldn't get our enrichment credit if one of the old people tripped over and broke a hip."

She managed a half smile at this.

Across the room, Sid winked at her, his arm around Glenis as they danced slowly, rocking back and forth. Over on the other side, Margaret was holding hands with grumpy Nurse Julia, who didn't look that grumpy, in fact, as she swung her partner's hands from side to side in time with the music. Some of the ladies had found cocktail dresses, and a couple of the men had donned bow ties for the event. And even though one or two were only wearing evening dress of the winceyette kind, ready for bed, they all had one thing in common. Every one of them looked happy, including one old codger who she'd never seen cracking a smile.

Her sadness lessened a little. Donna had been right.

"So, you going to dance or not?" Sid appeared at her side, having left Glenis to dance with one of Drey's young volunteers. "I think you'll have a queue forming soon. Thought I'd get in first. Might book you for a waltz later, too, assuming these folks know how to play one."

"Thank you, Sid. A dance sounds like just what I need."

He dipped his head in a half bow before reaching out and taking her hand, which he brought to his lips and kissed. She could feel tears welling up again, but she wasn't going to cry. She refused to.

He led her to the dance floor like she was thirteen years old again at the school disco. When he stopped and turned to her, she looked him in the eye.

"You keep those hands up, Sid."

"Good grief, I'm insulted. I'm a gentleman, you know."

"Yeah, right."

They grinned at each other, as they rocked back and forth. Holly was impressed. For someone his age he had no problem keeping to the beat, and in one unexpected moment, he even spun her around under his arm. She laughed momentarily, regaining her balance, and her eyes fell on the band.

Michael was sitting at the keyboard, singing into a mic. The drummer was nonchalantly keeping time, in that effortless way they do. And the third member of the band was standing, plucking at the strings of his double bass, looking straight at her.

"Ben," she whispered.

CHAPTER FORTY-SIX

*A*t any other time, she would have been able to cope with it. Or at least coped with it better than she knew she was about to. Seeing him again reminded her of the last time they'd been together, in the hospital with Verity. Darling Verity, who was now gone. Who she didn't even get to say goodbye to. She struggled to breathe and her eyes filled with tears. Blinking only made it worse. She looked at the ceiling and tried to think of something else, but they stubbornly pooled in her bottom lids before spilling over and down her cheeks, dropping onto the fabric of her blue dress.

"Sorry, Sid," she managed to say, before dropping his hands and wiping her face. It was taking every bit of will power not to run straight for the door. She wanted to, but there were too many people around her and Drey, Jamie, even the nurses, would spot her. So instead, she kept her head down, weaving through the couples as fast as she could, gasping for air as she reached the double doors of the Birch Room and the peach-coloured corridors beyond.

Normally, they'd be almost empty. But tonight there were

people milling around, talking to one another, holding glasses of the non-alcoholic punch. Why was it so hot in here? Surely it was too hot, even for an old people's home? She could feel sweat beading on her neck as she gulped down one breath after another. Now that she was away from the crowd, she picked up the pace.

She wobbled slightly as she raced past reception, swung open the front door and stepped outside. The cold air hit her like a blast from the Arctic. Why was she finding it so hard to breathe? She hadn't known Verity very long. Not in the grand scheme of things. So why did her chest feel like it was in a vice? Bending over with her hands on her knees to try and get her breathing under control again, she was suddenly aware of just how very cold it was. Her arms were already covered in goose-bumps and her legs were quivering. She couldn't stay out here for long, not wearing a dress like this. Her best bet would be to go back inside and find a quiet room, where she could wait until it was time to clear up. Yes, that was what she'd do.

Feeling chilled to the bone, she turned back to the door, giving her eyes another wipe. It was only when she looked up again that she saw Jamie standing there.

"Holly, is everything all right?" she asked, worry etched on her face. "What's happened? What's wrong? If it's about Ben being here, I'm sorry. Caroline said I should have told you, but I thought it was better this way. Michael couldn't get anyone else, and he didn't want to let you down, and you'd said you'd be okay being in the same room as him. I thought not telling you would give you less time to stress about it."

"Not everything is about Ben," Holly replied, sounding a little more rattled than she'd intended.

"Then what's happened?"

She sucked in a lungful of air, so cold it almost choked her.

"It's Verity. She died this afternoon."

She heard Jamie gasp and saw tears well up in her eyes.

"Oh no. I can't believe it."

"I saw her. She's gone."

Holly watched as the same pain she'd felt only half an hour before flooded through Jamie. And why wouldn't it? She'd been coming here for years, had known her for years. And she had a wardrobe full of Verity's clothes, for crying out loud.

"So, what do we do now?" Jamie asked, her breath fogging in the night air.

"I guess we carry on with the dance."

For the next few hours, the pair somehow managed to keep smiling. The only thing that made it bearable was seeing the residents dancing and laughing, like they were teenagers. She took another turn on the dance floor with Sid, then with Margaret and then with two others who came to her bingo nights. No one mentioned Verity or why she was missing. Was it that they already knew? Possibly. Perhaps they were just more accustomed to death.

At eight o'clock, Michael and the band finished with *Auld Lang Syne* and Holly felt her heart breaking all over again.

Then the atmosphere suddenly changed as Nurse Donna switched on the main lights.

"All right ladies and gents," she called. "That's your lot. Now, we've all had a lovely evening, but right now you need to get a wriggle on. We'll be starting our rounds in fifteen minutes. Please make sure you're in your rooms by then. If you need assistance, then just stay where you are, and someone will come and fetch you."

As she passed Holly, their eyes met.

"Thank you for tonight, Holly. A job well done, I'd say. Now you just need to get rid of all these bloody decorations."

With so many hands, it didn't take long. Justin, Drey's friend, insisted on taking all the stars down himself, so that they weren't broken. Michael and the band, Ben included, cleared out all their equipment, leaving Holly and the others to deal with shifting the chairs and removing the silver drapes and fairy lights. Within the hour, everything was packed away and only Holly and Jamie remained.

"Right, shall we go get a drink? I think we've earned one."

Holly looked around the room. How effortlessly it had been returned to its muted peach tones. Tomorrow, the residents would come in and it would be as if the whole thing had never happened. Maybe she could get some photos printed for them. She'd seen plenty of the youngsters with their phones out. Although there'd not be one pinned to a bedroom wall, next to a picture of a Christmas tree, she thought sadly. They turned off the lights and shut the door.

"I think I just want a long bath," she said. "But if you want to go, don't let me stop you."

Jamie studied her, then nodded. "I'll just go for one. I said I'd join Michael. As long as you're sure you're okay on your own?"

"I am."

For what must have been the hundredth time since moving to Bourton, Holly was grateful to have found Jamie and have her as a housemate. Someone who recognised when she needed space.

"Okay. Well, I'll drop you home first."

Stepping outside, she saw the sky was filled with the same heavy clouds that had been threatening snow for weeks.

"Actually," she said, "I think I'll walk."

"You can't be serious? It's Arctic."

"You've got your big coat in your van, haven't you? And

your wellies, too. I'll use those. I fancy a bit of fresh air. Honestly, I'll be fine."

Jamie sucked in a long breath.

"At least let me drop you at the pub. That way you're a bit closer to home. And if you change your mind, I can drive you all the way."

Holly thought about it. Yes, she could wear Jamie's wellies, but she only had tights on and her feet would end up freezing in them, if she walked all the way. Her offer seemed like a good compromise.

"Okay, then," she said, and clambered into her van.

A couple of minutes later, they were parked outside the pub.

"Are you sure you don't want me to drive you all the way?" Jamie asked. "It'll take no time at all."

"You don't want to keep Michael waiting. You go. I'm fine. I'll text you when I get in."

"And you'll go straight home?"

"I will. Promise."

CHAPTER FORTY-SEVEN

It was a promise she had fully intended to keep. Straight back, a candlelit bath with loads of bubbles and a glass of whatever was already open in the fridge. But as Holly strode over the bridge towards home, she found herself drawn towards the lights of the Christmas tree.

Tonight, they shone almost violet and reflected in the river below, mirror-like, the water was so calm. A lump came to her throat. She was glad she'd brought Verity down to see them being turned on. At least that was something. Her old friend had so wanted it to snow that evening. Had that been a clue? Had she thought it was going to be her last chance? Had she even been hoping Holly might see through what she was saying?

"Can we talk?"

His voice cut through the silence.

Spinning around, Holly glared. His coat was buttoned all the way up and he was wearing thick woollen gloves which, at that moment, she was immensely jealous of. She plunged her hands deeper into her pockets.

"I don't think we have anything to talk about."

"I think we do. Jamie told me about Verity. I'm so sorry. And I'm sorry I turned up tonight without telling you."

"It's fine. We needed a band. I understand."

He rocked slightly on his heels.

"I know that, perhaps, I may have distanced myself from you, but I want you to know … that … that …"

She was too cold to stand there and listen to him stumble over his words. He was the one who'd said he wanted to talk, after all. After another moment of silence, she shook her head in annoyance.

"What do you want, Ben? Because I'm tired of trying to work it out. And you obviously don't respect what I ask you to do. In case you don't remember, I said I didn't want to talk."

"I know. I realise I've messed it up. I've messed us up."

She laughed. It was a bitter sound and quite unlike her.

"There never was an *us*, Ben. It took two months to manage a first date. Maybe that should have been an omen. If we'd really wanted to make a go of it, it would have been easier and it would have happened," she said. "Friendship isn't meant to be this difficult."

Ben's chin dipped.

"I don't want to be friends," he said, so quietly she barely heard him.

"No? Well that's something we can finally agree on."

She twisted away from him, but before she could leave, he gently caught her by the arm. His eyes bored into hers, glinting in the lights of the tree.

"I was selfish, Holly. I was the worst kind of man. I was so focused on protecting my own heart, that I didn't think about yours."

Her scoff was as cold and brittle as the frost covering the ground.

"What did you think your heart needed protecting from? Me? I've never done anything to hurt you. Never. And I've never given you any reason not to trust me."

"I saw you kissing Dan."

"Dan kissed me. And maybe I got a bit lost in the moment, but as soon as I came to my senses, I sent him packing. You know that."

"Yes, but all those romantic gestures. I thought it would only be a matter of time before you …"

His words faded into nothing, but she wasn't going to let him get away without saying what he meant.

"A matter of time until what? Until I went back to him? You think so little of me?"

"No, I think everything of you, Holly. I think the whole world of you. I think you're amazing."

"Yeah, well you have a funny way of showing it."

He still had hold of her. She looked down and scowled at his hand, but instead of letting go, he ran it down her arm and drew hers from her pocket. She wanted to pull it away and leave him standing there in the cold, but she found her fingers instinctively entwine with his. She closed her eyes and took a deep breath.

"Tell me what to do?" he said. "How can I fix this?"

Her heart was aching. Why was he making this so damned difficult?

"You didn't even want to kiss me," she reminded him.

"What?" He stepped back, now letting go but keeping his eyes on her. "You're joking."

"You never kissed me."

"You never kissed me, either."

"Well, you can hardly blame me."

He shook his head.

"What about now?" he asked.

"What *about* now?"

"Can I kiss you?"

Of all the things Holly felt like doing, kissing him was, for once, not on her list. Hit him, certainly. Throttle him, perhaps. But kiss him? Definitely not.

"I'm not in the mood for games, Ben."

"When have you ever know me play games? Other than board games, obviously."

He was trying to make a joke. Acting like they were okay. But they weren't. His smile dropped. When he spoke again, it was with sincerity.

"I've messed up, Holly. I have messed up repeatedly and I realise it is all my fault. All I can tell you is the truth. Ever since I first saw you, standing outside the sweet shop the night you came back to Bourton, I haven't been able to stop thinking about you. You are always on my mind. And I'm a coward. I'm a coward because I was scared of you rejecting me one day because I wasn't funny or smart or spontaneous enough for you. So I tried to ignore my feelings because it could never work out, and we'd be better off just being friends. And when Dan turned up, I became even more convinced.

"But when I saw you tonight, when I saw all the hurt in your eyes, I hated that I couldn't run after you. I'd have done anything to take the pain away. I still would. I would do anything for you, Holly. And I don't want to be just friends either. I want to be everything to you."

His voice cracked, and she realised tears were welling up in his eyes.

"I get that it's too late. I realised that at the hospital. But I kept thinking about what you said there, and I wanted you to know you were wrong. I was never not into you. I was head over heels, Holly Berry. I still am."

He'd stolen the breath from her lungs. Her heart was hammering.

"They're just words. Everything you're saying, just words."

"I know."

He stepped forwards again, slipping his hand back into hers.

"But I hope you know me well enough to realise that I mean everyone one of them."

He was so close now that she could feel the warmth of his breath. What was she about to do? Setting herself up for more heartache, most likely, but there was something about the way she still felt when he was near. Something that made her feel calm and safe. In spite of her misgivings, she found herself speaking.

"Ask me again," she whispered.

"Sorry?"

"Ask me again if you can kiss me."

He lifted his hand and caressed her cheek.

"Holly Berry, may I kiss you? Please?"

She tilted her face up to his.

"Well, it is nearly Christmas," she said.

He pushed a wayward strand of hair behind her ear and then pressed his lips against hers.

How long they stayed like that, Holly couldn't have said. As his warmth flooded into her, time seemed to freeze. When they finally broke apart, she saw a nervous smile playing on his lips. She was about to kiss him again, when something stopped her.

"What is it?" he asked, a shadow crossing his face.

"Look," she said and stepped away from him.

It was so faint, it was barely visible in the muted glow of the streetlamps, and it took her a moment to be sure she wasn't imagining it. But after a few seconds, she was certain.

"It's snowing," she said, as the glistening white flakes started to dance before them.

When they reached the ground, they vanished, and that somehow made it all the more magical.

"Isn't it beautiful?" she said, watching as they danced over the river and around the Christmas tree.

"It is," he replied, slipping his hand around her waist. "Very beautiful, indeed."

They stood there in silence, as the snow grew heavier. Only when she let out an involuntary shiver, did Ben speak again.

"Maybe we should find somewhere a little warmer to continue this."

Holly grinned, with a giddy happiness that was only partly due to the snow.

"I think that could be arranged," she said and then kissed him again.

The end

TURMOIL AT THE SWEET SHOP OF SECOND CHANCES

Life has finally settled down for Holly Berry, but when things start to go awry for those around her, will she be able to come to the rescue?

Holly's family has always been there for her, and when her dad is made redundant she is only too happy to help out. But giving her father a job wasn't quite what she had in mind. Can she strike a balance between family and business, or will it all be a bit too close to home?

Make sure you don't miss out on the further adventures of your favourite sweet shop owner and pre-order your copy of ***Turmoil at the Sweet Shop of Second Chances*** today.

·

Order here

ACKNOWLEDGMENTS

To my wonderful editor Carol, whose patience know no limits.

To Cherie, for yet another beautiful cover.

My eagle-eyed beta readers Lucy and Kath, who continue to be the final gatekeepers in my war against typos.

Lastly, once again I want to mention Nina, my beloved sweet shop boss. She is one of the kindest, most sincere people I have ever met and I thank my stars frequently that you said yes to giving me a job all those decades ago. During my teenage years that tiny building was a second home and a sanctuary for me. This book is a homage to that time in my life that I will never forget.

ABOUT THE AUTHOR

Hannah Lynn is an award-winning novelist. Publishing her first book, *Amendments* – a dark, dystopian speculative fiction novel, in 2015, she has since gone on to write *The Afterlife of Walter Augustus* – a contemporary fiction novel with a supernatural twist – which won the 2018 Kindle Storyteller Award and Gold Medal for Best Adult Fiction Ebook at the IPPY Awards, as well as the delightfully funny and poignant *Peas and Carrots series*.

Her latest work include retellings of classic Greek myths and saw her win her second IPPY Gold Medal for the first book in her *Grecian Women Series*, the heart-wrenching *Athena's Child*.

Born in 1984, Hannah grew up in the Cotswolds, UK. After graduating from university, she spent ten years as a teacher of physics, first in the UK, then in Thailand, Malaysia, Austria and Jordan. It was during this time, inspired by the imaginations of the young people she taught, she began writing short stories for children, before moving on to adult fiction.

Nowadays you will most likely find her busy writing at home with her husband and daughter, surrounded by a horde of cats.

Eric sighed heavily. Suzy took his empty glass from his hand and swapped it for a full one.

'Maybe I should give it up. Let the church have it. I mean it's just a car. After all, we can always go and buy another vintage DB4,' he said.

Suzy gave him a withering look.

'I mean, we'd have to re-mortgage the house,' Eric said. 'And Abi would have to go to that school down the road where all the kids smell like baked beans and do their homework on used kitchen roll, but we'd get by.'

'You're not going to give it up,' Suzy said. 'We both know that.'

Eric thumbed the rim of his glass until it let out a deep, low hum. 'No,' he said. 'I guess not.'

'So, I guess we're all heading to Burlam this weekend?'

Twenty minutes later, Eric was sitting at his desk with Suzy peering over his shoulder. His laptop was open on the *Burlam Village Website*, specifically the Classifieds. The page contained various lists and headings in colourful blues and greens with a serene picture of the river and sailing boats set as the background.

'I'm not sure this is what he meant,' Suzy said. 'I thought you said *you* had to maintain the allotment?'

Eric continued typing away in the little rectangular box. 'This is just a short-term solution to buy us a little time. Anyway, I'm maintaining it. I'll just be paying someone else to do the digging.'

'I'm not convinced.'

'Trust me. This will see us all a lot happier. Mr Eaves included.'

With a satisfied smile, Eric clicked enter.

'There. All done.'

Half a second later his succinctly worded advert appeared on *Burlam Village Classifieds* page. *"Gardener wanted for allotment plot. Can grow anything. Will pay good money."*

'Now all we have to do is wait for the applicants.'

Peas, Carrots and an Aston Martin is a heart-warming novel from the Peas and Carrots humorous fiction series. If you like crazy capers, quirky characters, and brilliant second chances, then you'll love Kindle Storyteller Award winner Hannah Lynn's madcap tale.

Buy Peas, Carrots and an Aston Martin to ride into the weeds today on Amazon!

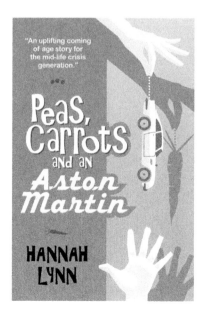

"**I absolutely loved this book**! It's funny, uplifting, contains a whole host of unforgettable characters and I can't wait to read the sequel! I was looking for something to cheer me up and this fit the bill. **A highly recommended 5 star read**."

"Peas, Carrots and an Aston Martin was **brilliant from start to finish** just downloaded the second book would **definitely recommend** to anyone."

"Will have you laughing one moment and misty eyed the next. This was **a joy to read**. Her characters a vividly drawn and strangely relatable. **Recommend**."

"**I loved this book**! Had me gripped from the first page. A real feel-good factor. Might need a tissue at some points. **Hugely recommended**."

STAY IN TOUCH

To keep up-to-date with new publications, tours and promotions, or if you are interested in being a beta reader for future novels, or having the opportunity to enjoy pre-release copies please follow me:

Website: hannahlynnauthor.com

Alternatively sign up to my newsletter and receive a free book.

Sign-up to Newsletter

REVIEW

As an independent author, I do not have the mega resources of a big publishing house, but what I do have is something even more powerful – all of you readers. Your ability to offer social proof to my books through your reviews is invaluable to me and helps me to continue writing.

So if you enjoyed reading **_Romance at the Sweet Shop of Second Chances_**, please take a few moments to leave a review or rating on Amazon or Goodreads. It need only be a sentence or two, but it means so much to me.

Thank you.

Printed in Great Britain
by Amazon